Taming the Cougar

Taming the Cougar

VONNA HARPER

APHRODISIA

KENSINGTON BOOKS
http://www.kensingtonbooks.com

APHRODISIA BOOKS are published by

Kensington Publishing Corp.
119 West 40th Street
New York, NY 10018

ISBN-13: 978-0-7582-2946-5
ISBN-10: 0-7582-2946-1

First Kensington Trade Paperback Printing: October 2009

10 9 8 7 6 5 4 3 2 1

Printed in the United States of America

Deciding who to credit with helping birth a book is both an easy and difficult process. The obvious culprits are my writing friends, my agent Laura Bradford, and my editor Audrey LaFehr, and I want them to take their well-deserved bows.

Less obvious, especially with this book, are my mother and husband. I have to laugh because both pretty much leave me alone to write erotica, occasionally giving me sideways glances as if assuring themselves that I haven't gone off the deep end. But several years ago, the three of us took a road trip through Arizona so I could research the locale for a historical novel I was writing. We drove through Hopi and Navajo reservations, gaped at the Grand Canyon, and stayed in remote towns made famous by Tony Hillerman. It was fall, the highways all but deserted. I was transported back in time as the land reached out to touch my soul.

So Mother and Dick, take your own bows.

1

Dark crouched at the far end of the canyon, ready to spring. Long accustomed to the totality of night in the vast network of sculpted sandstone passages, Hok'ee watched the death of another day. If he'd been fully human, night would have meant the end to his hunt, but he wasn't. As a result, even if he couldn't see the woman he'd been stalking, his nostrils would have kept him near her.

His bare feet moved soundlessly over the summer-dry land, sensing the life-giving moisture beneath the surface. A cooling breeze washed his naked body and sent fresh energy to joints that had been on the move since morning. Muscles carved from a physical existence easily kept pace with the need pulsing at his temples and deep in his groin.

He was thirsty and hungry with the need to hunt demanding to be filled as it always did, but the primal need that had claimed him from the moment he'd first caught *her* scent kept those concerns at the back of his thoughts. He was alive, senses charged, mind processing. One moment he focused on the danger she and her companion represented to his world, and the question of whether he should kill them. The next, her heat came close to consuming him.

He wanted her, would have her.

And when she had nothing more to give him, what then?

Lifting his head, he pulled in fresh oxygen. There she was, her erotic smell mingling with that of hot rock, the distant stream, cottonwoods, pinon, juniper, and sagebrush. The other human who'd come to the land he and his pride had claimed was male, stinking of sweat and determination. Growling low, he imagined tearing at the man with fang and claw, but to do that he'd have to change form, and that would terrify the woman. He didn't want to do that to her, yet. Maybe ever.

Stalk. Exist in the moment.

Another growl, this one born of long solitude, rolled through him. As if fighting his command to remain in the present, an image bloomed in his mind. In cougar form, he had run her down, slammed his weight into her back, and knocked her off her feet, onto her belly. Even as she fell, he brushed aside her long pale hair and touched his fangs to her soft, vulnerable neck.

Effortlessly holding her against the ground, he ripped at the worthless fabric she'd covered herself with. Careful not to injure her, he laid bare her shoulders, spine, and buttocks. Then, ignoring her screams and futile struggle, he flipped her onto her back.

The horror in her blue-gray eyes penetrated the mental haze that was part of being Cougar, and he commanded himself to become human. He did so quickly because he didn't want to give her time to try to escape.

Even before he'd completed the transformation, shock warred with her horror. Her stare said she didn't, couldn't, comprehend what had happened, but she had no choice because the truth loomed over her. Arms and legs limp, she stared as the man he'd become tore away at what remained of her clothing.

The moment he exposed them, her breasts called out to him,

compelling him to lathe the sweet, swollen flesh. Again and again, he teased her nipples until they became rocklike. Her moans and restless movements spoke to him, turned him even more savage. Grabbing her slim wrists, he forced her long arms over her head.

Although she struggled against his greater strength, he knew she didn't want freedom after all, because the scent of arousal emanated from her now parted legs. Containing her wrists with a single hand left him free to touch and tease and caress. She was silk against his rough, lean muscle, in contrast to his bulk, heat to his heat.

Whether she twisted from side to side or bucked beneath him made no difference. He claimed her neck and breasts, slim waist and flat belly. Although he needed to be the one in command, the curves of hips and legs, of buttocks and sex flesh, forced inhuman snarls from him, and he knew he was gone, done. He would fuck her, yes, bury himself in her richness, maybe die, and in the wondrous death find a reason to go on living.

Because of her.

Looking down, Hok'ee acknowledged the rod jutting out from him—a rod with nothing to house itself in. Gripping his cock, he held it through the worst of the lonely pain, then spilled himself on the ground. Back under a measure of control, he started walking again, his pace dictated by the speed of the two he was tracking. Their slowness sanded his nerves and tested his patience. At the same time, he savored the possibility of a protracted hunt. As long as it ended with the male vanquished and the female under his control, what did time matter?

His cock knotted again, making a lie of the question. Always before, when the fuck-drive threatened to overwhelm him, he forced himself into human clothing and made his way to the nearest town where he knew he could find a woman willing to accommodate him.

Those unions never lasted beyond one or two days because,

by then, his soul insisted he return to the canyons. The women, although they begged him to remain in their beds, had never comprehended that the only way he would stay in their lives was by their going back with him. And even if one had been willing, he'd never asked.

But now a female, a woman, had stepped onto his land—his and the rest of his pride's.

Shaking off thoughts of those with whom he shared the world that had been forced on him, he pulled the newcomer's essence even deeper into him. Her scent spread throughout him, touching veins and muscles, his mind even. Most of all, he felt her in his groin.

The cougar in him said yes, he'd separate her from her companion, killing the tall, ungainly man if necessary. If the female was incapable of seeing beneath the human surface to the beast deep inside him, she might willingly remain by his side, at least at first. But as night flowed into night, she'd undoubtedly learn the truth. And then?

How would he keep her with him once she'd seen the monster, and did he want that?

Unable to face the answer to the first question and not knowing how to respond to the other, he picked up his pace. A horned toad scrambled out of his way, its small claws and tail leaving tracks in the sandy soil. From where it stood on a ledge above him and to his right, a coyote watched him pass. Lifting his hand in salute, he acknowledged the lean, shy predator. According to what he'd researched during one of his forays into town, the Navajo who'd once made this land their home had considered the coyote both a trickster and a powerful being. They'd been right, at least about Coyote's spirit-strength.

I acknowledge you, brother. If you wish to walk with me, I welcome the company. Perhaps you will tell me why I find this female so intriguing.

Walk alone, Abandoned One, the coyote replied, calling him by the Navajo name his fellow Tocho had given him because, like them, he couldn't remember which one he'd been born with. *You need to travel with your thoughts if you're ever going to comprehend them. She intrigues because she is mystery. And because she has the capacity to touch you where you have never been touched.*

How can that be when she doesn't know I exist?

It doesn't matter, yet. What does matter is whether you will survive once she does. Whether either of you will.

The fading sky was placid and clean with not so much as a cloud or bird to distract Kai Tallon from the seemingly endless horizon. Even with Dr. Garrin Gentry within shouting distance, she felt alone, as she always did this time of day. The urge to haul out her digital and capture the approaching sunset was almost more than she could ignore, but she'd felt the same way yesterday, and the day before when they'd arrived at Sani, and if she didn't delete some of the images, the memory card would soon be full. The strange thing was that she had the sense that if she kept taking pictures, eventually one would reveal something unexpected. Otherworldly.

Giving herself a mental shake, she again focused on the ancient bone fragment she'd been holding since she'd uncovered it some fifteen minutes ago. It had finally started speaking to her, and although the voice wasn't yet strong enough for her to understand everything of what she believed had been a coyote had to tell her, it shouldn't take much longer.

If she could keep her mind clean enough to hear the message.

Propelled by a sharp pain in her left knee, she shifted so she was no longer kneeling. With most of her weight now on her right flank, the rocks no longer dug into her. Unfortunately, as soon as her focus was off the less than comfortable working conditions, her thoughts returned to unwanted territory. She should be catching up with Dr. Gentry as he returned to the tent camp the two of them had set up, not doing—what?

It was this remote canyon, its fault that her imagination had been doing whatever it was doing since she and Dr. Gentry had ridden their loaded quads in here the other day. With no worldly sounds, not even her favorite country and western music to keep her company, she shouldn't be surprised, but her unexpected inability to concentrate on her *gift* wasn't helping her earn her salary. Damn it, she needed to put every bit of mental and emotional energy she possessed into getting the bone fragment to spill its secrets, not . . .

I wish you were here, Dad. You'd love being with me. We could have a ball exploring this place. You'd love being away from rules and regulations. To be out here with me, away from the red tape—why'd you get yourself killed, Dad, why?

Giving up, she carefully set down the bone and stared at the dying line between earth and sky. Shut down thoughts of the father she'd loved with all her heart, and faced what she could no longer deny.

Something was out there. Something she'd never encountered in her twenty-eight years of life. Something with energy beyond anything she'd ever expected. Something that turned her restless, half-scared, and achingly alive.

She wanted to jump to her feet and run until her lungs screamed and her feet were shredded, until intellect and nerve spilled out of her. Left with nothing except exhaustion and clawing thirst, she wouldn't care about anything except creature comforts. She'd sleep the sleep of the dead, dreamless and peaceful.

But was that what she wanted? she asked herself as heat speared her. From the first time she'd touched an animal and comprehended that she could sense its emotion and see its world, her life had been dictated by powerful forces. Whether she fought her *sight* or embraced it didn't matter. The gift and curse was woven throughout her, part of her pulse and breathing. Was this newborn heat, this awareness of her body that different?

"I don't know," she moaned to the faint breeze and, hopefully, her father's spirit. "I don't know what's happening."

Now that she'd admitted how out of control she felt, facing the unknown seemed a little easier, although maybe the swiftly approaching night was responsible. Before long, darkness would assure there'd be no visual distractions, which meant she'd be pulled into herself, knotted into a tight, pulsing ball.

Determined to give the sensations a name, she tried to draw comparisons with what else she'd experienced in life. Fortunately, this primal energy had nothing in common with the tearing grief and anger that had engulfed her that day six months ago in the face of her father's death.

A longtime seeker of thrills, she'd parasailed at the Oregon coast on a day when the winds fought each other, steered a battered race car into a second place finish at a county track, and spent knuckle-whitening hours in a canoe caught in Colorado River class-five rapids. Those adventures had dried her throat and loosened her bowels and made her feel acutely alive, which had been her goal when she'd taken them on. In contrast, this—

Sex. Climaxing. Jumping a man's bones and riding him until he collapsed, until her spent body shivered and her pussy screamed to be left alone.

Was it as simple as that? She hadn't had sex in months. A little alone time with her fingers and batteries, and this *thing* she'd been feeling would slip away? Somehow she knew that wouldn't happen.

"Kai, where are you?" Dr. Gentry called out.

Wincing at the unexpected shout from the Arizona University archeology department professor, she tried to shake herself free of self-absorbed thoughts. "I'm coming," she replied, then mentally apologized to the living creatures she and Dr. Gentry had undoubtedly disturbed.

Dr. Gentry, or Garrin, as she was starting to call him, was the opposite of the absentminded professor. He could juggle an infinite number of balls at the same time, and if he ever dropped one, she'd seen no indication of it. In his mid-forties, he was said to be the obvious choice to replace the department head when Dr. Carter retired, which from what she'd heard wasn't going to be anytime soon.

As a new and temporary university hire, she wasn't privy to the political maneuvering, thank goodness, but she'd already sensed Garrin's frustration at having to bide his time. She also guessed he'd pulled whatever stings that needed to be pulled in order to be put in charge of this operation.

And, as he'd told her the day he'd called to all but demand she join the expedition, he considered her key to its success. The grant-financed salary he'd been able to dangle in front of her had caught and held her interest, but that wasn't why she'd agreed.

This remote network of canyons in northern Arizona hadn't interested anyone except the Navajo, and an occasional wilderness hiker, for decades until one of those hikers had stumbled upon a crumbling kiva in a cave about a year ago. That discovery had led to a number of pictographs being found in the cave, and ultimately became proof that the ancient Anasazi had once lived in what the Navajo called Sani.

Translated as The Old One, the ultimate rights to Sani's historic treasure was being fought in the courts. In the meantime, the university had convinced a powerful state senator—who just happened to be an alumni—to allow a handful of their personnel to establish a dig site. The public explanation had been that university presence was necessary to protect the fragile artifacts.

Any fool, and she was no fool, got it that the university was determined to claim first and only bragging rights.

So where did that put her on the greedy scale?

Nowhere, she answered, acknowledging that financial remuneration had little to do with why she was sleeping on the ground in a pup tent, and eating reconstituted dried food. From the moment she'd seen her first picture of the area, Sani had called to her in ways beyond her comprehension, powerful and heated.

Sani, or something in it?

2

*T*ocho. *Mountain lion.*

Hok'ee had changed into cougar form before joining the other Tocho in a cave near a stream that cut deep into the sandstone. No matter that he'd spent part of every day of his short memory with the four males, he greeted them with exposed fangs and sharp snarls. Despite the shared aggression that came with being Tocho, he couldn't imagine ever harming them, or they him. As the largest and most accomplished hunter, he accepted his role as leader.

As a Tocho, he became a creature of instinct. He lived to hunt and kill, and put survival first. But even when his mind went no further than filling his empty belly, he knew he and the other shape-shifters were different from their namesake. Not only did they live together in contrast to a true cougar's solitary existence, but there were no females among them. Uneasy in their bodies, they craved something different, something rooted in a past they couldn't recall. Taking on human shape meant a return to intellect, but it wasn't enough, because none of them could remember what they'd been or done before coming or being forced here.

Throwing off concerns beyond his feline comprehension, he nuzzled Anaba's neck. The younger Tocho nuzzled back, a slow and contented rumbling purr letting Hok'ee know that Anaba's belly was full. The necessary communication over, they stood side by side for several minutes. When they resumed human form, he might ask Anaba what and how he'd killed. As for whether he'd ask Anaba if he'd sensed the female presence—

On the tail of a long purr, Anaba headed toward the rear of the cave, where he spent most of his nights. Left alone, Hok'ee started toward his own occasional nesting place, only to stop and face the cave's opening. Although he breathed deeply, cautiously, he didn't smell anything except the familiar canyon scents that drifted in. Maybe he'd been wrong. Maybe there hadn't been anything—

Walking silent and slow, he returned to the entrance. Restlessness built upon restlessness to tighten his muscles. He needed to become human again. That way he'd be able to think, to truly feel, to comprehend. But if he did, there'd be no sleeping tonight. Lifting his head, he screamed, then listened as the sound echoed off the canyon walls. Lonely. So lonely. Trapped.

What was that?

Pretending the unholy sound hadn't scared the hell out of her would have been a lie, something Kai refused to do to herself. What passed for dinner was over, and she was near the campfire making notes on what she'd done and observed today. Saying he was having trouble getting a signal on his cell phone, Garrin had taken off for a nearby rise, flashlight in hand. Approaching blips of light let her know he was returning. He'd done the same thing last night, and hadn't told her who he'd been talking to, not that she needed to know everything he was doing—did she? Just the same, with only the two of them here until other university personnel arrived, she'd hoped for more openness from him.

Well, as her dad had always said, ambition does strange things to a lot of people.

Another haunting howl brought her to her feet. Ice clamped hold of her spine. Beyond all logic, sexual energy warred with a case of nerves.

"What was that?" Garrin called out.

"Maybe a Chindi," she blurted without thinking.

"A what?" He sounded closer, because he'd broken into a run?

"Never mind. I was trying to make a joke about Navajo spirits. Sorry."

"I didn't hear what you said." She spotted his silhouette on the opposite side of the campfire from her. "Whatever it is serves as a reminder of why we brought weapons with us."

A flash of memory distracted her from thoughts of the pistol she'd reluctantly strapped to her belt. She'd heard that sound, or one close to it, but where? Closing her eyes, she concentrated. Not a zoo, because she'd never gone to one; just thinking about the sight and emotions of caged animals appalled her. But she'd visited several wildlife preserves where she'd observed the *inmates.* Unknown to staff and other visitors, she'd tapped into what the creatures there thought and felt about their existence. So many impressions had come to her at once that the tumbling bits and pieces had exhausted her, making it nearly impossible to isolate a predominant impact.

A lion? No, but close. Several other big cats came to mind, but because this part of the country was home to cougars, she settled on that as the sound's source. And yet cougar wasn't quite right, either.

Why? Because there was another quality in the lingering howl, a humanity.

Although she tried to tell herself that her surroundings were getting to her, she remained less than convinced when she finally gave up and crawled into her tent, then slithered into her sleeping bag. Dressed in her father's T-shirt and her own practical underpants, she searched for sleep.

Despite her best effort, however, she wound up on her back with her knees bent and legs spread, a practiced hand heading for her sex. The moment she made contact, her cunt muscles clenched, causing her to throw back her head and gasp. Wet heat streamed from her, the flood surprising and unnerving her. Determined to draw out the experience, she tried a barely-there touch, but the slightest brush of nail against labia simply added to the waterworks. Inner muscles tightened and relaxed, only to tighten and hold.

What was going on? Hot and heavy she could understand, but it had never happened like this without a member of the opposite sex doing his thing. How long had it been since she'd bonked or been bonked anyway? This build-up of untapped energy—holy cow!

Closing her eyes, she concentrated on escaping the hot prison wrapped around her before she lost her ever loving mind. Mentally reaching out, she brought a familiar image front and center. The man looming over her was faceless except for dark-as-hell eyes, but his body—six-and-a-half feet of wrapped and ready muscle, a cock large enough for her to get stuck on, and so long she'd feel it in her throat, his arms outstretched and only inches from her. Demanding she give as good as she was about to get.

Beyond caring whether Garrin heard, she whimpered and plunged two fingers into her hole. She bucked, whimpered again, fingers assaulting. Almost before she acknowledged what she'd done, she came. Silent, maybe. Hard, yes. Fulfilling, no.

Stalking. Muscles meshing. Nostrils flared. Night slipping away as the sun bloomed in the distance.

He moved from one ridge to another, leaping if he had no choice, but choosing to repeatedly climb and descend. Although he was barefoot, thick calluses protected him. He hadn't bothered with clothing, and his deep tan allowed him to sink into the background. As for whether his prey knew she was being followed—

It didn't matter. He'd capture her. Nothing she might do would change the outcome.

Patient despite the hunger that had started him on this journey, he kept pace with the woman walking below him. Her pace told him she was comfortable on her feet, and the way she continually scanned her surroundings spoke of an intense awareness. Whenever she looked in his direction, he froze, watched, breathed, waited.

They had this part of the world to themselves, so if he'd wanted, he could have already charged and grabbed, possessed. Instead of giving into impulse, he taught himself patience while taking his measure of the lean, long-legged woman.

She was different somehow from the few he'd fucked since his half-life began, unaware of her femininity, at peace with her body, her mind going places he couldn't comprehend. She was a seeker, a student, looking not just for answers but questions as well, restless.

That's why he was here today, to expose her restlessness and tap into it, to see if it mirrored his.

And if they had nothing in common?

It didn't matter. He was male, she female.

A heaviness grew throughout him. He couldn't expel all the oxygen he brought in, which meant her scent remained in him. The longer he looked at her, the stronger his belief that she was here for a reason, his reason.

Instead of giving into fantasies of what he intended to do to her once she was his, he let his mind slip off into a place designed by the past. He might not know much about that life, but he knew he'd once been an ordinary man, educated and intelligent, ambitious, even driven. In that place and time, women had been both intriguing and disposable. Nothing had mattered more than his designs for his life, plans and goals, not that he could remember what they were. The one thing he did know was that his death had been violent.

Steeling himself against the never-ending impact of what had ended his former life, he grabbed his cock and shook it. The distraction worked. And when his self-imposed assault was over, he turned his focus back to the woman. She'd added to the distance between them while faint images had swirled around him like smoke. Picking up his pace, he sprang from one boulder to another. Now instead of hugging the ground so she couldn't see him, he stepped into shadow. She stopped and, with her hand over her throat, looked in his direction.

Her contemplative gaze confused him. Her eyes, big and deep and compelling, took him into her, but not far enough. She was thinking thoughts he couldn't comprehend, feeling things—

Her, naked. Beneath him.

Again propelled by what had driven him all day, he started down the slope. The rocks clinging to the hillside threatened to break loose, but he couldn't make himself slow down. Restraint became little more than a thin veil. A simple gust of wind would rip it from him and turn him animal.

He wanted to be animal, wanted her in his grip, fighting uselessly, giving him a reason to impose his greater strength on her. He'd force her down, envelope her, show her who her master was.

He moved faster and faster, gravity and the steep slope taking him as if he was nothing more than a leaf in a raging river. Although he struggled to remain upright, he wound up on his ass, still sliding, rocks tumbling around him, the dust he'd created swirling out like a wave.

She screamed.

Dismissing his body's limitations, he stood and concentrated on her. She was looking at him and yet she wasn't, making him wonder if she was seeing his human form or Cougar. Her hand was still at her throat, her feet lost within the practical hiking boots, the wind pressing her shirt to her trim body. Then something kicked him off his feet, and once more he started tumbling over and over.

Too long a stretch of time passed before the ride ended. Despite the punishment he'd just gone through, his skin wasn't cut. He wouldn't bruise. There were no broken bones, no sprains.

He'd landed against a bush, legs tangled in some branches, and more of them digging into his chest. Scooting back on his ass, he freed himself and stood. The sun sent heat to stroke his skin and remind him of his nudity. From where he was, he couldn't see her and didn't think she could see him, but she soon would, and when she did—

"Hello? Are you all right? Hello."

A strong feminine voice, not frightened, yet. He wanted to tell her there'd been no damage done, but he hadn't used his human voice for so long he wasn't sure he remembered how. Besides, he wasn't here to talk.

Dismissing the dirt and debris clinging to him, he cocked his head. Her breathing had picked up, rhythm gone and anxiety deepening it. He didn't want her afraid, and yet he did, because the emotion made her vulnerable. He'd feed off that vulnerability and turn it to his advantage, weaken her.

Because if he didn't, she'd never stay with him.

Suppressing a growl, he took off in the direction his ears had alerted him to. He cursed himself for being clumsy, but hadn't he warned himself not to tackle that slope? He'd ignored the whispered caution because the beast in him had been so strong.

There. Her skin close, warm and soft. He started to pant, only to force himself to stop, to listen and feel. Becoming Cougar would make things easier. That way he'd approach her as an animal, a predator. Her reaction and response wouldn't matter because he wouldn't care. But he knew what she'd do if she saw the power-ful jaw and massive teeth. She'd run screaming from him.

Did he want that, or something else? A gentleness, quiet mo-ments and touches, standing with their arms around each other, her breath sighing over his chest.

Made uneasy by the question, he dug his nails into his palms until pain made him stop. His awareness now centered around the self-inflicted pain, he increased his speed. The action seemed to make his heart swell, to give it something to concentrate on. And the harder his heart beat, the more the sound consumed him. He was back to stalking, to closing in on his prey. As for what he'd do after he spotted her—

There she was, standing still as the dead, with an outstretched arm and something in her hand. Not slowing, he focused, but even when there was no doubt she was holding a chipmunk, he couldn't believe what he was seeing. Canyon rodents were fear-ful and illusive creatures who slipped away the moment they spotted something they didn't trust, and they trusted nothing. He thought this creature would be injured or even dead. In-stead, its whiskers twitched, and it seemed to be kneading the thumb with its front paws. Dismissing the tiny animal, he turned his attention to the woman. Her eyes were alight with some-thing soft and gentle, that something crawling deep inside him, slowing his stride. The woman had inclined her head toward the chipmunk, and her mouth was moving, almost as if she was talk-ing to it. Beyond all reason, the chipmunk seemed to be doing the same thing.

Then, as if it had been struck by lightning, the rodent leaped off the woman's hand and onto the ground. An instant later, it had disappeared.

"Wait!" she called out. "Come back, please."

Her emotion, more than what she'd said, settled around him. He felt both trapped and liberated by it, as if he'd been handed an unexpected piece of her. He was trying to decide what to do with the gift when she turned and looked at him.

Slow and undeniable realization changed her soft smile into intensity, and then alarm. She didn't speak or increase the distance between them. He, whose existence depended on his physical body, envied her single-mindedness. Every atom in her being was focused on him. He'd become her world, her everything.

Just as she'd become his.

"What do you want?" she said after a length of time.

He'd opened his mouth before acknowledging that he didn't want to talk to her. She was female, and he male. Nothing else mattered. Reminding himself that she was indeed looking at a man and not a predator, he started walking toward her. Her gaze trailed down him in acknowledgment of his nudity, and he wondered what the female in her thought of what she was seeing. Was her pussy responding, her nipples tightening, need pushing past caution?

"What do you want?" she repeated. She stretched her leg behind her in preparation for flight.

With the move, something switched inside him. The man faded, and the animal roared into life. Even in human form, predator blood flowed through him as he crouched and sprang. His cock surged.

Silent, she whirled and ran. Then, even before she'd reached full speed, she stopped and faced him, her attacker. Her uplifted arms were reflex, as was her open mouth. Her eyes said a thousand things, and nothing.

Equally silent, he clamped his hands around her middle, lifted her off her feet, and threw her over his shoulder. Despite her wild struggles, he kept her against him, one arm wrapped around her middle, the other immobilizing her legs. Her long hair grazed his shoulder blade, quieting the flames that threatened to consume him. Instead of screaming, she gave off short panting sounds that said she hadn't come to grips with what was happening to her.

Shock, surely she was in shock. And disbelieving.

He should take advantage of her mental state, so that by the time she'd regained her wits, she'd be completely under his control. But because he wasn't sure how that was accomplished, he continued to stand on widespread legs while her heat seeped into him. She weighed less than he'd anticipated, but maybe the truth was, the animal in him made a lie of her substance. She repeatedly tried to rear up so her upper body was off him, but after a few moments, she collapsed again, treating him to the press of breasts and long fingers futilely raking his skin.

He needed this, had been waiting for this—maybe forever.

At length, she stopped trying to scratch him and beat her fists against his buttocks. Each blow resonated in his crotch. His breathing quickened, deepened, and although she tried to kick him when he released her legs, he couldn't stop himself from stroking her buttocks through the denim.

"No, no, no," she chanted, her words garbled by her upside-down position. Mindless to the risk of falling, she twisted about.

After increasing his hold on her waist, he went back to patting and stroking. Then he swatted her ass. Yelping, she struggled to rake her boots over his thigh. At first he ignored her attempts, but then something snagged his flesh. Pain entered his consciousness and triggered the crouching beast within.

"Don't!" he bellowed, reinforcing his command with a blow to her ass that reverberated throughout her.

Screaming, she clawed and kicked. Instead of trying to twist free, she snagged his shoulder blade with her mouth and bit down.

More blows, each harder than the last, shook her off him. Determined to teach her not to bite him again, he continued to spank her, altering ass cheeks as he did. He had no doubt he was reddening her flesh, an image that tightened his groin. He loved the rhythm he'd found, relished in her frantic but useless attempts to escape her punishment. She cried out repeatedly, twisting and kicking, raking his buttocks until sweat coated her body and sealed them together.

"*You do not fight me, ever. Do you understand? Because if you do, I will punish you. And go on punishing until you've learned your lessons.*"

"*Let me go, please, let me go. Oh, God, someone, please, someone. No, no!*"

She was weakening. Although she continued to fight his control and punishment, strength was slipping from her muscles. The more she weakened, the easier it was for him to remember that he was human, at least partially. Although he continued his lesson, he no longer simply spanked her. When he wasn't reminding her of what he was capable of, he ran his hand down her thighs, caressing and controlling at the same time. She went limp when he did that, sighing and maybe sobbing, sweating anew. Relishing and learning from her submission, he gradually changed direction until he only occasionally punished. The rest of the time he learned the feel and warmth of a woman's legs, and dreamed of when her clothing was no longer between them.

His attempt to slide his thumb along her crack frustrated him and fed his hatred of the denim. If only he had a knife.

Changing tactics, he moved his restraining hand up from her waist. Assured that his hold around her spine would keep her from falling, he slid his free hand under her blouse. His first taste of the sleek smooth flesh made his temples pulse. If she moved, he'd be forced to forgo this exploration, but other than trembling, she lay limp and accessible. Sweat coated her skin in places, not that he minded. In fact, this proof of her reaction to becoming his captive gave rise to thoughts of how far he could take her.

Maybe, eventually, she'd want to stay with him.

Shaking off what had to be an insane man's fantasy, he slid palm and fingers over flesh he had no right to. In contrast to his *earlier punishment, he stroked, gifted. He could be gentle, somehow. She would grow to love it, somehow.*

Still showing her what his hand was capable of, he surrendered his fierce grasp on reality. In his mind she was no longer simply a woman he'd run down and imprisoned. Instead, she became his willing partner, a woman who cared for him, who understood and accepted his complexity, who didn't recoil in horror when faced with the truth of him.

When he could no longer keep the beast at bay, she'd accept the change with gentle hands and mouth. She'd kiss his muzzle, run her fingers over his fangs, stroke his ears and powerful jaw, cradle paw and claws on her lap. Her naked lap.

And when he rose up on his hind legs and hung his paws over her shoulders, his sex sliding between her legs from behind, she'd drop onto her hands and knees and offer herself, a human, to him, a Tocho.

It would no longer be a dream.

3

Not bothering to look at her watch, Kai crawled out of bed. Despite the high-desert middle-of-the-night cold waiting beyond her tent, she stepped outside. After a moment, she reached back in for her slippers and jacket, and put them on.

The moon was somewhere between a quarter and a third full. Back in civilization, it wouldn't stand much of a chance against the never-ending artificial illumination, but here where only a handful of trees reached into the sky, the moon dominated. Instead of heading for the campfire with its faintly glowing coals, she sat on a rock.

She was grateful for the moon's quiet light. At the same time, she needed to see more of her surroundings. With most of the shadows chased away, maybe she'd have an easier time shaking off what had wakened her.

Disturbing didn't go far enough in describing her dream. Vivid was right-on, and yet it had been more than that. Mostly she'd run, her lungs hurting and her heart on fire. Something had followed hot on her heels; she just wished she could remember what that something was—or did she? She'd been beyond afraid, overwhelmed. In some regards it hadn't been that different from the time she'd lost control on black ice on a mountain road, spinning in one circle after another, the trees coming closer and closer, knowing she was going to crash, everything happening in slow motion.

Incapable of lying to herself, she faced facts. If she'd ever had a stronger physical reaction to a dream, she couldn't recall. True, the nightmares following her father's violent death had deeply shaken her, and still returned occasionally to shatter her attempts at sleep, but that was to be expected.

But this?

Trying to tell herself that communicating, or trying to communicate, with Sani's wildlife had overloaded her system briefly satisfied her. Then the sensation of being watched overtook her. Who, or what, if anything, was responsible? And did she have anything to fear from—

"Kai, you okay?"

For the second time today, Garrin had stomped into the middle of her thoughts, not that she minded. "Just can't sleep," she said, looking around for him.

Although she heard his whispered footsteps, he was twenty feet from her before she spotted him. He was wearing socks. Like her, he had on a jacket. Unlike her, his jeans covered his legs. Unable to do anything about her condition, she bent her knees and tucked them under her jacket.

"What about you?" she asked as he sat on an adjacent rock. "Why aren't you in bed?"

"I have a lot on my mind."

"I'm certain you do. With everything you need to do before the others get here—"

"That's not the only thing. I know I shouldn't let it get to me, but that scream we heard—it couldn't be anything except a cougar. I just didn't think one would come so close."

"That surprised me, too."

"We're hardly in the middle of civilization, which means I need to adjust my thinking. Just because I don't have to worry about getting mugged doesn't mean I can drop my guard." He paused. "Look, if you think my imagination's gone over the top, let me know, but you're someone who's uniquely tuned into your surroundings. Do you ever get the feeling we aren't here alone?"

She hadn't known him long, but Garrin had struck her as practical and pragmatic, the ultimate in revering logic, which was why she didn't understand why he'd wanted to bring her onboard.

"I'm sure we're not alone. We could have attracted the attention of an owl or coyote, even the cougar we heard."

"That's possible. But . . ."

"Are you thinking it might not be an animal?"

"I'm not sure. I was hoping you could—but wait, you have to touch something before your psychic ability kicks in."

"Unfortunately. Maybe it's the Anasazi. For all we know, their ghosts could still be around."

"Is that what you think?"

"To be honest, I'm not sure how to respond." As she pondered whether ancient spirits might somehow still call Sani home, the sensation of being under something or someone's scrutiny reawakened in her. Along with it came unexpected awareness of her body, particularly between her legs. What was her problem? Hadn't she recently satisfied herself?

"We'll never know everything, will we?" she continued when he didn't say anything. "I've been places, such as some of California's missions, where I had no doubt that something remained of those who once lived there. One time I was in what I thought was a courtyard in one of the missions. A powerful sense of sorrow gripped me. Later I learned I'd been in a Native American graveyard."

"Maybe what you felt was tied into your—whatever it is?"

Someday she'd have to give a name to her *sight*. "I can't an-swer that." Long accustomed to keeping emotional space be-tween herself and the rest of the world, she went in search of a way to redirect the subject. "Do you really think we aren't alone out here?"

Even with the inadequate light, she was certain Garrin was mulling over her question. Why was it so hard for her to open up about what she'd been feeling? Was it because if she admit-ted she half-believed she was being watched, she might have to confess that the wondering was turning her on?

"I'm an academic," he said. "I'm not accustomed to thinking any other way. That's why I'm puzzled by tonight's sensations. Maybe—quite possibly, the explanation is that I'm not used to being outside the academic setting. What do they call what I've become—a desk jockey?"

"Good point."

"In contrast, I'm certain you've spent considerable time in the outdoors. All the work you've done for the National Park Service—and if everything I've heard about you is accurate, as I trust it is, in many respects you exist in a realm that's anything but conventional."

He was right about that. "Maybe it is the Anasazi. Maybe Chindi."

"I can't believe you're saying that."

According to historic Navajo belief, when a person died, a ghost or Chindi was released with the last dying breath. It was always an evil force determined to avenge some offense. Com-ing in contact with a Chindi was considered dangerous and caused sickness or misfortune. Naturally, the Navajo took every possible precaution to avoid contact with one, especially the worst of the worst, Skinwalker.

"You asked. I simply offered up an explanation."

"That's no explanation. It's ignorant superstition."

Don't dismiss what sustained a people for generations. "Perhaps, but we both sense something we can't explain."

Garrin grunted.

He was quick to dismiss ancient beliefs as superstition but saw nothing wrong with trying to use her gift to his advantage. Did the man really think he could have it both ways? "If I remember correctly," she said, teasing him a bit, "Chindi are seen only after dark. They appear as a coyote, a spot of fire, whirlwind, mouse, owl, even human form, or an indefinite dark object."

"For crying—how do *you* know so much about them? It's integral to my career, of course, but—"

"My father," she said softly. "He wanted the two of us to learn everything we could about the areas he was assigned to. In fact he wasn't that far from here—Canyon De Chelly—when he died. It was his second assignment there, with a lot of years in between."

"I didn't know that."

Distracted by memories of life between the ages of ten and twelve, when she'd accompanied her National Park Service-employee father as work took him into the heart of Navajo country, it took her a moment to turn the conversation back to emotionally safer ground. "Dad homeschooled me some of the time. I was an eager student, fascinated by my surroundings. I read everything I could get my hands on about the area's geology. And the history, of course—the humans who lived there. I'm sure you know that sometimes Chindi are nothing more than sound."

"We aren't getting sound tonight."

"No, we aren't." *Just sensation.*

Neither of them spoke for the better part of a minute, then Garrin broke the silence. "With everything we archeologists and anthropologists know about ancient societies, there's a lot we don't have the answers to yet."

"Such as?"

"Such as where beliefs like those involving where Chindi come from. We can speculate. And if that speculation finds its way into papers and texts, eventually it becomes fact. Frankly, I've never believed in anything I couldn't see, touch, or analyze."

"Then why did you seek me out?"

Garrin shifted position, making her guess his butt wasn't crazy about being up close and personal with a rock. In contrast, she half-believed she could sit here in relative comfort for the rest of the night—unless a Chindi came calling.

"Simple. My investigation led me to conclude that you indeed have the unique skills you're rumored to have, skills I believe will result in far greater knowledge about this area than would be possible otherwise."

She liked Garrin, respected him. He was determined to make the most of the rare opportunity Sani represented, even if it meant hiring an animal psychic. What did he care if his choice resulted in his being the brunt of his colleagues' jokes, as long as she contributed significantly to knowledge about Sani.

Garrin was asking her how she'd become aware of her special ability. Because she owed him more than the standard spiel, she explained that she and her father had long wondered if losing her mother at just two years old had opened a door, or valve, or something in her head, heart, and soul.

"My father was wonderful about letting me express myself. He never questioned anything I told him about *conversations* I had, first with the family pets, and then with any and every living thing I got my hands on. I think if he'd discouraged me, I would have shut that door. At least I would have tried."

"So your father is why you've been working with the Park Service? You were following in his footsteps."

"Not exactly. He's—he was a career employee, while all I've done is contract work."

"Park Service brass thinks highly of your talent. I'm surprised you left them for this."

She'd known Garrin would eventually ask for an explanation, she just hadn't expected it tonight, with the night so close. "The money's incredible."

"You're also running the risk of notoriety I know you aren't interested in. Depending on what we uncover here, the media could go crazy. You must have given your potential exposure a lot of thought."

She had, and if she hadn't needed distance between herself and her father's untimely death, she probably wouldn't be here. Coming to trust and fully believe in her unique connection with the animal world had been a long process. Fortunately, her father had known who within the Park Service could be trusted to protect her. She had no problem sharing what she discovered about the animals that lived in various national parks with those entrusted with their safety. To her way of thinking, what was the point of having a gift if it wasn't put to use. She just didn't want her name on any text, or worse, handed to the media.

Sensing a too-familiar headache coming on, she gave an exaggerated yawn. "You're right. I gave your offer a lot of thought. I was going to say no until you sent me the video of Sani. To think there's a chunk of turf here in the United States that's basically gone unexplored and unexploited—it's incredibly exciting."

"So it was Sani, and not the salary that tipped the scales?"

"Garrin, yesterday I held an old badger skull, and *saw* the Navajo arrow at the moment it struck him. What if . . ."

"If what?"

Maybe Garrin already knew what she was about to say, and that was why he sounded so intense. "Maybe someday I'll pick up the skeleton of a creature killed by the Anasazi. What if . . .

I *see* the truly ancient man or woman responsible for the killing? Be given insight into the way they lived, like no one else ever has."

Something warm brushed the back of her hand. She started, then relaxed when she realized Garrin had touched her. He'd leaned forward without her noticing, his larger size both comforting and disconcerting.

"Tell me something, Kai. Do you think that's possible?"

"Maybe."

"Just maybe?"

"I don't know. I just pray I'll learn the answer—that the centuries can be gaped."

"Why do you think I wanted you here?"

Don't say that! I don't know how to handle it. "You're asking a hell of a lot of me."

"Am I?"

Unwilling to take the conversation any deeper, she stood and tried another yawn. After saying something utterly forgettable about needing her beauty rest, she headed back to her tent. She had no doubt that he was staring at her.

What she didn't realize was that he continued to study her tent long after she'd disappeared, or that his hands were so tightly clenched, his nails dug into his palms.

Fall asleep, damn it. What's so frickin' hard about shutting off your mind?

A spider had gotten into the tent and was making its way along a side seam. Although Kai couldn't see it, she sensed the spider's single-mindedness. One thing she'd learned about nature's living organisms, the majority operated according to pre-programmed mechanisms. The spider wasn't thinking about what it was doing. Rather, it crawled because nothing had told it not to. It would remain on the move until it came in contact with something that switched a trigger in its rudimentary system. Maybe the trigger would *tell* it to create a web, although it might head toward her, or the heat she gave off.

Losing interest in something that had little to tell her, she replayed what she and Garrin had talked about. Although they'd cleared the air somewhat, the conversation had left her with an uneasy feeling. She just wished she understood why she felt the way she did. Facing her gift was one thing, especially when it might lead to greater understanding of an extinct culture. Knowing someone hoped to capitalize on what she learned was another.

Thoroughly tired of her self-absorbed thoughts, she tried to make peace with tomorrow's agenda. The rest of those the university had selected for the initial exploration would be here next week. In the meantime, Garrin was insisting that the two of them cover as much territory as possible. Instead of thoroughly examining the land near where the kiva had been found, she and Garrin were to do a *quick and dirty* search. She suspected he'd prefer not to let her out of his sight, but with the others breathing down his neck, so to speak, he didn't have much choice. What she most objected to was his insistence that she document her every move and finding, and share her notes with him.

What she hadn't put down was anything about the indescribable sensations that sometimes washed over her.

Too tired to throw up any defenses, she sank into sensation. It didn't matter that she was alone, her body didn't feel alone. Quite the contrary, she'd almost swear she was sharing the confining space with something or someone, a creature or human with the ability to slip under her skin. The initial inroad made, *he* spread his impact throughout her. Her quick, hard climax— had she really been solely responsible? Usually self-satisfaction took time and effort, but tonight—

Hunger, that's what it all boiled down to—and energy. Even with her muscles worn down and the blood in her veins slowed, she was once again in the grip of something wildly alive. Granted, her body remained motionless. But the rest of her was under siege, alive, aching.

Slipping, sliding, oozing, reality weakening. Grateful for what she hoped was sleep, she opened her mind and welcomed the nothingness.

Then something touched her.

4

Hissing like the animal she'd become, she waited. Her hair fell in wild tangles around her face and down her naked back. Limp strands draped over her exposed breasts. Weary beyond belief, she acknowledged the ropes that prevented her from doing anything about her hair or about taking her from this place of waiting.

How she'd gotten here mattered only a little. Cotton clung to her elbows, forcing her arms behind her, her breasts out. More rope circled her belly. Knotted in back, it also circled her wrists and forced her tethered hands against her ass. Yet more rope tightly caressed her thighs and ankles and kept her in a kneeling position. Immobile. That's what she was, imprisoned not just by her bonds, but by whoever had done this to her.

She was utterly and completely naked, forced into a position of servitude. Instead of railing against her captivity, she embraced it. Her captor, whoever he was, desired her body. Otherwise he would have killed her.

With nothing to do except wait and experience, she closed her eyes. Behind her lids, she continued to see herself as her captor surely would when he returned from wherever he'd gone. Kneeling, arms wrenched back, breasts hard and hot. Thighs modestly together, or they would be if she could cover them. As long as these ropes remained in place, he couldn't get to her sex, but he could and would do what he wanted with her.

And she wouldn't try to stop him.

The thud of feet against earth opened her eyes. Lifting her head, she stared in the direction the sound had come from. There he was, he, the man who'd claimed her. Why was he in shadow when sunlight rained down on her offered body? His smell was unfamiliar, as was the tempo of his breathing. Even his shadow was unknown to her.

She should be afraid, should be begging him to free her. To not kill her. Should be digging through her mind for her past. Instead, she inclined her head.

"You understand," he said. "Understand what's happening."

"Do I?"

"I hope you will," he said after a moment. "So much depends on—you're beautiful, exquisite in your captivity."

"The ropes—you're responsible for them, aren't you?"

"We both are."

"That can't be." A sliver of fear sliced into her and awakened her emotions. Panic was a breath away. "I wouldn't have tied myself like this. It's impossible."

"You let it happen."

"How can you say that? I don't remember—"

"Silence!" Stepping out of the shadows, he slapped her cheek. She didn't feel pain so much as a throb of sensation. He could do this to her, couldn't he? There was nothing she could do to stop him.

Shoulders aching from the strain he'd put them under, she leaned away from the bulk looming over her. Feeling herself start to lose balance, she struggled to straighten. The lesson learned, she concentrated on this man, her mysterious captor. Some part of her said this wasn't really happening, at least not yet. But it was the only reality she had.

"I have made you mine," he went on. "You belong to me because I must have something, because I will possess."

"Why me?" By the time she remembered that he'd ordered her to be quiet, it was too late. She steeled herself for another slap, only to have him grab her hair and force her head back. Her throat was exposed; it would be so easy for him to slice it open.

Maybe he'd tapped into her thoughts because, still gripping her hair, he stroked the taut tendons. She shivered, and yet fear didn't consume her. Her upthrust breasts grew harder. If he touched them, what then? Would she beg him to let go—or to caress, tease her nipples, close his mouth over them?

Out of control, sensuality seeping through her. In the grasp of a powerful stranger.

"This is my place." He released her hair but kept his hand over her throat. "You came to my land, mine and the others like me. A gift from Skinwalker."

Swallowing cautiously, she took a chance on speaking. "Skinwalker? Why would a ghost give me to you?"

"Because he took everything from me. Now it is time for Skinwalker to give back a little—to hand me the one thing I want, you."

"You don't know me."

"But I will." His grip carried enough strength that she'd wondered if every breath would be her last. Now, perhaps because he'd made his point, he began stroking her flesh there. She'd learned the folly of trying to move; there was nothing she could do except present her body to him, to wait. Feel. "Just as you will come to know me."

She couldn't make out his features, so how could he say that? In contrast, she had no doubt that her face, and more, was fully exposed to him. It had to be a dream—a dream that included strands snaked around her elbows, wrists, belly, and legs.

"Where are we?" she tried.

"I heard you call it Sani, The Old One. To us it is Tochona."

"Tochona? What does that mean?"

"Land of the Mountain Lion."

A shift, something changed inside her. Although she remained acutely aware of her helplessness, she broke free enough so she could concentrate fully on her captor, if that's what he was. The sense, the gift that set her apart, was stirring to life. Perhaps she'd shoved it aside so she could deal with what was happening to her, but maybe he'd separated from that part of her mind and soul. Whatever the answer, she longed to embrace the familiar. To learn everything she needed to.

"Touch me," she said. "On my face."

A grunt made her wonder if he knew what she was trying to do, but what did it matter as long as he granted her request?

"What are you afraid of?" she asked when he didn't move or speak. "You think I can hurt you?"

"You aren't ready for this; neither of us are."

"Ready for what?" Straining to see his features kept her from crying out or letting fear overwhelm her. "And if not now, when?"

Another tightening of the fingers on her throat brought her back to reality. "I sense you, and yet I don't." She kept her voice low and her body still. "You're a man, and yet . . ."

Unspoken words backed up inside her. She was still trying to sort through them when he ran his rough fingers from her chin to between her naked breasts. Shivering, she acknowledged the new life in her pussy. To be turned on at a time like this—

Ah, his hand under her right breast, cupping and gripping so when he pulled it upward, she rose off her haunches as far as the leg ropes allowed. Instead of trying to back away, she turned into him and leaned forward, resting her breast in his palm. Something not human spread out from him to whisper of secrets kept. She wanted to explore what he'd handed her, but it would have to wait until the sexual creature in her no longer demanded her full attention.

"Is this what you wanted to happen?" She glanced down at her breast. "You captured me so you could manhandle me?"

"Yes."

"That can't be all," she managed once she'd worked her way around the lump in her throat. "It'd be so easy for you to force . . ."

"For me to rape you?"

Insanely, she wanted to thank him, because not having to say the word made facing it easier.

"I'd never do that," he said.

"Then why the ropes?"

His silence made her wonder if he didn't know the answer. The breast in his palm felt heavy, protected and tested at the same time. In contrast, her other breast was lonely, lost somehow. She couldn't say whether this body was still hers; maybe ownership had been transferred to him while he was restraining her. He'd taken her clothes, giving rise to the question of what she'd have to do or say in order to get them back. She sensed words would have little effect on him.

His thigh brushed her shoulder, making her jump.

Then he took hold of her hair again and pulled her head back, and she was looking at his cock. It was only inches from her face, hard and radiating heat. She wasn't the only one naked.

Acting on a message as old as time, she inhaled his scent. Yes, that was male, human and—something else.

Still cupping her breast, he slid his hand outward until his fingers bracketed her nipple. He tightened his grip. Eyes unfocused and burning, she cautiously turned her head from side to side until stopped by the fingers laced through her hair. Her thighs burned; pins and needles worked their way up and then down her immobilized arms. She felt her hair slide against her back, felt the power in him, felt her response.

All woman, helpless and lost, sanded down to something elemental and primitive. Smelling something that wasn't quite human, her senses struggling to make sense of it.

"This is what will bring us together," he said.

Before she could begin to guess what he was talking about, he released her aching nipple. Then he leaned down and ran his hand between her legs and against her crotch. Hissing catlike, she lifted herself again, parting her thighs as much as she could. His hand easily parted her flesh. Then deserted.

Her head was free again, her scalp still tingling from where he'd pulled on her hair. She was grateful for the ability to sit upright again, but she'd already learned that he was a creature of change and possession. He'd lay claim again. All she could do was try to be ready for him.

To tell herself she didn't want this.

Something pressed against her cheek, drawing her attention there. Almost before she'd realized that the something had been his cock, the touch was gone. Then he was on his knees next to her.

"You're beautiful," he whispered. "Mine."

Was it as simple as that, a few ropes and touches, and she belonged to him? But for what purpose?

"What if I don't want—"

"But you do."

"How can you say—"

There was his hand again, resting on her thigh, leaving no doubt of what it was capable of doing. She started to clamp her legs together, but the strength for that washed out of her. She was a piece of merchandise, gift wrapped for him. No, she admitted with her temples pounding, she was hardly an unwilling participant.

His fingers went on the move once more, burying themselves between her thighs, sliding against her mons, coming closer and closer to her labia. Widening her stance once more, she let her head sag. Now her hair slid over her shoulders as if trying to shelter her. She wanted his hand where it was, and her body locked in place.

From where he was, he couldn't enter her, but her cunt must not know that because it wept for him, oozing and hot. She was becoming loose-limbed, all bundled nerves and not enough thought.

"You're ripe, Kai. Ripe and ready." He turned his hand so it was palm up, and pressed relentlessly against her sex, demanding she make herself even more accessible to him. Ignoring her protesting knees, she slid them along the ground until she was obscenely spread. She kept her head down and eyes closed, breathing deep but quick, trying to sort through the impressions but learning not enough.

It was her body's fault! She couldn't possibly begin to make sense of what or who he was with her temples pulsing, belly knotted, pussy streaming.

"You can't, you can't . . ."

"Yes, I can. And by the time I'm finished, I'll know I can trust you."

Him, trust her? Shouldn't it be the other way around? "That's why—the ropes?" Two, then three breaths before she trusted herself not to throw herself onto her back so her pussy was open to him, fully and wildly open. "So you can—what—remake me?"

"Not that. I don't want you to be anything except what you are."

How could he say that when she'd never known this wild child lived inside her? Deep breaths failed to cool her. If anything, the damnable dangerous flames leaped higher than they had a moment ago, all because he continued stroking—stroking.

"What—what are you?" she sobbed, cheeks flushed, breasts feeling as if they'd explode. "Who?"

"Hok'ee."

"I don't under—"

"The Abandoned One."

Then he was gone, his hand no longer sending sensual messages throughout her core, his cock not brushing her skin, that deep half animal voice silenced.

Shaking and sweating at the same time, she forced open her eyes and looked around. Night greeted her, night with its secrets and deep shadows, and the memory of the creature who called himself Hok'ee.

At length the ropes fell away, but she didn't try to stand. Neither could she stop her tears, or still the hand now cupped around her sex.

"You sound tired. I thought you were used to sleeping on the ground."

"I am," Kai told Dr. Carter. Cell phone reception had been spotty, but the head of the archeology department was coming through clearly this morning. She just didn't understand why he'd punched in her number instead of Garrin's.

"Better you than me," he said. "My back would never make it."

"I always use a certain air mattress. Expensive, but an occupational necessity. Did you try calling Garrin? Maybe you'd like me to find him."

"No, no, that isn't necessary. He's already out and about then?"

"We both are," she explained, although at the moment Garrin was in his tent. "There's so much territory we want to cover."

"So he kept telling me. Kai, I want you to be honest. He isn't pushing you, is he? I have to ask because it isn't yet eight o'clock."

Granted, she hadn't expected to see Garrin eating breakfast when she crawled out of her tent this morning. Fortunately, she'd put on a sweatshirt first. Otherwise—her attention strayed to the rope marks on her arms. Rope marks? From a dream? "I'm fine." She wasn't sure who she was trying to convince. Maybe herself.

"You aren't having second thoughts about what you're doing here?"

Dr. Carter was intense. At first she'd taken him for the stereotypical absentminded professor because of his long graying hair, whiskers, and ready for the rag bag clothing, but she'd learned he simply didn't give a damn about his exterior image. In many respects, she understood. After all, what took place between her ears was much more compelling than whether or not she had on makeup.

"Not second thoughts so much as wondering about my ability to sort through all the impressions I'm being hit with," she admitted. *And that's the least of it.*

"I hadn't thought about that. Of course I have no idea what it's like for you."

Dr. Carter's voice was the only connection she had with the world beyond Sani. She didn't want to lose it. Thinking about him reminded her of his prominent Adam's apple, which looked as if it could slice through the spare skin covering it. Unfortunately, she was also reminded of the big, strong hand that had been on her throat last night. She hadn't imagined that, she hadn't! Maybe.

"I'm sorry we didn't have the opportunity for a decent conversation," Dr. Carter continued. "I wish I knew more about your psychic abilities. Kai, hopefully it goes without saying that I agreed completely with Dr. Gentry's decision to hire you."

"I'm glad to know that." She sipped on her coffee, then shuddered. Tomorrow morning she wouldn't let Garrin get near the pot.

"I trust you didn't have any doubts. Frankly, your ability fascinates me. My world is cut and dry, nothing but reality. Then I meet someone who, what, talks to animals?"

"I haven't had what I'd call a conversation with anything four-legged," she said, trying for a light tone. "Maybe I'm stepping out of line, but I'd like to know something."

"Of course."

"Do you believe what I do is the real deal? Maybe I'm a convincing con."

"I don't know," he answered, thankfully without pausing first. "Being able to communicate with animals—I've never come across anything like that in my twenty-plus years of academia. The important thing is what you're able to do with whatever's going on inside you."

I don't know what's happening to me, why I have those marks on my wrists and ankles, why I could swear a man's hand was on my sex last night.

"Thanks for being open-minded. I appreciate it," she said. "I might need more than just Garrin vouching for me."

"He's Garrin to you?"

"That's what he told me to call him, why?"

"Nothing." In the silence that followed, she imagined Dr. Carter sitting at his large, old, sparse desk in a room that begged for a desk half that size. "Kai, I've known Dr. Garrin for many years, although perhaps *know* isn't the operative word. He's an ambitious man in an ambition-driven line of work. As I'm certain you know, the competition among academics can be fierce. And as such, the competitors are reluctant to play their hand around each other."

"What are you saying?"

He sighed loud enough for her to hear, despite the distance between them. "Sani is the most exciting thing to happen to the archeological world in many years. And for the site to be practically in the university's backyard is doubly exciting. Be glad you weren't around to witness the posturing that took place while the president was deciding who to put in charge of the expedition."

"It was fierce?"

"Exceedingly. If it wasn't for this knee of mine, I would have pulled rank. Kai, I called because I don't want you to lose sight of the fact that ambition can do some amazing but not necessarily honorable things to people."

"You're saying what?"

"Exploitation," Dr. Carter said softly. "If Garrin can exploit any of us on his way to fame and fortune, I fully expect him to do so. Him, or anyone in this position. It's human nature."

"I guess."

"No guess to it, Kai. I'm serious. Keep your eyes open."

5

Dr. Carter's warning remained with her the rest of the morning, not because what he'd said hadn't occurred to her, but that, coming on top of things that had happened over the past few days, it had her feeling as if her world were slipping out of control. Up until now she'd managed to convince herself that she'd been making good and valuable use of her time by going wherever the muse or her mind, or whatever it was, took her. She trusted her instinct. Said instinct coupled with her psychic ability might well result in something remarkable, maybe earth-shattering.

But that wasn't it at all, was it? Truth was, lack of purpose and outright hesitation had kept her from letting Sani's creatures truly open up to her.

Sani? Her *dream* man had called this area Tochona.

Land of the Mountain Lion.

Initially Garrin had wanted them to remain within sight of each other, but she'd finally convinced him that his presence wasn't helping. She needed to be alone. He'd argued that it wasn't safe for her to be on her own, especially because of the unreliable cell phone reception. Mindful of Dr. Carter's warning, she'd stood fast. If she'd been a man, she'd pointed out, he wouldn't be saying what he was. Then because even that hadn't made the desired impact, she'd asked Garrin whether he trusted her to share whatever she learned with him.

Not bothering to respond to his insistence that of course he trusted her, she'd fastened her water bottle and pistol to her waist, and tucked her cell phone in the rear jean's pocket that didn't hold her digital. She told him she was heading for an upper canyon about a mile away, where hopefully ponderosa pine and gamble oak provided shelter for any number of living creatures. She promised to be back by dark.

Guessing he was watching, she headed down the valley floor until she reached a sloping canyon wall and started climbing it. Then, taking advantage of the cracks and crevices in the wall, she slipped out of sight. When she was certain he couldn't see her, she started down again.

Just thinking about her true destination did unwanted things to her nerves, but she'd put off examining the summer-thin creek a half mile away long enough. Yes, the upper canyon held possibilities, but sooner or later, every living and once-living creature needed water.

The sheer number of creatures might make it impossible for her to sort through the din, but she wouldn't be doing the job she'd been hired for if she didn't give it her best shot. The creek had changed course over the hundreds or thousands of years it had been in existence, but she might be able to trace those changes. As for the reasons behind her hesitation—bottom line was that if anyone except her and Garrin was in Sani, that person or persons wouldn't venture too far from the only water source around.

So what, she chided herself as the sun made the back of her neck itch. What did she think was going to happen? Just because she'd had the unsubstantiated feeling that someone or something had been following her—

That was it, wasn't it? Alone she was vulnerable.

And alive, she admitted, as awareness of both her world and body spun through her. Wonderfully, excitingly, even frighteningly alive.

Placing her hand over her neck to protect it from the heat, she studied her surroundings. It took almost no imagination to fill the area with the ancient Navajo who'd once made this area their home. According to her research, the tribe had lived in harmony with this seemingly arid land. Not only had they kept livestock, they'd successfully planted the moisture-seeking corn that had been their staple food, and had developed a complex civilization. In contrast, modern people, even the Navajo, had little use for this area because of the minimal rainfall and remote location. Otherwise it would have been developed, or exploited.

Why was she faulting the generations that had come after the original Navajo? After all, Sani had remained a time capsule of sorts.

Chiding herself for allowing herself to get distracted, she turned her attention to the ground. She easily made out the prints left by birds in the sandlike soil, and unless she was mistaken, that meandering track had been the work of a snake. Birds and snakes. Who else were her fellow residents?

At the question, an unwanted possibility resurfaced. What if she was sharing the land with her stalker?

"Are you out there?" she called out, surprising herself. "And if you are, what are you waiting for?"

Surrounded by heat and the smell of sage, Hok'ee studied the woman below him. His senses had already told him that she was new to this land, and yet she carried herself as if she was accustomed to walking in the wilderness. Tochona didn't yet love her, but the promise was there. Maybe that's why she fascinated him, because she saw and felt things the handful of other out-siders who'd come here didn't.

That wasn't the only reason.

Muscles taut against the sex-beast that longed to claim his soul, he nevertheless risked his sanity by continuing to watch her. She'd been by herself before but never this far from the man, and he'd understood that she was leery of something.

Maybe him.

He needed her under his body and control, needed his hands on her, his cock buried in her.

What was it Anaba had told him as the two had watched her earlier—that if he fucked her, he might never be the same. He'd asked his companion, his friend, how he could say such a thing, and Anaba had replied that as Tocho, they needed to make their peace with solitude. Instead, the woman was making him question his solitude, even fight it. But it was a useless battle because eventually she'd leave.

Unless he kept her here.

Dropping to his haunches, he accepted the dark energy wait-ing at his body's edges. Staying in human form took effort and eventually exhausted him, which was why he never spent more than a night or two away from Tochona. No matter how hard it was, he'd never allowed one of the city women he bedded to see the beast beneath the civilized façade.

Although he'd given into the beast long enough to hunt and kill last night, when he was done, he forced himself back into his human skin. All too soon he'd be spent, helpless. If she saw—

There, her scent sliding into him, making his cock stir once more.

Earlier he hadn't bothered with clothing, and his nudity had given him an excuse to remain hidden, but this morning Anaba had handed him a pair of jeans in silent challenge. When he'd refused to take them, his friend had asked what he was afraid of.

Nothing, he'd retorted. His hand still extended, Anaba had

ordered him not to lie, because they both feared their future. The question was if he had the courage to try to bring a woman into that future.

Running his hands down his thighs, Hok'ee acknowledged the age-softened denim covering them. He hadn't bothered with a shirt, but boots meant he didn't have to watch his footing. Several lengths of stolen rope lay curled in his pockets.

There was no reason not to approach her, nothing except that once he had, there'd be no going back, no more simply losing himself in Cougar-thoughts.

Shaking himself like an animal caught in a downpour, he stood and started down toward her. Keeping to the shadows, he refused to answer the question of what he intended to do once he'd revealed himself to her. He didn't know, that was the hell of it. He didn't know.

About to increase his pace, he stopped and studied what she was doing. She too was no longer walking. Instead of looking at her surroundings as she'd done countless times, she'd dropped to her knees and was digging at a boulder. The change from prey behavior surprised him. Only a few minutes ago, she'd exhibited the wariness of a deer or antelope. Now she seemed to have forgotten who and where she was.

The rock weighed over a hundred pounds and was half-buried. What could she possibly want with it? Her behavior reminded him of a fox intent on uncovering a burrowing rodent, but even with the smells and sounds of food nearly within reach, a fox remains aware of his surroundings. In contrast, she risked breaking her nails as she worked to expose what he couldn't imagine her having any interest in. She concentrated on one spot, digging deeper and deeper. When she stopped to wipe her forehead and work discomfort from her back, excitement brightened her expression. Then she went back to her task.

Struck by an idea, he descended until he'd reached the flat area she was on. Not giving himself time to change his mind, he closed in on her. Despite her hunched-over position and the dirt on her jeans and across her forehead, she was beautiful.

In his mind, he stepped behind her so he could rest his hands on the small of her back. Looking over her shoulder at him, she'd spread her legs and place both hands against the ground. All that was left for him to do was to unzip her jeans and pull them and her underpants down as far as they'd go. That accomplished, he'd drop to his knees and bury himself in her waiting hole. They'd fuck.

Something crunched under his boot. Tense, she straightened and scrambled around, looked at him. Surprise erased her earlier excitement. Then she fixed her gaze on his naked chest, and surprise turned into caution.

"What are you—I didn't know anyone—who are you?"

He'd once had a human name, at least he must have, not that he remembered it. Although he could have lied and handed her one of the names he used when getting a woman to agree to have sex with him, he didn't. "What are you doing?" He indicated the rock.

"I sensed—look, you must know you startled me." Using the rock for leverage, she got to her feet. "I didn't know anyone was around. How long have you been watching me?"

Time meant little to him, not that he was going to tell her that. After days and nights of watching and thinking about her, being this close shouldn't have him so off balance. But not only couldn't he think how he might answer, a stirring deep inside him served as a reminder of how unreliable his human form was.

"Even if you fully exposed that"—he indicated the rock— "you won't be able to move it."

"I'm sure it looks strange. But I'm serious, have you been watching me?"

More than you'll ever know. "It's been interesting."

"I'm delighted you're amused," she snapped. "But it's time for you to go back to whatever you were doing." She frowned.

"You're a hiker? Where's your backpack? No one goes hiking around here without—"

"I live here." All his fantasies were behind him and here he was, not knowing what to say or do. Despite her small stature, her forearms were muscled, and from watching her walk, he knew the same was true of her legs. Good. His mate should be prepared for a physical life.

Mate? What was he thinking?

Another powerful and dangerous stirring in his core forced him to concentrate on remaining in the form she wouldn't find terrifying. Once he had her under his control, it wouldn't matter so much, but until then—

"We were assured there were no permanent residences in Sani, and I've certainly not seen anything that would change my mind." She sounded as if she was accusing him of lying.

"Sani?"

Something more than puzzlement spread across her features. She ran her hands into her back pockets, her gaze fastened on him. Instinct told him she was a heartbeat away from running. For the first time, he noted that she carried a pistol. "The name given to this area," she said slowly. "Surely you know that."

"Not Sani, Tochona."

One second became another as she remained frozen. At the same time, her expression deepened, almost as if she were looking inward. "Tochona," she whispered. He sensed she'd heard or said the word before. "Land of the Mountain Lion."

He'd been wrong to believe there was nothing between them. As for what that something was or could become, he couldn't be sure, and clamping down on what he knew was insanity, he nodded. The inner power he had such little control over was locked in battle with the man he'd once been. That power, that beast, needed to fuck. Her.

"What?" she asked, her voice strangled. "You keep staring at me."

He blinked, then went back to doing what she'd just accused him of. His sight was becoming keener, his ears more sensitive, and he had to struggle to think of anything to say. It was her woman-smell, the scent of sex.

And his animal hunger.

"I'm going to leave now," she said.

Although he heard the words, they didn't register until she took a step backward. The instant she did, muscles bred to stalk and attack woke. He wouldn't let his prey escape. More comfortable in his skin than when he'd been trying to pass himself off as an ordinary man, he kept pace with her retreat. His fingers and toes tingled in anticipation of becoming claws. He wanted to close his fangs around her neck.

Then she pulled her hand out of her pocket, and her fingers curled around her weapon.

"I'm not going to hurt you," he said, although he wasn't sure he could keep his promise.

"Sorry." The pitifully small pistol held high and aimed at him, she backed away. "But I'm having a hard time believing you."

A worthy opponent, countering with more than panic and foolish flight. He liked that; it challenged him. The longer he studied her, the more he became aware of feline possibilities. She might be woman complete with breasts made for his hands and mouth, but she was more than that. Given time and skill, maybe he could draw the animal inside her to the surface. Wrapping himself in the question of how he'd accomplish that, he lengthened his stride and cut down on the distance between them.

"I'm not alone. My companions—all I have to do is yell, and they'll come running."

"Not if I don't let you," he said, and sprang.

Turning his upper body at the same time, he slammed his

shoulder into hers. She stumbled, struggled to regain her balance, stumbled again and fell.

She landed on her buttocks, hands back, slamming against the ground. Her weapon flew free. Before she could reach for it, he stepped on it. Her mouth opened, and her throat worked. Intent on what had to be done, he dropped to his knees, closed both hands around her neck, and pushed back until her arms collapsed under their joined weight. As her face reddened, he considered choking her into unconsciousness, but what if he was too strong, or the beast took over?

Measuring his self-control in seconds, he released her neck only to clamp a hand over her mouth. She flailed at him, punching and scratching, twisting so violently he wondered if she didn't care whether she injured herself. Maybe she was too terrified to think.

For a cougar, taking advantage of a prey's panic meant doing what needed to be done while the prey was paralyzed with fear. Ignoring her attempts to wound him, he grabbed her shoulders and flipped her onto her belly. Keeping her face-down prevented her from screaming while he pulled rope out of a front pocket.

She continued to fight, her breathing quick and loud. When he tried to grab a wrist in preparation for pulling her arm behind her, she yanked it free. She kept trying to lift her head. Even with his own breathing matching hers and his head roaring, he made his decision. The next time she lifted her head, he was waiting with the rope. It pressed against the underside of her nose, prompting him to tug it lower so it settled into her open mouth. Quickly knotting the strand behind her, he looped it around her head two more times until her mouth was filled with it.

Silenced. Trying to bite her gag.

Victory surged through him to swallow more of the man. Another cotton length landed in his left hand, his right clamping down on a small wrist, forcing her arm up and against her back. Switching his hold to her forearm gave him the necessary leverage to secure her wrist. That done, he used the loose end to hold her arm in place while he captured her other arm.

Hissing, she struggled to turn over, prompting him to straddle her hips. His knee landed on her water bottle, popping the lid and spilling water on the thirsty ground. The hot feel of her battle ran into his cock. His world started turning red; his skin was becoming too small.

Hurry, hurry, he ordered as he lashed her wrists together, one over the other so her elbows remained deeply bent. He could barely see her wrists under the multitude of strands, but he liked it like that. The sense of power was like being drunk, and alive. More alive than he'd been since his *awakening*.

A quick, sharp blow to the small of his back reminded him that her legs were capable of inflicting damage, albeit minimal. Besides, he had to immobilize her while he still had hands and not claws.

Spinning around, he snagged a jeans cuff and pulled it toward him, keeping her leg bent while placing a loop around her ankle. Her boots were so short they didn't get in the way, and her socks assured he wouldn't cut off her circulation. He thought she'd give up once he'd knotted the ankle restraint, but she didn't, prompting him to grab the other jeans cuff and bend that leg toward him.

Clamping an arm around both limbs and pressing them against his chest while roping her ankles in place ate up what remained of his ability to plan and execute. Even when he was sure the knots were adequate, he added another. Then, shaking almost as much as she was, he let her go.

She bucked under him, shuddered. Then, making a sound he'd never heard, her legs dropped to the ground. Much as he wanted to get off her so he could truly see what he'd accomplished, he remained with his buttocks against the small of her back. Her crack was mere inches away, her cunt separated from him only by their clothing. He started to lick his lips, only to bite down on the lower one in an attempt to distract himself from the ever expanding creature just beneath his surface.

He'd done it. Captured her.

She was his.

6

Her head felt like it was about to explode, and if he didn't get off her, she wouldn't be able to get enough air into her lungs.

Funny how she could focus on the minute details when her world had been turned upside down, Kai thought, even as her mind banged into one barrier after another. She'd never once in her life been unable to move. A stranger to hospitals, even laughing gas at the dentist's office, she'd taken control of her body for granted. Now she no longer had that, and what—her brain had quit?

Rope was jammed in her mouth, making her drool, her wrists were crisscrossed at the small of her back, and her legs had been forced together. Most of all, the stranger who'd done those things to her was sitting on her.

Stranger?

Not entirely. The thought slid away into the swirling mass of her mind, only to resurface again. She'd known what he was going to call Sani before he'd said the words because, damn it, because she'd dreamed—

No! Not just a dream. Something more.

Making no sound other than his ramped-up breathing, he slid off her. Her back sighed in relief. Not considering what she was risking, she turned her head so her face no longer pressed into the ground and she was looking at him.

Not a stranger, not completely. She'd seen him before. In her dream.

That's what she needed, for it to be night with her in her sleeping bag, bits and pieces of impressions mixing as dreams usually did. She didn't want these details, or to be watching the way his chest lifted and fell as he breathed. Most of all, she needed use of her arms and legs, to be able to speak, to yell at the top of her lungs.

Those things weren't happening.

She'd never been studied with such intensity. But maybe—maybe noting what she looked like wasn't what he was about. After all, he could have simply asked to take her picture.

Immobilized. Rendered helpless by some man who'd carried the necessary ropes to make that possible.

A man who'd told her his name in her dream.

Hok'ee, The Abandoned One.

Feeling even more overwhelmed, she closed her eyes. The moment she did, she knew she'd made a mistake. What if he tried to do something she didn't want done?

What was she thinking? He'd already tied her up. Whether she watched or didn't made no difference. She'd become his to do what he wanted with.

Red-blooded male said everything and yet not enough about him. Strangely, admitting that was somewhat liberating. She no longer had to pretend he had motives other than the obvious. He hadn't kidnapped her for ransom, she was no political prisoner, no bargaining chip. He wasn't some crackpot who'd taken a dislike to her for reasons known only to him.

Sex. This was about sex.

A line of fire shot down her spine. It settled in her crotch to weaken her legs and kick up her awareness of her breasts. When it suited him, he'd strip off her clothes and get down to business. He'd have to untie her legs before he could make certain obvious use of her, wouldn't he? Maybe not. Maybe he'd stand her up and lean her over something so her ass was displayed. He'd have already pulled down her jeans and panties around her ankles, hobbling her even more than she was. Her shirt would be in shreds, fabric flapping in the wind, bra straps sliced, breasts exposed to the sun, and him.

More fire lapped at her. As it threatened to consume her, an even greater heat cupped her sex and held on.

Not turned on, damn it, not! Fantasizing about forced sex was one thing, a way of helping her get off when it was just her and her toys. The real thing—damn it—she didn't want!

Did she?

Unable to answer, she finally thought to open her eyes. From what she could tell, he hadn't moved, which made her wonder how long he could remain motionless and catlike.

As the word catlike expanded inside her, she opened herself to something that had happened while he was tying her up. She'd been consumed with fighting him, of course, but even as she struggled to free herself, his hands had hinted at deep and vital messages. She had something to learn from and about him, somehow. Beneath the surface waited more than a man.

That, more than her helplessness, robbed her of the ability to anticipate. She was still trying to come to grips with his feline element when he rolled her onto her side. By bending her legs, she managed to remain in position. To wait.

He was extending a hand toward her, the movement utterly graceful and confident. Wishing she could say something, anything intelligible, she lifted her head, only to let it fall. His fingers slid over her jawbone before reaching her throat. Instead of being afraid he intended to choke her, she wrapped herself in waiting and became his possession. There was nothing she could do, no reason to struggle, and no voice for screaming.

His fingers weren't gentle, but neither did he cause her pain as he caressed her neck. It dawned on her that perhaps he was trying to erase whatever marks he'd left there, and she wished she could thank him.

The ropes had no give to them. There was no way she could alter the position he'd placed her in, only being what he wanted.

The time of existing and floating ended when he stopped stroking and started to unbutton her shirt. Maybe because she'd already made her peace with the inevitable, she simply studied what she could see of what he was doing as button after button gave way. He left her breasts covered, her bra untouched.

More of her will stripped away. More of his taking over.

Cheeks flushing and lungs demanding more air than she could provide, she offered no resistance when he sat her up. She would have tumbled over if he hadn't straightened her legs. As it was, she had to lean over to keep her balance. Unable to watch him any longer, she sagged in her bonds like a toy waiting for its owner.

She had to stop thinking that way! she chided herself as her gaze locked on her bound ankles. What had happened to her will and determination, her fight? She didn't want this, damn it. She'd prosecute him to the ends of the earth once she was free.

If she was ever free.

The notion that she might remain within his grasp forever sent her mind to spinning again. At the same time, her forced-together legs shifted her attention to what was happening between them. Pressing her thighs together had long served to get her sexual juices going, and she'd occasionally fantasized about ropes around said thighs. This was far different from make-believe, though, deeper, cleaner somehow, more elemental.

Still kneeling, he took hold of her shirt and pulled the two halves apart. Not content with that, he tugged the fabric off her shoulders and then down her arms until the well-worn thing was against her wrist ties. Another step taken, one more step closer to her becoming his. Completely his.

The fire hit again, between her legs this time. She had no choice but to clamp them together and to feed off the flames, to give into something she'd carried in her since puberty. She wanted to be a man's possession, this man's possession. To have her will stripped away and hunger exploited. She needed to scream out forced climaxes, to kneel before him, and take his cock into her mouth.

Maybe most of all, she needed to be shown how to give and receive pleasure.

He wasn't speaking, wasn't touching her. A downward glance reinforced what she already knew. Her breasts spilled out of the top of her bra and heaved like a romance heroine's. He watched, his eyes narrowed and catlike.

Shaken out of herself, she focused on his expression. Although he'd slipped back into motionlessness, she sensed an inner struggle. Something was happening to him that he didn't want, and yet he did. His nostrils had flared, and his hands were clenched, his eyes nearly rolling back in their sockets.

That's why she needed her freedom back, not so she could run away, but so she could run her hands over his taut-as-hell body. Over and over again, she'd stroke his flesh, and in the end he'd give up his secrets. She'd know who or what he really was.

An errant thought distracted her from her desire to learn all she could about her captor. Garrin didn't expect her back for hours, but if she didn't return by dark, he'd grow concerned. He'd first try to contact her via cell phone, and when she failed to answer, his concern would grow. He might contact Dr. Carter, and they'd debate whether she'd injured herself, whether she might have lost or broken her cell.

As for when people would start looking for her, that would

probably be Garrin's decision. The problem was, she'd lied about where she was going, which meant they'd search in the wrong place.

Mentally berating herself for her role in her predicament, she turned her attention back to her captor. He still hadn't moved, and yet something seemed to be rippling through him. Emotion, maybe?

Having rope in her mouth was more than uncomfortable; being unable to communicate was nearly as disconcerting as her inability to move. She'd already tried to come to grips with what he could and might do, now that he held the upper hand, but studying the mysterious man brought reality back in spades. This wasn't an idle daydream or a sexual fantasy she could bend and mold to meet whatever her imagination wanted. Sitting here with her shirt gone and her limbs useless was reality.

She started shivering. Panic nibbled at her nerve endings. What if her kidnapper was a killer?

She'd started to lean forward in preparation for curling in on herself when he stood up, only standing didn't say the half of it. Sleek and beautiful, his body glided effortlessly from one position to another. Once again she acknowledged his feline qualities.

He stepped into her personal space, widened his stance, took hold of her elbows, and pulled her to her feet. Unable to balance herself, she started to tip over. He kept her upright by snaking an arm around her waist and offering his hip as support. She couldn't bring herself to look up at him.

In his grip, belonging to him, surrounded by him. Swimming in sensations he was responsible for. Wanting something she shouldn't, something dangerous. And heavy with the word sex.

Turning her a little, he switched his hold from her waist to her hips. His other hand closed over an ass cheek. He loomed toward her, his breath damp and warm on the side of her neck as she tried to lean away from him.

His hands weren't cruel, just *there*. And she didn't fear his breath so much as its ability to unnerve her. This wasn't suppose to happen. In a civilized world, liberated women didn't turn their bodies over to strangers.

Liberated? Not anymore.

Hell, she didn't even have water anymore.

Feeling his muscles tense, she tried to anticipate but couldn't, because his body was speaking to her, saying things she needed to hear.

Then he pushed her away, reached behind her, and un-snapped her bra. A blur of movement and her bra was up and off her breasts. Lightning sizzled in and between them, then rolled through her belly before heading lower. The lightning, strong as ever, lapped at her pussy. Out of control? She was just beginning to comprehend the concept.

Her knees buckling, she had no choice but to lean toward him for support. He caught her as he had before. That done, he held her tight against him, his cock grinding into her belly. Her pelvis dipped toward him, and his grip tightened, pulling her even closer.

She couldn't feel her feet, couldn't think about them. Her thigh muscles clenched and started to tremble. And her cunt, her damnable cunt, screamed to be let free. Fairly dripping sweat, she stood like the hot animal he'd turned her into while his mouth came closer and closer to her throat. At the last moment, somewhere between self-determination and contact, she lost courage. Although she leaned as far to the side as she could, it wasn't enough.

Too-short moments later, his teeth raked her neck. She shivered and moaned behind her rope gag. Although her knees were useless, she struggled to put distance between them. Even when his hold tightened and his teeth closed lightly over a tendon, she whimpered and fought. As for whether she was trying to escape him or herself, she couldn't say.

A sound she'd never heard penetrated the swirling confusion in her brain. At first she thought she was responsible, then there was no doubt the growls came from him. The sound had a hard rhythm, all base and drum, putting her in mind of rolling thunder. He was demented, out of his mind. Wasn't he?

Incapable of beginning to answer her question, she stopped struggling. Her entire body vibrated, and was hot and cold at the same time. She felt both separated from her body, and deeply linked with it. Whatever she was feeling was more than her system's response to something beyond all comprehension. She was also tapping into him, finding her way through his layers, identifying even more layers, and digging into them.

This was familiar territory because she'd done the same with animals countless times. Granted, none of them had been as complex as what she was now encountering, but the similarities kept her going. There was something rich at his core, incredible, erotic, and yet more.

A sharp burn at the side of her neck distracted her from mind probing. Yelping into the ropes, she risked whiplash trying to break free. For long seconds she feared he wouldn't release her, but when she yelped again, he opened his mouth and pulled back. Her freedom was less than complete because his hands were still on her and his cock pressed against her.

Fighting fear and more, she twisted and looked up at him. This close, his features were blurred, but she swore his contours had changed. His ears were now higher on his head and had become pointed. His jaw resembled a muzzle, and his neck had all but disappeared. A golden light filled his eyes.

Shock gripped her. She, who never screamed, let go with something that might have wakened the dead if she hadn't been gagged.

"No!" he ordered, his voice more growl than command. "Not—yet."

What was he talking about, and why, despite everything, didn't she want him to release her? Time beat between them. With each passing moment, she came closer to a truth she wasn't sure she had the courage for.

After standing her upright, he stepped away from her, and she briefly thought he was going to leave. Instead, he walked over to where her pistol lay and tucked it in his front pocket. Then he returned.

Another growl and he lifted her off her feet. She had just enough time to ponder what he had in mind when he threw her over his shoulder. A powerful arm looped over her waist to hold her in place. She gave brief thought to trying to kick him where it counted the most. But if she brought him to his knees, he'd drop her. With no way of cushioning her landing, she might break a bone, or worse.

His shoulder felt massive under her, broader than a man's had a right being, and densely muscled. She sagged where he'd placed her, her head and hair trailing down his back, her chest and belly sealed to him. The arm around her waist tightened in silent reminder of his greater strength. Mostly she thought about her exposed breasts flattened against his back, and him breathing.

Then he placed his other hand over her calves, and she knew he'd won this round. She couldn't, wouldn't fight him, whoever or whatever he was.

7

Too close. Self-control held by a thread. Some part of her penetrated his outer shell and reached for something he didn't understand, something vulnerable. No matter which defenses he threw out, she kept digging at them. She was worming her way into him, circumventing barriers, and going ever deeper, prodding—

He had to get into his private place before it was too late.

Her weight pressing against his shoulder, her warm breasts flattened against his flesh, her calves under his hand, and her thighs giving off a dangerous heat, he walked as quickly as he dared. With each moment a little more of the human he'd once been slipped away and Cougar gained strength. Most times he embraced the change, because when in cougar form, he didn't question, resent, or fear the existence he'd been thrust into. He simply existed.

Now he was taking those irrevocable steps into that simple and inescapable world, but taking *her* with him, because she refused to let go.

It wasn't yet noon, but the sun seemed to be trying to burn

the top of his head. The longer he held onto her, the warmer her flesh became. He needed to let her down and make her walk. And yet he'd waited so long to experience sensations like this.

He'd done it, captured not just a human female so he'd no longer be alone, but this one. What he hadn't anticipated was that she might slice through his layers and maybe expose what lay in the middle.

Did he want that? Could she handle what she discovered?

Maybe he could answer both questions if he was safely and fully in his human body, but thanks to her, he'd lost control over that part of him, and he didn't know when he'd get it back. The possibility that he'd never return to his human self half-chilled him, but then she tried to lift herself off him, and he lost the thought.

He tightened his hold until she gave up and sagged, but soon after she tried again to straighten. It occurred to him that blood must have pooled in her head and she was looking for a more comfortable position. He could grant her that one simple thing.

Stopping, he looked around at the only world he felt at peace in. He loved Tochona's quiet hues, with the steep cliff walls seeming to reach for the sky. He also loved the valley floors and the bushlike cottonwoods that rooted wherever there was enough moisture. Losing himself in the familiar surroundings, he set her on her feet. As she'd done earlier, she started to tip to the side. Her head hung, maybe to counter the dizziness he was certain she was feeling.

Carefully keeping his gaze off her pale, soft breasts, he positioned her on a boulder and crouched before her so he could adjust her ankle restraints. He had no intention of giving her a chance to run because if she did, Cougar might see nothing except his next meal.

Creating enough slack so that she could walk at a slow pace, he started to stand. Then the back of his hand brushed her shin bone, and he remained crouched. Repeatedly stroking her leg through her jeans quieted a little of the energy. If he kept touching her, claiming her, maybe he could contain Cougar. But if that wasn't possible, she'd see.

Why hadn't he considered that before jumping her?

A woman's leg, encased in denim, her top dangling from her tethered hands, and her breasts exposed. Her long and luscious hair had fallen forward to bracket her face and soften the impact dust and sweat had made on her cheeks. Closing his hands over her knees, he pressed his thumbs against their insides. As her legs parted, an unmistakable scent entered his nostrils. Cougar twitched.

"You want sex," he said. He had to work at getting the words out.

Although she repeatedly shook her head, she didn't take her gaze off him. Keeping her legs apart, he returned her look. No expert with a woman's emotions, he couldn't say what she was thinking. Her heavy lids seemed to speak of hunger, but maybe she was trying to keep secrets from him.

Determined to break through her defenses, he ran both hands up the insides of her legs. Even as he imagined tearing her jeans to shreds, he lost himself in the future. Once he'd taken her to his lair, he'd begin the process of making her his. Step by step, touch by touch, he'd bring her under his control until little remained of her except sex hunger. Keeping her sexually stimulated without risking his own sanity wouldn't be easy.

No matter how many times he'd tried to make his plans over the endless days and nights of his existence, he'd been forced to come face-to-face with the truth. Under this pale and hairless skin he wore, he was an animal.

Cursing the beast, he returned his attention to his captive. His hands still rested against her inner thighs. Concentrating on her crotch, he pondered whether she easily climaxed or needed lengthy foreplay. He might have once known how to bring a woman to the edge of her control—he wasn't sure—but surely that talent belonged to men who cared about the woman or women in their lives.

He only wanted a resting place for his cock.

A willing one, his human half insisted. *It doesn't matter,* Cougar returned.

Abruptly changing position, he cupped a hand over her mons, his thumb reaching as far between her legs as possible. A strangled cry slammed against her gag, and she struggled to twist to away. Her unexpected rebellion served as a vital lesson. She was no simple animal in heat.

Just the same, he wanted to hand her a lesson before pulling her back to her feet. By increasing his hold on her left thigh, he kept her anchored as he rubbed a thumb against the taut fabric over her core. His intention had been to impress her with how easy it was to invade her privacy and give her a hint of her future, but as he continued his massage, she stopped straining to get away.

"You want this?" Drawing as much of her mons as he could into his palm, he shook it.

More head shaking. The rest of her, however, remained motionless. He wanted to say something to her, speak words that had the power to break down the barriers between them, but she'd started panting and suddenly he couldn't think beyond the sound.

Leaning closer, he worked his hand even farther into the warm cave, stopping only when the boulder he'd placed her on got in the way. Releasing her thigh, he cradled a breast. His thighs had begun to protest, but the discomfort was nothing. He'd waited so long for a moment like this, sometimes doubting it would ever happen, or that even if he captured a woman, she wouldn't understand.

Was it possible? This woman knew what he was about?

Risking more than he wanted to admit, he again looked into her eyes. Her lids sagged, yet she returned his gaze. Unable to read her expression, he nevertheless told himself she wanted this moment and for the world to be about the two of them.

Floating in a current of need, he sought to wrap his mouth around her breast. But as he closed in on her, his left thigh threatened to cramp. Wise in the need to remain strong, he gathered his legs under him and stood. Doing so forced him to release her.

Kneading the knotted muscle, he continued to watch her. She'd already drawn her legs together and had sucked in her breath as if trying to put as much distance as possible between them. Her eyes remained heavily lidded, her nipples hard.

He shifted his weight. As he did, she leaned away from him, turning to the side at the same time. Whatever spell he'd managed to cast over her was fading. She was no longer wrapped in her primitive nature, and had become a captive again, a woman who wanted nothing to do with what was happening to her.

She feared him, maybe hated him.

Something cold and hard seeped into him. The more wary her expression, the more he wanted to strip it from her. Breath whistling, he slapped her. Her head snapped back, and she made a half-angry, half-frightened sound. The strangled cry put him in mind of a dying prey. Once again the inner animal shuddered.

"Get up!" Not giving her time to obey, he hauled her to her feet and shoved, thinking to get her walking. Instead, she stumbled. He could have helped her right herself. Instead, he watched, not caring as she fell. She landed on her knees, but without her hands to brace herself, she tipped forward until her upper body rested on her left shoulder.

Fingers repeatedly knotting and releasing, he studied her naked back. Her backbone and ribs were silhouetted beneath flesh that seldom saw the sun, her arms worthless. As Cougar, he sometimes crippled a catch and watched it struggle to drag itself away. Cougar cared nothing about a creature's pain or fear, but when he returned to human form, he had nothing but loathing for what the beast was capable of. Then he did it again.

This time the man had done the crippling.

Swallowing against self-loathing, he helped her stand but was careful to keep her back to him so she couldn't read his expression. Still fighting himself, he gave her a gentle push. After a few false tries, she found a mincing gait that kept her on the move.

When he'd matched his stride to hers, he closed a hand around an elbow to remind her of his presence. Her breasts shuddered with every step, and she kept dropping her head, only to jerk it upright. A warm breeze seemed to be following them, and every time it blew her hair about, it took all he had not to take hold of the pale length so he could feel its warmth.

Not looking at her was easier on his nervous system, yet he couldn't keep his attention off her for more than a few seconds. He kept telling himself it was because he'd finally accomplished what had long been a horny man's fantasy, but that wasn't the full truth. Giving into thoughts both revealing and dangerous, he acknowledged that he was drawn to not just any female body, but hers.

The faintest of memories told him he'd had considerable experience with women before he'd been wrenched from that all-but-forgotten world. His captive was attractive, not as lean and long-limbed as a model, but healthy, without exploiting her physical body. His brief exploration of her sexuality made him wonder if he could exploit it, and yet even that didn't touch what made her unique, did it?

There'd been something in her glances, a penetrating quality, a determination to dig deep into him. Despite her fear, she remained clearheaded. She was searching for more than the obvious. She wanted to understand what made him the way he was. Maybe she'd glimpsed or sensed Cougar. Much as he needed to throw up his defenses, part of him ached to let her in.

But first and foremost, he vowed to turn her into what he needed.

Unless the beast overpowered him.

Thank goodness, Hok'ee had finally gotten rid of the damnable ropes around her ankles. That done, he'd refastened her wrists so her arms were no longer forced into such an unnatural position. She might have taken that as a sign that he'd regretted kidnapping her, and would eventually release her, if he hadn't fashioned a collar out of the former ankle rope and used the loose end as a leash so he could haul her behind him.

To hell with him! He might treat her like a dog, but she'd be damned if she'd act like one. No matter what he did to her, she wouldn't cower and tuck her nonexistent tail between her legs.

What were his plans for her? Unfortunately, the answer was as clear as his broad, tanned, naked back. She'd have to be a fool not to get the message in the way he'd manhandled her after plunking her down on the boulder.

He'd gone right for her crotch. And although her jeans prevented him from reaching her sex, between shaking her mons and rubbing her labia, he'd given her a vivid demonstration of his intentions.

Why then wasn't she fighting?

Staring at the rope running from her neck to his hand, she nearly laughed. Like resisting would accomplish anything. Eventually they'd reach wherever he was taking her, he'd remove her gag, and give her something to drink, at least she reverently hoped he would. The moment she was capable of speaking, she'd . . .

What? Would she really ask if he was going to rape her?

Maybe it was the sun, wind, thirst, and her wearying body, but although the word spread throughout her, she didn't try to shove it away. Rape meant being taken against her will, which had already happened. How she'd react to the ultimate in violation was up to her, at least she hoped that was true.

What gave her doubt was her response to his hand between her legs, and another on her breast, and his fingers on her ass. When he'd done those things, she'd no longer been aware of her imprisoned body or useless shirt. Everything had revolved around the pressure against her cunt and the big, rugged man responsible for that pressure.

Swallowing, she tried to count steps, and when that failed to distract her, she tried to imagine where he was taking her. However, despite her need to stick with reality, her mind painted fanciful possibilities.

Her captor had taken her to a clear, slow moving stream where he removed her boots and jeans. Then he led her into the water, laughing when she gasped at the cold. Deeper and deeper they went until they stood in the middle, water lapping at her breasts. Her hands were still tied, albeit in front now. The gag was gone.

When he placed his hands on her shoulders, she believed he intended to help her maintain her balance. Instead, he pushed down and forced her underwater. Before panic could swamp her, he pulled her back up. Then he gently washed her hair and face before turning to the rest of her body. His movements were slow and sensual, making her feel as if she was floating, even when she wasn't.

When he was satisfied he'd thoroughly cleaned her, he closed his hands around her waist and lifted her, guiding her legs around his hips. She placed her arms over his head and around his neck to keep from losing her balance. Then she floated with eyes closed and mouth open as he ran his erect cock into her. With his hands on her buttocks providing the necessary support, she demonstrated her devotion to him, her captor, by drawing him deep. Again and again she pulled back, only to dive at him until they were both panting.

Although she'd been shivering since going into the water, she quickly warmed herself on his cock. She barely felt her arms, and her legs seemed capable of gripping forever. Her pussy loosened, swelled, embraced, then slid unrelentingly toward release.

He came first with sharp, hard thrusts, and a cry like a wild animal. Goaded by the primal sound, she caught up with him, gasping as everything spiraled. Sex muscles clenched, collapsed, clenched again.

And as her climax died, his cry echoed inside her.

Blinking, Kai brought herself back to the here and now, but even as she reacquainted herself with her aching insteps and jaw, she heard that wild animal sound. A warning from deep inside told her not to question, not to open herself up to something she might not want to know, but just as she'd never been able to ignore her connection with living creatures, she couldn't turn her back on this step she'd never imagined she'd take.

A thread of life ran from his hand, along the rope and into her veins. It pulsed with energy and mystery, fascinating and frightening her at the same time. When she gave herself over to it, she caught bits and pieces of images with little meaning. Once she'd reconciled herself to the fragmented blips, she pulled what she understood around her. The blips weren't unrelated snapshots of nothing after all. Instead, much as if she were working with puzzle pieces, she began constructing a whole.

She was watching an animal, a predator. Because it was night in her mind, she couldn't be certain what she was looking at, just that the creature was a member of the cat family. It moved with the supreme grace of one whose existence depended on silence and stealth. Every muscle was finely tuned, each step silent. She didn't have to touch that sleek and powerful body to know it feared nothing and felt nothing for whatever it was stalking.

The image sharpened, putting her in mind of a camera lens being adjusted. The feline form took on definition, and she was closer to it now, so close she could hear the creature breathing. Despite the possibility that it might attack, she focused on shape and size, color and energy.

Weighing upward of two hundred pounds, the animal had a disproportionally small, round head. Dark markings ringed its eyes and muzzle. Its ears were erect and in constant movement as it took measure of its world. Powerful hindquarters briefly distracted her from the powerful forequarters, neck, and jaw. Its paws were large in proportion to the rest of it, and the claws were capable of clutching, ripping, and tearing. The thick tail reached to the ground and slowly lashed back and forth, reminding her of a house cat signaling its intention to pounce.

Swallowing against fear and more, she returned to what she had to do. When the beast opened its mouth, revealing potent fangs, she admitted her admiration for a creature created for ending life. In strange contrast to the deadly body, its thick, rich coat was a soft tawny color that faded to blond on its underside, jaw, chin, and throat.

It wasn't looking at her. Just the same, she sensed the beast was aware of her presence and prepared to leap should she try to flee. Determined to learn everything she could about the creatures she was in tune with, she'd researched the various big cats. But even if she hadn't, she would have known this was a cougar. After all, hadn't her dream man told her?

Dream man? No longer, because she'd become his captive.

After assuring herself that she was still walking, and the ground ahead of her was level, she forced herself to take her thoughts even deeper. When she studied the masculine back ahead of her, she saw a man. When she drifted into what existed inside her mind, she saw a massive cougar. But when she concentrated on both, they became superimposed one over the other, first one form and then the other taking control.

Man and predator in the same body? Maybe sharing the same soul?

Head throbbing, she waited for horror and disbelief to wash away the insane thought. Instead, conviction settled over her. It was impossible, of course. A man couldn't also be an animal. But if they shared the space, sometimes the predator would demand that space. Then when it had accomplished whatever it needed to, the man would emerge.

Much as she needed to close her eyes so she could concentrate, she didn't dare. Telling herself to accept this new reality, she continued to study the dark naked back. Hok'ee—she had no doubt that was his name—was beautiful in a harsh and untamed way, and confident in his body. And yet she'd sensed an inner struggle. Saying that anyone capable of shape-shifting had a lot on their mind was simplistic.

What did he want from her? Sex, obviously. But it had to be more than that, didn't it? A rational human being didn't rob another human of her freedom simply because he craved a sex partner. Especially not a man who could bed any woman with a look and a touch.

What if he somehow knew she was different, in tune with his animal nature? Was that why he'd captured her? But for what purpose?

Her head ached, forcing her to stop searching for answers she might never find. Wherever he was taking her was more than a mile from where he'd brought her down because they'd already traveled that far. Either that, or she'd lost track of time and distance. It didn't matter. He'd do what he wanted, when he wanted.

Feeling herself slipping into a strange nothingness, she tried to pull free by concentrating on Garrin and the others who would be joining them, including Dr. Carter. Although she vaguely remembered what Dr. Carter looked like, Garrin's features eluded her. Garrin was take-charge. He'd organize a search party and come looking for her.

But where would he look? Would she ever see any of them again?

Maybe she'd die like her father had.

8

Although he spent considerable time with his pride, Hok'ee had fashioned a *home* for himself in what had once been an Anasazi apartment. A long-ago earthquake had collapsed most of the stone walls, but a few spaces remained intact. When he'd first spotted the cavelike opening, he'd been hesitant to enter it, but a thorough examination had convinced him it was solid. Protected from the elements, it needed little in the way of refinements, beyond a bed made from stolen blankets. Two folding chairs, taken from campsites, provided him with places to sit. He occasionally pondered what the campers thought had happened to their chairs.

Because he'd spent little time inside the cave, he hadn't concerned himself with making it more comfortable, but he'd need to before winter because as much as he loved the other Tocho, he must have been a solitary human because he craved solitude.

Winter, snow, and cold, and long days and nights when the weather would keep him inside with his thoughts and loneliness.

Maybe for the first time, he didn't hesitate before ducking

his head and stepping through the low opening. Tonight he wouldn't be alone.

Straightening, he turned and studied the woman. She'd come in far enough that she wasn't in danger of hitting her head on the low entryway ceiling but had stopped without his permission. Instead of looking around, she stared at him. Because daylight was behind her, he couldn't read the look in her eyes. She was gnawing on the rope in her mouth, and her stance was wide. Her breasts seemed to sag more than they had earlier, alerting him to her bowed posture.

Puzzled by his concern for her comfort, he let go of the leash. It slid between her breasts and legs, the end draped over the dried grasses he'd brought in to insulate the stone flooring. Half-expecting her to run, he folded his arms across his chest and planted his weight on the balls of his feet. His heart rate picked up.

Aware that Cougar would soon demand freedom, he looked around for a way to keep her here. The cave walls were jagged in places where ends of slab stuck out. He could tie the rope to one of them.

But what if she panicked when she saw what he became? She might choke herself. Thoughts of anything digging into her soft throat penetrated his fading brain, and he shook himself back to awareness. An instant of self-loathing shot through him, then was gone.

"Come here," he said, indicating a spot in front of him. After a moment, she shuffled forward. Then she sagged again.

Alerted by his own body's needs, he knew he had to give her something to drink and let her rest. Thinking about removing the gag made his fingers twitch. Taking hold of her elbows as he'd done before, he turned her so her back was to him. Warmth from the sun radiated off her. Caressed by her heat, he untied her gag and pulled it off her.

Pivoting on her left leg, she faced him. Doing so caused the leash rope to curl around her legs. She licked her lips and worked her jaw muscles. He waited for her to scream, but she remained silent. When she continued to lick her lips, he acknowledged the self-restraint it took for her not to ask for water.

Leaving her, he stepped over to the stone and wood table that had been here when he found the cave. He kept his water supply in a five gallon plastic bladder he'd taken from a sporting goods store. Filling a ceramic cup with the water he'd gotten from a nearby creek, he held it to her mouth. Not taking her gaze off him, she downed it. He gave her another cupful, then drank himself.

The necessary chore over, he leaned against the table. Every time he looked at her it was as if he'd never seen a woman's body before. Her youth and strength, and slim, healthy body spoke to him, but even more, he embraced the thought that she belonged to him. Unlike the strangers he fucked when he had no choice, he wanted to know everything about her. He needed to hear her voice, to touch her hair, to draw her breasts into his mouth, to plunder her pussy.

He also needed to know what was different about her.

A painful knotting in his groin captured his attention. No matter how much he tried to ignore his swollen cock, it was controlling more and more of his mind. Cupping the hard organ, he fought its power. At the same time, he made no attempt to hide what he was doing from her.

"That's what this is about, isn't it?" she softly asked. "Sex, whether I want it or not."

"I smelled your cunt. You're alive."

"Of course I am! As for the scent, haven't you heard—fear and sexual need are both powerful emotions."

In many respects, he was like a naïve boy. Unfortunately, his adult body wanted more than his mind comprehended.

"What I don't understand," she continued, "is why you kidnapped me. You—you're attractive. You can't have trouble getting—" She looked around, mouth slack and eyes widening. "Where are we?"

"My home."

She shook her head, the long hair brushing her shoulders. "No. It can't be."

Much as he wanted to know what she was talking about, the explanation would have to wait because he'd put off Cougar's demands as long as he could. Even now Cougar screamed and tore at him to be let free. Jaws clenched, he pushed off the table and ended the distance between them. She started to take a backward step, only to stop and glance down at the rope around her leg. Then he reached for her throat and she moaned softly. His fingers were becoming numb, his nostrils keener. Feline muscles pushed against his flesh.

Working quickly, he freed her legs, then removed the rope collar. After dragging the end of it off her leg, he led her over to the table and bent her over it with her head down. She moaned again, longer, higher. Freeing her wrists took a long time because his fingers refused to work, and he struggled to think how to resecure her without giving her the opportunity to fight him. Keeping her against the table, he drew her arms over her head, pulling off her shirt and bra as he did.

Remembering how to tie knots took up more time and mental energy he didn't have, as did positioning her under a slab some seven feet above the ground and tossing the rope over the slab so he could secure her to it. He left enough slack that she could stand flat-footed, and bend her elbows somewhat.

All but panting in relief, he stepped away. His vision was blurring as it had countless times. Although he rubbed his eyes, she remained shaded and shimmering. He had to get out of here, go where she couldn't see what he became.

Too late! His legs lost strength, bringing him to his knees. He managed to yank off his boots and jeans and stand again, but the effort left him too weak to make it to the entrance. Despite his battle to slow the change, his body shifted, stretched, bones thickening and taking on new form, flesh becoming covered in short hair. His mouth expanded, teeth lengthening. He stared without seeing as his hands morphed into claws. Then, surrendering to the inevitable, he bent forward and his newly emerged front legs bore Cougar's weight.

Kai couldn't close her mouth, couldn't think how to blink. "My God. My God," she blurted without knowing she was going to speak.

On an instinctive level, she'd known something like this was going to happen, but watching a man become a cougar was beyond her comprehension. With no more than five feet between them, she felt the predator's strength in every molecule of her being. During the change, he/it hadn't looked at her, but now yellow eyes locked on her. They harbored no humanity.

Fighting terror, she yanked on her bonds, but there was no give to the rope. Much as she needed to scream, she didn't, because the sound might prompt what Hok'ee had become to attack.

She'd been wrong, terribly wrong to think she'd been grabbed simply because her captor wanted sex. Had the truth been that the man provided the cougar with food, and she was about to become tonight's dinner?

No, that didn't make sense. Did it?

"Can you under—" Her throat contracted. "Can you understand me?"

If he/it did, the cougar gave no indication. She didn't know whether to study its expression, mouth, or legs. Neither did she know what to do with the overwhelming sense of being trapped.

The terror she'd been battling pushed up from her belly to spread over her throat. Fighting soul-deep fear, she ground her teeth together. She'd never been a coward, a crier, or a screamer, not even the day she'd found her father's bloodied and broken body. If she gave in to any of those things now, they'd overwhelm her.

"I knew—earlier I sensed what was going to happen. At least that something would." That said, she didn't know how to go on.

She'd thought Hok'ee was beautiful. If anything, the predator he'd become was even more so. Yes, the cougar was too large for the space, which was more than disconcerting, but she couldn't help but admire its graceful yet strangely designed form. She understood the need for powerful hindquarters, but why hadn't the predator been designed with a head in proportion to the rest of its body. And that oversized tail—

You're losing it.

"What do you want from me?" The moment she asked her question, she wished to hell she hadn't. The thick tail was working back and forth as it had in her imagination, or whatever had taken place on their way here. The expressive ears twitched, and it lifted its head so they were looking eye to eye.

This incredible place Hok'ee had called his home was locked in shadow, but she now saw something in the pale feline eyes that reminded her of the man. He wasn't gone after all, not completely. Some remnant of him, hopefully his intellect and compassion—not that she'd seen much of that—remained.

"I don't know how to reach you. I want to, but I don't know what words to use."

The cougar blinked, slow, measured. Then its muscles contracted, tightened, gathered. She'd opened her mouth to scream when it sprang. Instead of attacking her, it raced toward the opening and disappeared.

Come back! Please, come back.

Kai had lost track of time. Her world went no further than her weary legs and the strain in her arms. She could hear the wind push against some bushes just beyond where she'd been left to hang, but that was the only sound. Much as she'd wanted to call out for help, she hadn't because she was afraid only the cougar would hear.

A cougar! The man disappeared and a predator—

How long before *it* returned, and what would happen when it did? No matter how many times she tried to deny the questions, they kept pounding at her. Well, why shouldn't they? It wasn't as if she had anything else to think about, and there was nothing she could do.

He/it would return. It made no sense for Hok'ee to have gone to the effort he had, only to abandon her. Of course if the cougar refused to relinquish control—

Stop it! Just the hell stop it!

Hok'ee had given her all the water she wanted, and he'd gone to the effort and care to tie her hands in front, thus allowing her a more natural stance. She kept telling herself that echoes of him had remained in the cougar. She just wished she fully believed that.

She was hungry, had to go to the bathroom, and might kill if that's what it took to get a massage. Damn it, his jeans with her pistol in a pocket were so close. If she could get her hands on the weapon, a great deal would change. Granted, she was loopy, but the more she thought about it, the easier it was to contemplate murder in exchange for a massage. Granted, such creature comforts were in short supply here, but since the fantasy was all she had between herself and insanity, she'd turn it in whatever direction she needed.

That was her fantasy, but she was in Hok'ee's home.

She should have realized where she was before now. Much as her surroundings resembled a cave, it was more than that, much more. To begin, she'd studied the exterior as she was being led into it. She'd seen the stone slabs that made up the walls, slabs that had been set in place thousands of years ago.

The Anasazi were responsible! Those long-dead and almost

mystical people had created multi-storied tower houses during what historians called the Great Pueblo period. Most of those unique structures had given way to time and weather, but a few remained.

Canyon De Chelly had become a national landmark because of places like Mummy Cave, Antelope House, and Junction House, all incredible ruins left behind by the Anasazi. With her father, she'd photographed, studied, and touched the monuments. They became more than structures to her, more than testaments to The Ancient Ones. They were life, albeit frozen in time.

And now she had proof that what had made Canyon De Chelly rich also existed in Sani, or should she say Tochona. University staff had been thrilled with the kiva the hikers had found, and had hoped to find other Navajo artifacts, but this— this was magical and mystical. Maybe there was more than this single space. Maybe it was part of an *apartment* complex.

Excitement caught her unawares. For a few moments she forgot what had been done to her, and what lay ahead. If only her father were alive. Not only would he share her awe, he'd know how to protect what remained of The Ancient Ones.

Damn you, Dad. Why'd you go and get yourself killed? I need you now, maybe more than I did after Mom died.

A sound. Soft.

Her thoughts shattering, she faced the entrance. Something was coming toward her, but she couldn't be sure what. Either that or she was putting off facing reality for as long as she could.

Home, she thought. Home was wonderful! Granted, a leased condo without a square inch of lawn to call her own was far from a palace, but it was *her* space. She could lock the doors and shut out the world.

Not a cougar. A man. Hok'ee. Taking one slow step at a time. Coming closer. Naked and shoeless, a thin, bloody scratch along his belly.

Relief warred with tension and cut a line from her throat to her crotch as he straightened and fixed his gaze on her. Insanely, she wished she'd combed her hair and put on something decent. Then she remembered he'd taken away her shirt and bra, that he wanted her like this. Tied. Waiting.

He smelled of energy, of excitement, reminding her of the year the college softball team she'd been on took the state championship. They'd gone undefeated, each game filled with determination. She'd lived for early morning practices, late night strategy sessions, the feel and smell of her glove and the power that ran from her bat to her hands. A single up the middle with a teammate on third had been as good as sex, while a home run put every climax she'd ever had to shame.

That's what Hok'ee was feeling; the scratch told her why. As a cougar, he'd killed.

Let me go, she wanted to say, but she wouldn't beg. Instead, maybe because she was feeding off his emotion, she refused to back away. He was all fierce power; she wanted to be the same. His gaze raked her from the top of her head to her toes. It lingered first on her breasts and then the space between her legs. Her nipples puckered, and something that wasn't quite pain brought tears to her eyes. Wet heat sealed her panties to her cunt. The time of waiting was over. He'd soon take what he wanted from her.

In a space created by the ancients.

Fight. Give in. Whatever her decision, the outcome would be the same.

Pinpricks danced over her skin, making her squirm. Maybe she was fighting herself when she tugged against her bonds; maybe she was assuring herself that she'd remain where he wanted her until he wanted something different.

Taken against her will? Maybe. Maybe not.

Naked with dark eyes, hair, and skin, he was more than

beautiful, beyond magnificent. Every one of his two hundred pounds spoke of male animal, yet he was human—at least right now he was.

"Where have you been?" she asked. Her voice rasped, forcing her to swallow.

"Hunting."

The clean admission caught her off guard. She didn't know what she'd expected, certainly not this truth.

"You were successful?"

"Yes."

If she asked more questions, would he tell her all the gory details? Knowing she wasn't ready for that, she simply nodded. It was funny in a bizarre way. Here she was strung up and waiting for whatever he had in mind, but pushing him like some nosy wife, demanding to know why her old man had been out all night.

Seeming not to care that she was watching his every move, he reached up and untied the rope over her head. Sighing in relief, she let her arms drop. Her shoulders ached but not as much as her legs did. How long had it been since she'd been allowed to sit?

Allowed?

How long then until she had control over her body back?

"Take off your jeans."

"What?" she stammered.

"Either you do it, or I will."

Fuck you! Knowing better than to engage in a tug of war, she didn't try to jerk the rope out of his hand. But neither was she going to go down without a fight. Squaring her tired shoulders, she glared at the man who exuded pure sex.

"I'm serious."

"So am I. Look, Hok'ee, I have no intention of—"

"How do you know my name?"

"How—" she started, then stopped. If she told him about

her dream, he'd think she was either crazy or lying, but she'd gotten his name right, and he couldn't deny that. "There's something about me you need to know," she said, although she was far from sure she was doing the right thing. "I have this ability to—I can read minds."

"I don't believe you."

"I don't blame you, but I'm serious. I'm a psychic, for lack of a better word."

"A what?"

"I can get into minds. Only it's animal thoughts I reach, not human."

The way he kept shaking his head, she knew he hadn't bought her explanation, not that she blamed him.

Neither of them speaking, she took stock of her world and the man dominating it. He couldn't have exemplified sex any more if the word had been tattooed to his chest. She'd seen men like that before, of course, raw and rugged. To her way of thinking, too many women didn't care whether those studs had anything between their ears as long as the package from the neck down was damn near perfect. Granted, a lot of those men were the product of Hollywood or some advertising machinery, although there'd been a handful of jocks who'd flip-flopped her belly. He was the real deal, rough around the edges, and dangerous as hell. What did he care about laws or social conventions?

Nothing. Because he was more than human.

Quick as a striking snake, he hauled her to him, turning her from him at the same time. She was still trying to make sense of what he'd done when he pushed her against the wall and held her in place via a forearm to the back of her neck. Pent-up power flowed from him to her, and when he went to work one-handed on her wrists, she knew better than to test his self-control. He freed one hand, only to wrench it high behind her back. Then he let go of her neck so he could bring the other hand up to the first. A handful of seconds, and her arms were lashed behind her again.

Then he stepped back. Holding her breath, she faced him.

"I gave you a chance to comply." His eyes daring her to argue, he grabbed her waistband and deftly unhooked the fastening. "Now we'll do it my way."

"We've done it your way from the beginning," she said in a tone better suited on a small child.

"Not me. What I've become."

A world of regret, accompanied the simple words. If she could have escaped at this moment, she wasn't sure she would have. Her world had shifted and changed form because of him. Because of him, she wasn't the same person she'd been this morning.

Hands on her shoulders again, and she was being spun so her back was to him. Waiting and wondering. Not afraid so much as alive. Hotly alive.

Then he took hold of her hands and forced them up until she had to lean forward. He easily kept her off balance and her arms high, reinforcing his mastery as he unzipped her jeans. Reaching around her, he dug into her rear pockets for her cell phone and digital camera, which he dropped to the ground. Had he broken them?

Snagging her waistband once more, he first worked the denim down over her hips, then her buttocks. He settled the jeans around her knees and then did the same to her panties. Apparently satisfied, he released her wrists and let her straighten.

She was free of him, not that it made any difference. Where was she going to go with her hands tied behind her and her clothing roping her legs?

"I wasn't defying you," she started, then stopped. If she began apologizing now, how long before he'd stripped her down to nothing. She had to stay strong somehow. Only what did it matter, since he in essence owned her?

Crouching in that graceful way of his, he loosened her boots and tugged them off one at a time while she struggled to remain on her feet. He did so in such a matter-of-fact way that it took a moment for reality to settle in. Barefoot meant she stood no chance of outrunning him. He'd as good as hobbled her. Mentally cursing his seemingly indestructible feet, she acknowledged how easily she'd accepted his nudity. Well, why shouldn't she? His body was his tool, whether he was man or cougar.

"What do you want from me?" she asked. He'd stood and stepped away so he could do what he'd already done too many times, study her. Was he seeing an ordinary woman, a captive to play with, to fuck when and how often he wanted? Or was there more to this kidnapping?

Either he hadn't been listening when she asked her question, or he had no intention of explaining. Fine, fine. She'd learn moment by moment, and step-by-step.

And when she'd understood everything there was to know, who and what would she be?

"You're thirsty," he said.

"Yes," she admitted. "And I have to go to the bathroom."

"Hmm."

He was still staring at her, damn him, his gaze washing over her every inch until she half-believed he could see her swollen bladder. Always a private person when it came to bodily functions, she now stood barefoot with her belly, crotch, and buttocks exposed. And her breasts. Don't forget her breasts.

She was melting, becoming insignificant and losing substance. Every bit of her was or could be under his scrutiny. She had no secrets left, no way of hiding her reddish pubic hair or the slightly smaller left breast.

Showing no emotion, he planted his hand over her belly and pushed her back against the wall again. He kept his hand in place, pinning her while she shuddered and tried to keep her breath from whistling. The pressure on her belly increased, then settled. "I smelled something earlier," he said. "Your cunt."

Unnerved by the crude yet telling words, she kept her head high.

"Because you're afraid or me? Or because you want me?"

"I'm not going to answer that."

"Yes, you are."

9

She was a deer he'd run down, a rabbit too startled to move. Bit by bit he'd stripped away what made her a civilized woman. A little more, and she'd be the same as him, naked.

Then the real work would begin.

Feeling her shiver again, he knew he wouldn't wait after all. He couldn't.

He screamed each time Cougar took over. He did so now, albeit silently, but the sound wasn't the same. This was even more primitive, male and not animal. Keeping her against the wall, he slid his free hand between her legs. This time there was no denim in the way. Instead, he touched satinlike flesh and heard a woman's low, soft murmur. Her eyes were wide, and she lifted herself onto her toes. Except for what was between her legs, her whole body was tense.

Making no secret of his fascination with her expression, he turned his hand to the side so his thumb glided over her core. His goal was to reach her sexually and, if possible, sand away her resistance.

During the million or more times he'd dreamed of today,

he'd told himself only his needs mattered. His reasons were simple: if he had any chance of holding onto what remained of the human in him, he had to bring another human into his world. A female.

But the more he'd dreamed his dreams, the more he'd realized keeping her with him wouldn't be enough. He needed to be privy to all her emotions, not just her fear.

Fear was what Cougar got from his prey.

So stroke away her fear. Show her his human side.

If he was capable.

After letting up on the pressure against her belly and waiting for her breathing to deepen, he bent his thumb and gave her the only gift he possessed, himself. He invaded a fraction and retreated, stroked and stroked that soft, wet flesh again, sometimes long and slow, other times using a quick, short gliding movement along her labial lips.

Her breathing picked up, stopped, quickened even more. Her head had fallen back so the wall supported it, and her eyes were now hidden behind her heavy lids. She had incredibly long lashes, almost like a deer's. When she stopped trying to keep her mouth closed, her lips seemed to swell. What would they feel like around his cock?

No, not his needs! Not yet.

Fighting frustration and impatience, he took the next step. His thumb found her entrance, dipped in and let heat surround him. All but panting with the need to bury his cock in her, he waited out the dangerous moment, then escaped. As he did, he ran his thumbnail over her clit. Shuddering, she jerked upright.

He stopped, thinking to give her time to relax, but when she didn't, he went after her again. A memory far older than those stranger-to-stranger nights since he'd become Tocho said he was doing the right thing. If he continually touched and stroked and tested, she'd stop thinking of anything except him. She'd need only him.

He'd come this far in the only journey that mattered to him. All those solitary days and nights, the countless times Cougar had taken over, and finally he wasn't alone. He'd found her, a woman who'd known his name.

"Hok'ee," she whispered as if reading his mind. "I can't— oh, God, I can't . . ."

"What?"

"Wait, please."

For a moment he couldn't make sense of the single word. Then he realized she must be talking about her full bladder. Grunting, he dropped to his knees and yanked off her unnecessary clothes. When he was done, she took a step toward the entrance, then stopped and watched him stand. The beast he'd forced into hibernation took a breath. Not taking the time to battle it into submission, he laced his fingers through her hair and led her outside. She walked with her head high and still, her steps slow.

"It's afternoon," she said. "Late afternoon."

"That matters?"

Although she merely shrugged, he sensed it was no casual comment. And though he should have questioned her, the only thing he wanted to do was guide her toward the nearest bushes. Was she embarrassed by her nudity? Maybe he'd already taken her past such unimportant considerations. Matching her pace while limiting her freedom fed a need for power, and made him wonder what it would take for him to let her go. Right now he couldn't conceive of a time when he wouldn't want her beside or under him.

When he stopped, she tried to look around, but he kept his grip firm. Then he pressed down on her shoulder, indicating she could relieve herself where they stood. She gave a shuddering sigh before widening her stance and squatting. She would have fallen if he hadn't provided the necessary balance.

Finished, she continued to squat until he hauled her upright. They'd shared something not intimate so much as private, and in the sharing, maybe she'd taken another step toward turning her will over to him.

"You're a bastard. I hope you know that."

"Yeah, I do."

"Why is this happening? That's what I don't understand."

"It doesn't matter."

"The hell it doesn't!" She tried to swivel toward him, prompting him to pull her against him via her hair. "All right, all right! I'm sorry I said anything. That's what you wanted to hear, isn't it? For me to grovel."

It wasn't, but the hell of it was, he didn't know what he wanted from her. Or maybe the truth was he longed for words he knew she'd never say.

"There." Releasing her hair, he shoved her away. She stood with her back to him and her roped hands touching her ass. Her fingers were clenched, her toes dug into the ground.

"Go on, run," he challenged.

"Get the exercise in futility out of my system, you mean." Other than her spine straightening, she didn't move. "You'd like that, wouldn't you, to chase me down, just like the cougar you became chased down whatever it killed."

"I'm not—"

"That's what this is about isn't it?" she interrupted. "Not just sex, but having prey for the next time the beast comes out."

"You think—"

"I think I'm a creature you've put in a cage and intend to toy with before tearing my throat apart? You're damn right I do."

If she truly believed that, then she was the bravest woman he'd ever known.

"Say something," she hissed. "Anything. This not knowing or having answers is making me crazy."

"Not yet."

"Why not?"

Her tone had changed from fierce courage to something he

couldn't wrap his mind around. Softer and less intense, her tone cut through the walls he'd built to preserve what remained of his sanity. This time, when he took hold of her thick hair, it wasn't so he could control her but to give her a small piece of himself. Turning her head so they were face to face, he stroked her cheek. Her eyes widened, and her nostrils flared, but what captured his attention was the way her lips parted.

Running his hand from her cheek to the back of her head, he kneaded the tight muscles there. He still had hold of her hair, and his ropes were on her, but if he could believe her softening expression, she'd remain before him even if she was free.

He wanted that with every fiber of his being. To wake to the sound of a woman's gentle breathing and her head on his chest, to touch her and have her nestle against him.

And although he knew that would never be, he lowered his head and covered her mouth with his. She started shaking, and her breathing, like his, was quick and shallow. How soft her lips were, tentative and questioning.

Of course they were, and yet despite everything he'd done and robbed her of, she was letting him kiss her. Deeply thankful for what he needed to believe was her gift, he wrapped his arms around her and lifted her onto her toes. Although he towered over her and far outweighed her, he felt as if he'd just escaped an attempt on his life.

She was dangerous; that's why he felt the way he did. But along with that danger came breasts and belly and shelter for his cock.

And, in his most insane of dreams, understanding.

Bending her backward, he pressed his lonely lips against hers. Instead of trying to pull free, she met him square on. Her mouth parted even more, and her tongue slid out and between his lips. His vision clouded, and his needs hummed. Even with his cock aching, the kiss became everything. He'd never allowed himself to think it could be like this between him and the woman he chose to protect him from a lifetime of solitude. They'd have sex of course, hard and urgent, driven by the inner animal. But softness? Caring?

When she swayed, he relaxed his hold so she no longer had to stay on her toes. Her mouth opened yet more. Responding to the silent invitation, he ran his tongue around the insides of her lips.

She belonged to a world he'd lost contact with, and maybe that's what he most needed from her. Hungry, he lapped at her sweet moisture. Instead of being satiated, he needed more. Whispered words of love and a body freely given would have shattered his protective walls.

Even with his heart telling him he'd never hear those words, or her legs willingly parted for him, he slipped into a space painted by sensation. She tasted of life and promise, two things she'd willingly share with him. He had little to give in return, only his body, but she was content with the gift, and demonstrated her appreciation by taking it over and over.

They'd become simple creatures ruled by heat and need. Day would fade into night, and night would give way to dawn, and they'd still be together, their bodies joined, kissing endlessly.

Then a distant scream jerked him back to reality. They straightened as one, the closeness shattered.

"What's that?" she asked.

"A cougar. Hunting."

As if reinforcing what he'd just told her, the predator screamed again. The sound echoed, causing his teeth to ache from the urge to be the one proclaiming a successful kill.

"A real cougar or—are you the only one? Are there others like you?"

He hadn't wanted to talk about his shape-shifting until they'd had sex, but neither was he willing to lie to her any more than he already had. "There are others, at least four."

A shudder rolled through her slight body, and then she'd stepped out of his embrace, leaving him with not enough memory of what she felt like. "When are you going to tell me what's happening?"

Never, he wanted to say, but hadn't he just acknowledged his need to tell her the truth? "I don't understand everything," he admitted. "Neither do the rest of the pride."

"Pride?"

"We live in the moment. No matter how hard we try to remember, the past remains a mystery."

Hok'ee's tone had changed. For the first time, Kai heard hesitation and confusion from the man. Even with his body dominating her world, she sensed the child he'd once been, the lonely boy. Other things had started to come to her while they were kissing. Like blips of light from lightning on a moonless night, she'd seen bits and pieces of where he'd gone, and what he'd done after he'd taken on cougar form. Although he'd been pure animal, a killing machine, a current of humanity had remained. That's what she needed to focus on somehow.

But first she'd have to shake off his physical impact.

Her lips felt bruised, and her pussy ached. No matter whether she acknowledged his cock or struggled to keep her thoughts off it, it dominated her mind. "Maybe," she finally thought to say, "you're deliberately blocking out the past."

"Why would I do that? If there were holes in your life, wouldn't you try to fill them?"

Anger, quick and raw. "Of course. I'm sorry. I didn't mean—"

The distant cougar screamed again, and although her heartbeat didn't jump this time, the cry distracted her. "You said there are at least three others—what should I call you?—shapeshifters. Do you know which one that is?"

He shook his head. Then he blinked, and again shook his head as if trying to clear his mind. Laying his hand on her shoulder, he let his gaze travel down her. He was so slow with his scrutiny it was almost as if he hadn't looked at her before. She might have wondered if he was going to change form again if she wasn't staring at him in the same way. He truly dominated her existence, but not just because he'd stolen her freedom. Even if she still had the use of her hands and believed she might be able to outrun him, this was where she belonged.

For now, she amended. For now.

"We're going back inside," he said.

And then?

They hadn't walked that far from the ancient structure he'd turned into a crude home, but returning to it seemed to take forever. Of course she felt that way, she told herself as he directed her via a work-honed hand on her elbow. She was being led to something she'd never forget. Although she barely heard her feet as they settled on the warm ground, each step closer to where he lived had a finality about it.

Silence had been forced on her almost from the first moment she'd seen him. He'd removed her gag, but then he'd turned into something shocking and had disappeared. Even while he was gone, it seemed as if they'd carried out countless conversations. Either that, or the moments they'd spent kissing had—

She had been a willing participant. Not an overwhelmed captive, not even a woman caught in lust, but his equal, at least for those moments. Now that the moments and emotion were behind her, her mind was clearing. He couldn't know it, of course, but in some ways he'd opened his soul to her.

Even with lightning dancing on her skin and her pussy alive, her understanding of him had grown while they kissed. She'd *seen* him stalk the prey he'd killed and eaten, but that wasn't all. For no more than a second, she'd *seen* a boy speeding down a country road on a bicycle.

Wondering how much of the boy remained, she looked over at him, but then they entered the testament to the existence of the Anasazi. It was cooler in here, and she heard, or thought she heard, a quiet growl. Alerted, she stopped. Yes, there it was. Even when Hok'ee forced her over to what she'd determined was his bed, she fixed her mind on the sound. It was, or rather, it had been a dog.

Using a technique she'd perfected over the years of living with her talent, she closed her eyes. Without the cave distracting her, it didn't take long to locate the far corner of the cave where the growl was, or had come from.

In her imagination, she slowly approached the dog. It wore no collar, and its long yet sparse hair looked as if it had never been brushed. A mutt, its back came as high as her thighs. Its head appeared too large for the rest of its body, but maybe if it wasn't so scrawny, everything would have been in proportion.

The mutt wasn't aware of her presence, not that that surprised her, because in her *visions,* she floated above whatever creature she came in contact with. By concentrating on its breathing and heart rate, she soon determined that it was experiencing equal parts fear and anticipation. Its belly was empty, and it salivated. This wasn't the first time this had happened. In fact, wanting to be fed, but not knowing if it was going to happen, was part of the fabric of its life. Much as she longed to study what the dog was looking at, that wouldn't accomplish anything. If she wanted to learn more, and she did, she had to wait for the creature to do the revealing.

A part of her was aware of Hok'ee's hand on her elbow, and his confusion as he tried to determine what she was doing.

Ah, the dog was slowly lowering itself to the ground, and its growls became anxious whines. The hairs on the back of its neck stood up, and it pulled back its lips to reveal yellow teeth. Strangely, it started wagging its tail. Sorry for the creature, she pondered why its emotions were in such conflict. In her world, most dogs were loved and cared for, but she'd been sucked far into the past.

How far? Where was she?

History expanded. She smelled wood smoke and roasting meat. Like the dog, her mouth filled. She might have been distracted by her hunger if not for the sounds. Now she was securely inside the mutt's body. She saw what it did, smelled what it did, heard the same things, and reacted as the dog did.

Several people were talking in a language unlike any she'd ever heard. The predominantly male voices consisted of a series of clicks and grunts, along with occasional sounds that came from deep in the speaker's chest. She'd heard Navajos speaking among themselves while at Canyon De Chelly, and knew that wasn't what she was hearing.

Who else had made Sani their home?

A thrill of comprehension slammed into her. She had to fight it in order to keep her focus on the mutt. Quivering in excitement, she slipped back into the mutt's body. It was still wagging its tail, still prepared for danger. It had settled onto its belly with its head high, nose twitching, spittle running from both sides of its mouth. Suddenly a blur of movement flew toward the dog, only to drop to the ground a foot in front of it. Moving with the speed of youth and need, the dog snatched up whatever it was and swallowed.

The mutt was being fed scraps from whoever was teaching it how to live among humans. And not just any humans, but those who'd lived here thousands of years ago. She'd heard them, could duplicate some of the sounds!

"What is it?" Hok'ee demanded. His hold on her shoulder tightened.

"What?"

"You're shaking, and you keep staring at the same spot."

The image faded. Nothing remained of the roasting meat smell, and Hok'ee's voice was now the only one she heard. She wanted to scream, to cry out and beg the dog and humans to return.

Even as she reluctantly turned her attention to her captor, she had no doubt of what had just happened. If she could do that again, take more time and pay closer attention . . . "I can't explain," was the only thing she could think to say.

"Neither can I."

"You're talking about what happened to you earlier, aren't you?" Her arms were useless; she was naked. But she had to do everything she could to connect with him. "It—it's going to happen again, isn't it?"

"Yes." He slid his fingers down her arms, warming them.

"You can't stop it?"

"No."

She should ask him more questions, maybe warn him that she was determined to slip into his mind the next time he became a cougar. Instead, she fixed her gaze on his chest. He was still stroking her arms, his fingers lighting small fires wherever he touched. It wasn't fair! She should have the freedom to do the same to him, to show him she was capable of turning him on. She'd wordlessly let him know she no longer feared him. Yes, he was equal parts human and predator, but that's what excited her. He'd become precious to her.

No, not that, damn it. Just because he'd stolen her self-determination didn't mean she was going to let him do whatever he wanted with her.

Lay her down? Stretched out on his bed with her arms reaching for him, her legs splayed, her cunt exposed and waiting.

He had to stop touching her in that possessive way, and had damn better hand back ownership of her body, because she needed . . .

Needed what? she tried to ask as he finger-combed her tangled hair. She should have taken time to put it in a braid this morning, should have had the unwieldy mass cut before coming to Sani, but knowing she'd be living in primitive conditions, she'd clung to that one piece of femininity. And now it was being used against her, reminding her of what it was to be a woman.

But she loved the slight tug against her scalp as he continued working her hair. Maybe the gesture said he found the badge of femininity attractive and couldn't keep his hands off it.

When had he last touched a woman?

10

Before she could so much as think how she might answer her questions, Hok'ee's hold tightened, and he pulled her head back. She tugged on her bonds, only to forget what she was doing when he cupped a hand around her right ass cheek. Although he released the meaty flesh before his hold became painful, the aftershock headed straight for her sex.

She stared at the stone ceiling, barely seeing it, waiting for his next move. She had no doubt he was looking at her breasts. They ached for his touch, to be massaged, even pinched. That's what she needed, to be manhandled.

Anasazi? Who cared?

Her throat felt stretched, and she was starting to have trouble breathing. Comprehension of how fully he controlled her awoke a now familiar fear. Then apprehension changed and became hot anticipation. She had to be patient, had to wait out his silence.

He was good with silence, wasn't he? It became his tool, and yet another way of pulling her into his world, perhaps unknowingly. Earlier today, he'd demonstrated how easy it was for him to rob her of speech. That, coupled with the loss of her clothes, stripped her down in ways that went beyond nudity. His hands would claim her when he wanted, his cock would plunder her when he was ready, and his world would become her reality.

She might see Cougar again.

Another tug on her hair had her gasping and leaning against him. Bringing his mouth close to her ear, he exhaled a long, slow breath. Heat spread over her to erase memories of what she'd been before today. Even when the tension on her head let up and she was no longer in danger of falling, she continued to be his.

There, his hand back on her buttocks. Only this time, instead of grabbing and compressing it, he lightly slapped the too-receptive flesh. Again and again he smacked her until, unnerved, she tried to move away. Her rebellion earned her another warning tug on her hair. The gentle spanking continued.

She should know to remain where he wanted her to, but with energy building everywhere and mostly between her legs, she started walking in place. Lifting a foot, only to set it down so she could lift the other, gave her something to do, some way of controlling her response to the assault.

"Don't, please, please, don't. Oh, God, I can't. Please, stop."

"Not going to happen. Not until I've accomplished what I need to."

He'd been focused on her right cheek, heating and heating it until she swore her flesh would catch fire. Then he stopped and blew into her ear again, and she sobbed.

"What's that?" he demanded. "Something you're trying to say?"

"Stop, damn it, stop."

"You don't mean it." The words said, he lit in on her again, this time targeting her left side. She counted, tried to anyway. Tried to lock her knees and keep her feet from moving. But he kept after her, a light quick slap building on the one that had come before. She couldn't remember where she'd been in her counting, so she tried to start over. At the same time, her legs slid apart a few inches, her lips buzzed, and her temple pulsed.

Being trained, taught, controlled.

"I can't, can't—it hurts, please, it hurts."

"You're lying."

"No, I'm—"

He pinched the flesh he'd been attacking, gripping and twisting a little at the same time. Yowling, she rose onto her toes, only to settle back down when he released her. It vaguely registered that she could turn her head a little, and the pressure along her throat was gone, but she couldn't put her mind to how she might test the limits of this new freedom.

Was he done punishing her?

Afraid to ask, she concentrated on slowing her breathing and trying to get her mouth to close. She might have succeeded if he hadn't pressed something, probably the heel of his hand, against her tailbone. As if that wasn't enough, he rotated his hand from side to side, the pressure building.

"What . . ."

"What am I doing?" he finished for her. "Reaching."

That made no sense, or maybe the truth was his few words made terrible and irrevocable sense. In her mind, his hand became his cock. It was pushing through her layers, finding her core, entering her, and claiming ownership.

He, owning her?

Instead of the fury she needed, her legs weakened. His fingers were on the move, heading south, finding her crack and sliding into the hot, close space. Trying not to make a sound was so damnably hard, and she couldn't begin to think how she might send strength to her legs. All she could do was stand there like an animal about to be slaughtered.

No, not slaughter.

His thumb, she reminded herself—keep track of it.

Oh, there it was, pushing between her ass cheeks. His nail touched her puckered rear opening, retreated, touched again. She tried to prepare herself, to throw up a civilized woman's defenses, but hearing herself bleat like some lost lamb, she knew she'd failed.

"I've thought about this for a long time." His mouth was near her ear again, his breath like butterfly wings on the incredibly sensitive flesh. "What I must do if I'm going to succeed."

At what? What are you trying to do?

"I don't know what it is to be a woman," he told her with his short, smooth nail unraveling her. "So all I can do is try to put myself in your place. You hate what I'm doing, don't you?"

Yes. No. I don't know.

"I know what hate feels like. I live with it every day of my life."

His voice had dropped to a low, harsh whisper that pulled her out of herself. Not moving, she began a slow, relentless surrender. This man she'd be wise to loathe had stepped into her personal space. Not only had he taken control of her physical body, he'd begun touching her at a deeper level. She cared about him, that's what it boiled down to. She cared.

"What is it you hate?" she asked, despite the pressure against her ass.

"Being alive the way I am."

"Cougar and man, you mean?"

He didn't answer, prompting her to ponder whether to repeat her question. She suspected she'd already gone further than he'd anticipated, and as such was forcing him to reassess their relationship.

What relationship? She was Hok'ee's plaything, his sexual possession. He wanted and intended to use her for sex. Maybe he had no other interest in her.

Being afraid of her body's weakness was an overwhelming sensation. For someone who'd always taken pride in her intellect, what she'd become seemed impossible, and yet she couldn't deny the truth. On a summer afternoon, she stood naked and restrained while a powerful stranger laid siege to everything she'd ever believed about herself.

His large and rough thumb was no longer simply at her rear entrance, it plundered there. Pressure built upon pressure. Her ass muscles protested by clamping down. At the same time, she needed to know what total invasion felt like, to test her limits.

To be ass fucked.

Why that instead of *normal* sex? Was it part of some diabolical plan to shred her self-determination? Or his idea of a gift.

"Why this?" she managed. She tried to pull away, then sagged back against him. "Oh, God, why this?"

"What's your name?"

"I—Kai Tallon."

"You know your name."

"Of course, who doesn't? What are you talking about?"

Once more he gave her only silence. Her mind was filling with dark heat, a thick nothingness mercifully blocking all shame. *This* was happening. There was nothing else.

Gone. Pressure missing. Her ass muscles tightened as if trying to find something to grip. Before she could think how to make them stop, he ran his fingers over her sex lips. She became lost in the sensation, heat rolling through her, and her breathing stopped. Eyes open or closed? She couldn't tell which, and didn't care.

A shift in his body brought her back a little. He was no longer behind her, but at her side with a hand back on her hair. A too-familiar smell awakened her nostrils, and she knew he'd brought his fire-drenched fingers close to her nose.

"You want this, Kai Tallon," he said. "At least your body does. Taste yourself."

Driven by what might be her last shred of resistance, she shook her head and clamped her teeth together.

"All right," he said, when she thought, and maybe hoped, he'd punish her. "But whether you taste or not, we both know the truth." That said, he ran his hand down her cheek, leaving behind a sticky trail.

Suddenly angry, she glared at him. However, with him close by her side and her head still immobile, all she saw was a blur. "How far is this going to go?" she demanded. "What do you want, me on my knees begging you to . . ." Unwilling to continue, she struggled not to acknowledge the proof of her arousal he'd left on her cheek.

"It'll go as far and for as long as I believe it needs to."

For maybe two seconds, she believed he wasn't going to go after her sex again, but then her thigh muscles jumped. Trying to shake her head only earned her a tugging sensation. Looking front and center like some felon about to have her mug shot taken, she willed her legs to relax, but how could they? That damnable hand of his was on her labia again, taking unacceptable liberties, gliding over heated flesh, stroking her repeatedly. One finger after another slid along her opening, touching lips and clit.

Her legs again threatened to go out from under her, forcing her to widen her stance. Of course that only increased his access, and ratcheted up her vulnerability. A swimming sensation floated around her, hot and alive and peaceful at the same time. She existed between her legs and wanted nothing except to have her cunt caressed. Vaguely aware of how quickly the floating sensation could suck her down, she nevertheless gave only scant thought to how she might protect herself from drowning.

This was warm afternoons and sensual music, a man's talented hands on her electrified body, languid foreplay.

Mouth opening, she arched her back and thrust her buttocks at him like an in-heat mare welcoming a stallion. She had only one thought, one reason for living.

Her pussy was swelling, blood pooling and adding to her

pleasure. This time, instead of trying to deny the vulnerability that came with a dripping cunt, she silently thanked her woman's body. And Hok'ee. She was so grateful to him for, what—understanding what she needed?

As her cunt overflowed, her mind slipped away and became all instinct. Soon, oh yes, soon the balance would be tipped. There'd be no going back, nothing except rushing. She'd cry out, saying things that made no sense. Her pussy would tighten, and then tighten even more. The explosion, the incredible, life-affirming explosion—

No! Where had his hand gone? Just a second more, another heartbeat, and she'd—

"Taste yourself."

Opening her mouth, she let him lay his wet fingers on her tongue.

"Suck."

She did that, too, closing her lips around three fingers and not gagging despite the pressure at the back of her tongue. She drank of herself, tasting sex and him. Deeply hungry, she ran her tongue between his fingers, licking until she'd cleaned everything he'd gathered from her cunt off him and taken the truth about her vulnerability deep into her throat.

"Good," he told her. "Now we're going to do it again."

He was right. Five, six, then seven times he replenished himself from the bottomless well of her hunger and placed her offering in her mouth so she could, like a dog licking her master's hand, lap and lick. Her empty stomach recoiled, but she continued to feed off herself.

Unexpected pressure on her shoulders lifted a bit of the mist she'd slipped into. The pressure continued, leaving her with no choice but to bend over. As she did, she mentally stepped behind herself and studied her naked buttocks. Then there was no need for imagination because he'd placed his forefinger against her ass. Concerned she might lose her balance, she flexed her knees and turned her feet outward. What did she care about dignity when she'd already left it in the world she'd once lived?

Releasing her hair, he looped a hand around her tethered wrists and lifted her arms. At the same time, the finger against her rear opening made a fresh inroad. Dangling in his grip, she tried to fixate on muscles and bone, but her mind—if that's what it was—cared about only one thing, his finger.

"You're a woman, a sensual woman," he muttered. "And that's your greatest weakness. Your body needs what it needs. It will learn I satisfy those needs. Only me."

"What—what do you want?"

"Everything."

Everything? As an infant, her parents had been her world, but since then she'd assumed ownership of her body and mind. Now this man was determined to turn her into a child again?

No, not a child, something even more elemental.

Fight! Don't let him do this!

His finger, working even deeper into her, curving and turning, stroked and explored her rear passage. Another finger teased flesh that all but wept for him. He'd stepped beyond her final defenses and laid waste to self-determination. The plundering finger asked no questions, waited for nothing from her, took, and took, and took.

And yet it wasn't enough.

Her nerves shimmered and shook. Her arms, legs, breasts, and belly became part of an inescapable whole. She existed as a cunt, Hok'ee's cunt.

"Who owns you?" he asked.

Desperately holding onto what shreds remained of the woman she'd been this morning, she refused to answer.

"Who owns you?" A finger, it didn't matter which one, flickered over her clit.

"No! No—no!"

"I asked—" Another lightning stroke and the invasion to her asshole ending. "Who do you belong to?"

"Damn you!"

"I'm already there." A third touch to her clit, quick and light and lifting the top of her head. "Who is in charge today?"

"You. You."

The admission brought a sense of peace with it. There were no more battles to be waged, no more desperately protecting her trembling body. She'd surrendered.

For now.

"That's right," she heard him say from a great distance. "You're mine."

Something about his tone touched a nerve, but she couldn't hold onto the sound. What a slut she'd become, a willing and eager whore. Her dignity for a climax, that's what it all came down to, didn't it? Relief and release before she could think again.

"So long," he muttered as his fingers continued their exploration and her legs quivered. "So long."

She should ask what he was talking about, turn the conversation to accountability on both their parts.

Later.

Her cunt was a river, a swollen, flooding river. Proof of her insanity ran down the insides of both thighs. Irrational pride for what her body was capable of made her smile. At the same time, she ached to distance herself from the primitive. Was she reacting this way because Hok'ee was primal, half man and half animal?

Didn't matter. Not now with her head about to explode, and need screaming through every inch of her.

"What are you doing?" Throwing what strength she had behind the question, she closed her sex muscles around the thumb that had slid into her. "What the God damn hell do you think you're doing?"

He chuckled, and although she cringed at the sound, she couldn't blame him. Once again blood rushed to her head and her temples throbbed. No matter that she was willing, even eager to stand here like some malleable sex toy, she needed relief. She tried to straighten, but his hold on her wrists tightened. No, he wasn't done with her.

Get it over with. Bring me to climax.

Giving herself over to the only thing she wanted out of life, she focused on the living invasion. She was being fucked, albeit finger fucked, but fucked just the same. She'd ride him, buck and twist and in the process, push herself into space.

And after . . .

There, clenching and releasing, fighting to suck him even deeper, muscles burning, screaming even, everything building. One more second, almost there, that final leap!

No! Not withdrawing!

Too late, she clamped down with every bit of strength in her. He was already gone, escaped. Screaming in fury and pain, she struggled to look back at him. If she could reach any part of him, she'd make him bleed.

Wait! What—ah, a finger on her again. Drenched by her liquid heat. Once more tapping at the entrance to her bowels.

Panting, she willed herself not to move. He waited a moment, pushed against her rear hole, went still, pushed again. She opened under the assault. Muscles designed to protect and defend lost their will. She was welcoming him in, giving him permission to invade and conquer. Deeper and deeper he plundered.

In, he was in again, his finger surrounded by tissue he had every right to.

When the pressure against her temple decreased, she realized he was helping her straighten. For a moment the lessening strain in her arms distracted her from what was happening to her ass. Then a fireball rolled through her belly.

"Ah, ah!"

He pulled her hard against him, the hand gone from her wrists, his arm now compressing her breasts.

Locked in his embrace. The fireball spinning out of control, igniting her entire body on fire, screaming again, loud and wild.

Climaxing.

And in the moment of climax, seeing something that made her shudder in fear.

11

Her head down, Kai sat cross-legged on his bed. He'd retied her hands in front so she could eat, but although she nibbled on the apple and granola bar he'd given her, she reserved her enthusiasm for water. She had the look of a woman who'd spent the night fucking, complete with limp hair clinging to her cheeks and throat, and a still-swollen pussy. If she was aware of how much he could see of her cunt, she gave no indication.

He'd done that to her, shaken her so deeply she had no choice but to rest. Unfortunately, resting was the last thing he could do. Not only hadn't his erection given any indication of fading, his self-disgust was growing.

Bastard, that's what he was, a damnable bastard. And all because he was scared to death he'd lose her otherwise.

There had to be another way, something laced with tenderness and compassion instead of hard sex. A caring and intuitive man would know what that something else was, but he was neither of those things. Instead, he existed in a world rejected by both humans and animals. He didn't even know what name he'd been given at birth.

Anaba's scream earlier had reminded him that he wasn't completely alone, and as soon as he could, he'd let his friend know he was grateful for the contact. Because Anaba lived in the same dark world, the other man/beast would understand why he'd thrown his ropes over a woman.

Now what? Certain steps had been taken that would forever define his relationship with Kai. Even before he'd seen her, he'd believed he would have to do what he had. Otherwise, whatever woman he chose would flee. But he hadn't spent enough time examining the steps he and the female he'd haul into his world would take in this journey.

That was why he was on edge.

That and his inability to shake off the unfathomable look in her eyes as her climax ended.

Putting down the crumpled granola bar wrapper, she looked at him. Her eyes were saying the same thing they had a little while ago, not asking questions so much as telling him she'd found answers. If only he could comprehend what that was.

"I'm not afraid of you," she muttered. "Maybe I should be, but I'm not."

"I don't want you to be."

"Don't you?"

She was right; he was familiar with fear. Because a terrified prey was easy to bring down, he screamed and snarled while attacking. Then in sharp contrast to those moments of strength, he'd lain awake too many nights because his future frightened him.

"That was your intention when you first grabbed me. I know it was," she went on. "But maybe your agenda has changed now that you know a little about me. Very little."

She'd been locked on him while she was talking, but now she dropped her gaze to her lap. Tipping her head a little to the side, she placed her hands between her legs and touched her swollen sex.

"Is this what you wanted? To push my buttons? Once I was turned on, you figured you could get me to do whatever you wanted? Maybe follow you around like some pet."

Watching her unself-consciously stroke her labia, he wondered whether she was trying to stimulate or soothe herself.

"Maybe your agenda will work. All I know is, I'm not in control of my body." She held up her tethered hands. "And not just because of the ropes."

It wasn't suppose to be like this. He'd assumed instinct would tell him what he needed to do and why once he'd brought a female under his control. Maybe he should have never let her speak.

"I saw something," she went on after a short silence. "Right after I went off."

"Saw?"

"Maybe that's not the right word. It isn't easy to explain. It's nothing I can point at or take a picture of, but it existed in my mind just the same."

He was suppose to be the one with depth and secrets. He'd become resigned to skin that didn't fit. Now, maybe, he was learning his *captive* had secrets of her own.

"Tell me, please."

"Please? That's not a word I expected to hear from you."

"It's not one I thought I'd use."

"But you did. All right." She sighed. "I think you need to know this. It's up to you to decide whether you believe me, or if it makes any kind of sense."

"All right," he said hoping to get her to continue.

"Earlier I mentioned my ability to connect with animals."

"I remember." Although the desire to touch her chewed at him, he sensed she needed to be alone with her thoughts.

"And I know what you become."

Such simple words, and yet maybe the most complex he'd ever heard.

"A cougar."

"Yes."

"Yes?" she echoed. "Just like that, no denial on your part?"

"What would be the point? You saw it happen."

"Yes, I did," she whispered. "All right. In my mind I was standing on a bluff looking down into a valley. I'm sure it's part of Sa—of Tochona. There was a cougar—you. I had absolutely no doubt I was looking at you in cougar form. You were half-awake. Not looking for something to hunt, just existing. But . . ."

When the silence stretched out, he placed a hand on her ankle.

"You weren't alone," she continued. She didn't seem to notice the touch. "There was something around you. Dark and foglike. I sensed energy and anger in the fog, a possessiveness. It scared the hell out of me."

His throat tightened. "Around me?"

"It was as if you'd been surrounded by a storm cloud. That's as accurate a description as I can give you." She started to touch his hand, only to pull back and cover her sex again. "That anger was directed at you."

A half-lost memory laced with fear coiled through him. "Emotion, from a cloud?"

"You have to know what I'm talking about," she insisted. "I'm not saying anything you aren't aware of, am I? Hok'ee, I've sometimes touched animals that have just been killed. Even though they're dead, I know what they experienced and felt during the final moments of their lives. It's the last thing I want to do, but I believe I owe it to the creatures to acknowledge those emotions. I see how they died." She shuddered. "It's more than that. I've felt a bullet penetrating a deer's heart, a car striking a dog."

"I'm sorry."

"So am I. That's when I'd give anything not to be psychic, or whatever you choose to call it, but I believe I've been given my gift for a reason. I have to take the bad with the good."

"I'm not so sure it's a gift."

"There are times when I couldn't agree more." Her eyes were hollowing out. "Like the time a barn fire trapped . . . At least what I experienced helped convict the bastard who lit the hay on fire. He'd been fired. That's all, fired. He'd somehow convinced himself . . . I hope he never gets out of prison."

A few more words from her, and he'd clutch her to him until the pain was gone from her voice. Change their relationship, not that it hadn't already morphed into something he hadn't expected. "You don't have to do this. If it's too hard—"

"Yeah, I do! There are answers for you in the fog. I'm convinced of it."

"What kind of answers?"

"You honestly don't know what I'm talking about?"

Walk out of here. Take back your space. "There are so many holes in my past. Hell, I have no past." He couldn't believe he'd just admitted what he had. "No matter how much I try, I can't remember anything except living here, me and this inner cougar that threatens to take over."

She nodded, squeezed his hand, then let him go. "How long has it been like that?"

Although he questioned the wisdom of telling her more, he nodded. "Not a full year. I have memories of winter and spring but not fall. Anaba—he's the same as me—says I wasn't here when the leaves last changed color. One day I wasn't part of him and the others, the next I was."

"So you had another life before that, were someone else."

Don't say anything. Don't let her get close. "But who, damn it?"

"Trying to find answer threatens to drive you crazy, doesn't it?" Her whispered question stood in sharp contrast to his outburst. "Even if you don't know what it was, you want the life that was taken from you."

Before he could decide what, if anything, to tell her, his muscles started to heat. Cougar was stirring. If he didn't find a way to quiet the beast, it would soon take over. Not trusting himself, he released her ankle and pressed his hands together. His nostrils flared, his chest expanded.

"It's happening again, isn't it?" she asked him. "The need to change. Because of what I said?"

"I'm not sure of the reason."

"I think you are, Hok'ee."

Determined to remain in the world he shared with her, he stared. However, her edges were losing definition, and she seemed farther away than she'd been a few minutes ago. Cougar flexed his muscles again, promising an end to human burdens.

"I'll tell you what I think is happening," she said. "The beast will do everything he can to keep you from hearing what I'm trying to tell you."

The last time Cougar had assumed command, Cougar had run until his lungs and legs burned. After he'd made his kill, he'd shredded the creature's body. "Talk," he ground out. "I'll try to listen."

12

She might be looking at a man, but a predator waited just beneath the surface. Acknowledgment made, Kai started to close her eyes so she could concentrate on what she'd seen. Then, despite the risk, she grabbed Hok'ee's wrist and brought his hand to her breast. She waited until he'd flattened her flesh, then mentally slipped into him.

Instead of the contact between them helping her see the fog scene more clearly, she caught a glimpse of something new. An athletic looking man wearing leather pants and jacket walked over to a shiny black motorcycle. After putting on a helmet, he straddled the bike and brought it to life. Large strong fingers gripping the handlebars, he looked around, and she guessed he was making sure nothing was in his way. He seemed at ease, looking forward to a ride.

Leaning forward brought her close enough to Hok'ee that his breath warmed her throat. The image in her mind momentarily darkened and then became clearer. A cell phone rang, and the man pulled off his helmet and reached into a jacket pocket. Whatever the other person said prompted a smile from him. He was on his way, he said, would be there in a few minutes. He listened, his smile fading a little. Then he said he'd get there as soon as he could. After a little more listening, he said, "All right. Good-bye."

After returning the phone to his pocket, he put the helmet back on. Seconds later, the bike started rolling forward. Then it reared and came down screaming. Man and machine disappeared.

"You had a motorcycle," she said. "A powerful one."

"What are you talking about?"

"I'm telling you what I saw. I know it was you; I have no doubt of that. The bike represented something important to you, maybe the way you approached life. The scene—Hok'ee, it might have been the last day of your life."

"How can you say that?"

"Because that's what I asked for."

He started to release her breast, prompting her to tighten her grip. Doing so caused the rope to rub against her wrists.

"Don't be afraid," she said. "And don't fight Cougar. The closer he is to the surface, the more I'll be able to see of what you once were."

"I don't believe you."

"Yes, you do! And you want your past returned to you, don't tell me you don't."

When his breathing quickened, hers followed suit. Images continued to flash. Sometimes she saw fog slip around the cougar. When that happened, the cougar bit and clawed at it. Other times, she hovered overhead while the cyclist sped down a late night highway. Sexual energy interlaced both scenes.

"Cougar," he ground out. "Tell me what's happening to Cougar."

Was that him talking, or the other half of his being? Alerted to that possibility, she struggled to block out the man. "He's standing up, backing away, but the mist keeps following him."

"Is he afraid?"

"I—I don't think he knows what fear is. It's more like an innate caution, maybe a self-protective mechanism. Cougar is comfortable in his world, but when that world becomes something he's never experienced and can't control, he leaves. Only this time he can't."

"What is the fog?"

"I don't know." *I want to.* "It's cold, terribly cold." A sudden thought made her shiver. "Maybe—this is going to sound insane, but maybe it's you, the man, the other half of him."

"I'm turning into fog? Hardly."

"I know it doesn't make sense, but why else would Cougar want to get away? You're the only threat to his existence."

"Cougar threatens me, not the other way around."

Wondering if Cougar would say the same thing, she held onto him with every bit of strength she had. "The two of you share the same body, you *have* to work together."

"The hell—you try living any kind of life, not knowing when you're going to be trampled into nothing so some beast—"

"What about when you trample Cougar? Hok'ee, that has to be what happens when he's in control. Otherwise, the human side would never come out again."

When Hok'ee didn't respond, she hoped it was because he was considering what she'd said. Although she wanted to wait him out, she didn't fight when something began pulling at her. Still holding Hok'ee's hand, she returned to the hill and looked down at Cougar. If the predator had moved, she wasn't aware of it. In contrast, the fog had become denser and was so cold ice had started to form on the nearby plants.

Cougar was an incredible beast. He carried himself with unconscious grace, his keen hearing and eyesight as remarkable as his muscles and fangs. She not only admired him, she would give a great deal to be able to touch him.

Mentally moving closer, she pushed into his space. Because

she was used to an animal's simple and yet complex makeup, nothing of what she found surprised her. Cougar saw, he heard, he smelled. His mind filtered the various impressions, casting off the unimportant and focusing on what he needed to know in order to survive.

But unlike the other predators she'd *examined,* Cougar had feelings and emotions. He might just be standing there watching the fog, but he'd already accepted it as a foe he couldn't master. Resigned to his fate, whatever it turned out to be, he nevertheless longed to put it off as long as possible. In addition, he was determined to learn everything he could about his surroundings and hold those impressions close while he existed only as a memory. That way he'd be ready when Cougar broke free again.

It went deeper than that. Instead of simply gathering impressions and knowledge, Cougar ached to live fully and forever in his world. He loved the hot, sage-scented wind, the sheer canyon walls, the call of birds, the Anasazi ghosts.

Anasazi?

Shaking herself free of Cougar, Kai stared at the man sitting across from her. "Hok'ee?" Her voice squeaked, prompting her to try again. "Hok'ee, do you sense anything about the first people to live here?"

"What? I thought you were—"

"I know, but something just happened. Maybe it was just a thought, but—what do you know of the original residents?"

"The Anasazi, you mean?"

"Yes. I was in Cougar's mind, at least I was making my way into it. Then suddenly they popped into my mind."

"They're still here, their ghosts anyway."

You truly believe that? "Ghosts? That's how you think of them?"

"Yeah. Why?"

Although she hadn't thought of Garrin in hours, she wished

she could share this moment with him. Instead, she had Hok'ee. "You aren't the only one who feels that way. So does Cougar."

"He's an animal, a killer."

"He's more than that, and I think, on some level, you know it. Have you ever wondered if there's any way the two of you could peacefully coexist? Instead of resenting each other's presence, you could work together to increase—"

"He wants me dead."

About to disagree, she closed her mouth. In essence Hok'ee shared the same physical and emotional space with Cougar. In contrast, a few hours ago she hadn't known either of them existed. But given time and cooperation from both entities, could she bring them together?

With animosity and distrust gone, could they serve as the link to an extinct people?

Fairly shaking with excitement, she tried to hug Hok'ee. Damn the ties around her wrists. And damn him for believing he had to treat her this way.

But if she was the one with a rope, wouldn't she try to capture man and animal?

Head throbbing, she dragged his hand off her breast. The cool cave air dried her flesh but did nothing to lessen the deep-seated heat.

"What about Cougar?" he demanded. "And the fog."

"I think you'd like to have me tell you the fog killed him, but I can't. I want him to live. How does that make you feel?"

She was wrong, she had to be! All the times he'd battled Cougar for control, Hok'ee had never sensed anything except raw animal. And if—no! He wouldn't entertain the possibility that Cougar had a soul, he wouldn't!

Furious at this woman who'd tried to change him, he grabbed her shoulders and pushed her down onto the bed. She started to twist away, prompting him to clamp both hands around an ankle. Lifting her leg into the air, he anchored her in place. Her sex-scent drifted to him, and he rested her leg on his shoulder so he could slide closer. She scratched his chest. He growled.

"Who's doing this?" she challenged. "You or Cougar?"

Growling again, he slapped the breast he'd been covering a short time ago. When her nails dug in and drew blood, he slapped her other breast. Far from looking frightened, she reared up and reached for his throat. He easily pushed her back down.

"It doesn't matter," he belatedly answered, "because either way I'll win."

"Win what?"

You. Determined not to answer, he used his knee to shove against the inside of her the leg. Instead of resisting, she let him spread her. Her wide eyes and the throbbing vein at the side of her neck said she was already turned on. Maybe she'd never climbed down from that state.

He was in control, his stronger body ruling her sweet and soft one. She was like water, like a breeze, formless.

Was he any different?

Cougar shifted inside him, not trying to break loose for once, but so he could share in what was going to happen. Instead of resenting the invasion, Hok'ee felt himself stepping aside to make room for the beast. Then, studying her with eyes belonging to man and predator, he dragged her hands off his chest.

"Your eyes," she said. "He's trying to come out again, isn't he?"

"Yes."

"If he succeeds—"

"I won't let him."

What if you can't stop him? her eyes asked. He didn't bother to tell her that he was determined to sense the shift in power in time to walk away from her. Cougar had no interest in fucking a human female. But if the beast wanted to shed blood—

Power. Fighting. Never giving up control.

Driven by the thought, he slid off the low bed, but remained on his knees. Then he dragged her to the edge and bent her knees, spreading her at the same time. It would take nothing to spear her, least of all her cooperation.

The thought of taking her against her will made Cougar's muscles flex, but that wasn't why Hok'ee thumbed her entrance. Fragments of memory hinted that he'd once been a gentleman, a civilized and politically correct male, but that creature had died along with the life he'd led before everything shattered. Only Hok'ee remained. And Hok'ee wanted sex.

Her eyes drifted close, and her head rocked from side to side. She didn't try to draw her legs together. Leaning low over her, he took a breast into his mouth. The moment he did, she tried to pull her arms free. Pressing down, he kept them trapped between their bodies while he ran his tongue over full, heated flesh.

She kept tossing her head. Her mouth was open, as were her eyes. This close to her and intent on her captured breast, he couldn't make out her expression. All he knew was that she'd stopped flexing her arms and had started pressing her legs against his flanks.

Her breast, his. If he wanted—if Cougar won this round—he'd bite and chew and there was nothing she could do about it.

Cougar shifted, muscles strengthening. Not fighting the other half of his being, Hok'ee pulled more of the soft, full mound into his mouth.

"Stop it."

She spoke to the man, but Cougar heard. Energy ran through the predator. Gathering strength around him, Cougar took in the scent of woman. It curled through him to touch the man.

Shaking himself back to awareness, Hok'ee straightened so Kai no longer had to bear so much of his weight. But although he should release her breast, he couldn't. She'd climaxed earlier, not him. She'd found release, not him.

The swollen flesh changed form inside his mouth as he sucked, adding to instinct and need. She was his, possession and property, raw sex. Surrounded by temptation, he relaxed until only her nipple remained in his damp cave. He ran his teeth over the hard nub, somehow keeping the touch light.

"Oh, God. God."

She'd started to shake, nothing frenzied but neither, he sensed, was it anything she had control over. Cougar, conditioned by a lifetime of dominating prey, smiled. He'd run down some creature and had crippled it. Whatever it was lay under him, alive and yet standing on the path to death. Cougar had no conception of another animal's pain, and didn't care if it was terrified.

No! Don't let it happen.

Trying not to snarl, Hok'ee pushed back and up, releasing her nipple at the same time. Even as he fought his own darkness, he realized Cougar was no longer trying to take over.

But soon . . .

13

Did he know how much he was revealing, Kai wondered, watching Hok'ee's jaw clench. Studying him despite her loosening body, she wasn't sure whether she was looking at the man or animal. Maybe both.

In some respects, it was like watching two movies at the same time, one superimposed above the other. Hok'ee might represent the dominant film, but the other was much more than a shadow. Cougar—she wondered if he had any other name—put her in mind of a creature trying to shake off hibernation.

Remembering her earlier thought about the possibility of the two working together to pull the Anasazi into the present distracted her from what she was experiencing. Then Hok'ee ran his hands over her thighs, and only his touch mattered.

"You're all right?" she asked. "Cougar won't—"

"I can handle him."

"Stop saying that! All I have to do is look at you to know the truth."

He started to shake his head, then stopped. "It's never been like this. Always before, I know when Cougar needs to hunt.

So we won't fight, I step aside so he can do what he must. Right now there's another kind of battle."

"Am I responsible?"

Instead of answering, he stroked her thighs. She managed to remain still until his fingers reached the join between leg and torso. Gasping, she lifted her buttocks off the bed. She couldn't think what to do with her hands.

"I didn't know this was going to happen," he said, his fingertips resting on flesh so sensitive she could hardly stand it. "If I had, maybe I would have left you alone."

"But you didn't."

"No, I didn't."

"Because?"

Instead of admitting to his loneliness, he pressed both thumbs against her labia. Shuddering, she tried to slap them away. Laughing at her feeble effort, he increased the pressure.

"Not fair. Not damn fair."

"Tell me you don't want this. Maybe I'll stop."

Silence, that's what she'd give him. Otherwise she'd lie and he'd see through it. Giving up, she lifted her arms over her head. She shouldn't trust him with her body, but whether she did or didn't wouldn't change the outcome, would it?

Besides, on some deep and inaccessible level, she did trust him.

"What does it feel like, coexisting with an animal?"

"It's the only thing I remember; I have nothing to compare it with."

The only thing I remember. But given enough time and Cougar's essence beating inside Hok'ee, she might be able to reconstruct his past for him. Maybe she'd be able to do the same for Cougar.

"I asked a question," he said, his body curling over hers, his cock stroking the inside of her left thigh. "Do you want me to go away?"

On the brink of saying no, she held back. Everything was so complicated, except for her body's responses. It wanted only one thing. Him. Now.

"What does my answer matter?" she came up with. "You've already changed everything."

"Just as you've changed me."

She needed to touch him, to embrace and curl around him as he'd done to her. At the same time, she loved being stretched out beneath him. He'd turned her into his possession and could do whatever he wanted to her. Of course he'd stop short of harming her, but maybe he'd slap her breasts again, and when they were red and aching, he'd run his teeth over her belly.

She'd moan and twist, prompting him to tie her hands to something to hold her down. Maybe he'd spread her legs and snake ropes around her ankles so she couldn't move. Hissing, sometimes growling, even screaming, he'd slide a hand under her buttocks and lift her. Finding her core, he'd ram into her. Sweat would stream from his straining body as he humped his writhing captive.

Awash in fantasy, she stared at him. She couldn't think how to move her arms, forgot she'd put them over her head. A vessel, that's what she'd become, waiting to be filled.

"Do it! Damn it, do it!"

"Shut up!" Clamping a hand around her jaw, he forced her head down. "I'm in control, not you."

"I know, I know."

"Then be quiet."

He punctuated his command by pulling on her legs so she was in danger of sliding off the bed. She'd started to dig her feet against the stone flooring when he arched her upward. About to beg him to fuck her, she remembered his command not to speak. Sweat pooled at the base of her spine, flames licked along her slit.

Power. His. The **fingers on her hips** holding her in place.

Halfway through a deep breath, she stopped. For an instant, she simply existed. Then understanding and acceptance ran through her. His cock head touched her entrance. She had no memory of her earlier climax, no awareness beyond his bold strength grazing her inner channel. He slipped in, easy and smooth, stretching her.

There was nothing civilized about him, only animal fucking animal.

Fear touched her, running along her sides and into her throat. He was so damn big, so strong. He might split her apart, the animal in him surging to the surface. No matter how fiercely Hok'ee fought Cougar, the beast would win. She'd be the ultimate victim.

Finishing her breath, she raked the back of his right hand. She tried to twist to the side, only to have him clamp down on her thighs.

"Not going anywhere." He leaned back, then ran himself even farther into her. "You're—not—going . . ."

Another change, fear fading beneath her sudden and raging hunger. He more than filled her—he consumed her, possessing every quarter-inch of her pussy.

Patting where she'd scratched, she lifted her ass as far off the bed as she could. His cock shifted inside her. Then it pulsed as if gathering energy from an inexhaustible source.

He was on the move again, sliding out a little before plowing and plundering. Quick, he was so damnably quick, she couldn't possibly keep pace. Reaching deep inside herself, she found her own tempo. They worked as one, lost touch, ran off at their own pace, then came together again.

She'd found satisfaction earlier, she reminded herself. He hadn't. His release came first, took precedent.

The hell it did! There was only her straining, screaming body and this terrible, wonderful burning. Let him grunt and groan. Let his muscles shatter and his cock catch fire; she didn't care.

Then she did again.

"Now, now, now," she chanted, trying to time the words to his full and fierce strokes. She couldn't move and talk at the same time, couldn't push her body to its limits while putting his needs first.

"Now, damn you, now." That said, she ran out of breath.

He kept after her, punishing, hot, wet power searing her channel. Even as the hard explosion caught her, his cock's contours changed, lengthened.

And his sounds, no longer the cries of a man in the midst of climax, but longer, coming from a deeper chest.

"Hok'ee! Hok'ee."

Too late. Gone. She was gone, spinning and slipping, her body swirling.

The pieces of her started to come back together. Always before, she'd hold onto her climax and draw out the sweet, overwhelming sensation, but this time she gathered up the shards and slapped them together. Her eyes were open, and although she knew better, she tried to wrench her wrists apart. She wanted to touch Hok'ee's hand, but was afraid. What if it had become a claw?

Calm down. Don't lose it.

The cave roof was the same dark gray as the rest of the stone. Strangely, she wondered whether the original residents had wanted something different, livelier maybe, softer.

Shaking off the question took time and energy, but when she'd accomplished her task, she no longer stood on the edge of self-control. The man/animal who'd spilled himself in her still knelt between her gaping legs. His pelvis occasionally jerked, and his cock was shrinking slowly. With her cunt numb, she couldn't tell whether his cock belonged to a human, or beast, or maybe a bit of both.

She wanted to say something that would prompt him to

speak but couldn't think what the words might be. Maybe she didn't want to hear his voice after all.

No longer interested in the cave's color, she closed her eyes. Male weight pressed on her thighs and male bulk kept her legs apart. Who or what had just fucked her was having trouble controlling his breathing.

Flashes. Impressions of something.

Thinking she might be returning to the scene with the motorcycle, she went deep inside herself. Instead, she found herself in an unlit living room. A woman was sitting on a pale couch, leaning forward with her hands clutched in her lap. She was looking up at something, prompting Kai to do the same.

A man, wearing black leather and holding a helmet.

"It was my decision," the woman said. "I knew what you'd say. You'd try to change my mind. But my life—"

"*Your* life," the man spat, and she knew it was Hok'ee, or rather whoever he'd once been. "What about the one you just ended?"

"Don't put it like that. If you'd had any idea how hard—"

"No, I don't have any concept what you went through making your damnable decision, because you didn't allow me to be part of it. You shut me out, damn it!"

Hok'ee was angry, but another emotion lived beneath his outburst.

"We're lovers, Ryan, that's all," the woman said. "Scratching each other's itches. Nothing was ever said about spending the rest of our lives together."

Hok'ee, or Ryan, let go of the helmet. It thudded to the carpet. "I wouldn't have walked out on you. I'd be there for our— surely you know me well enough to—"

"I don't know you at all, just as I'm a stranger to you." The woman buried her face in her hands. "All that crap I fed you about being a modern broad in charge of her sexuality . . .

Look, I don't blame you for our *accident*. After all, I insisted on handling birth control. I thought I had, that this wouldn't happen."

"I wore a rubber, except that one time."

"When we'd both had too much to drink." She started rocking. "I was less than two months along. The abortion—I hardly felt anything."

Hok'ee dropped to his knees and pulled the woman's hands off her. Then he rested them against his chest. "*You* didn't feel anything."

"Don't!" She tried to pull free. "Damn it, don't! It's been a nightmare. The last thing I need is to have you kick me while I'm down."

"You just said you hardly felt anything."

"That's not what I'm talking about, and you know it. I want children, just not now."

"Or with me."

The woman said something, but Kai couldn't hear. Although the couple's body language left no doubt of what they were going through emotionally, Kai felt herself being drawn away from the scene. No matter how she fought, she couldn't stay. Reluctantly, she opened her eyes. The dark gray ceiling waited for her.

"What is it?" Hok'ee asked. "You—what happened?"

They'd just had sex. What they'd both known would happen had. Contentment filled him, and she wanted to sleep next to him, nothing else.

Unfortunately, that wasn't possible.

She had to sit up and tell him what she'd just learned, give him a fragment of his past. But because she didn't know how he'd react, or how much of Cougar stirred inside him, she studied her surroundings instead.

Thousands of years ago a mysterious and mystical people had found shelter here. They might have lived a primitive existence by today's standards, but surely their emotions had been no less complex than what modern people felt. They'd cried when their children died. Men had hunted with hammering hearts while women prayed those men would return alive. And when a husband or father died or was killed, their families faced an uncertain and sometimes frightening future.

That's what she longed to pull out of the past, with Hok'ee's help. And Cougar's. Archeologists might be content with physical proof of the ancients' existence, but she had an incredible opportunity to paint the ancients as human beings—with help.

From a man who'd been robbed of a child and had died shortly after?

"Kai? Are you all right?"

When she didn't respond, he took hold of her hands and pulled her upright, compelling her to look at him. This close to him, she could see deep into his eyes. Yes, there was a faint yellow cast to them, proof of Cougar's existence. "Does the name Ryan mean anything to you?"

The beginnings of a frown turned into puzzlement. Still looking confused, he drew his dying cock out of her and massaged it. "I'm not sure. Why?"

"I *saw* something, an image from your past. Maybe more of the last day of your life."

"What happened?"

How could she answer right now? Not only did her body continue to hum with the aftermath of the sex they'd shared, she didn't want to cause him pain while Cougar's heart beat next to his. "I'm not sure this is the best time to—"

Shaking his head, he released his cock and ran his thumb over her drenched labia. "I'm with you, if that's what you're thinking. Me and not Cougar."

"He was here while we were having sex. He still isn't completely gone."

"I know."

"Were you afraid?"

"Of him breaking free? The only thing my cock cared about was staying inside you."

"That's not what I asked."

"I know." Watching her, he ran his thumb into her opening. Then he withdrew it, only to bring his hand to her mouth. "Taste yourself again, Kai. Admit I'm responsible for this."

He didn't want to hear about her vision. If he had, he wouldn't have tried to distract her the way he had. She sucked his thumb into her mouth, licked cum and more off him, and swallowed everything. That done, she did what she knew she had to.

"You were going to become a father," she told him. "But your girlfriend—I think that's what she was—had an abortion."

"How do you know?"

Sparing him nothing, she detailed the conversation she'd *overheard*. "You didn't say much, but you didn't have to. It was obvious the news hit you hard. You wanted to take it out on her, maybe you did."

"You don't know what happened after that?"

"No. Things faded away, probably because of this." She indicated her still-red pussy. Then, feeling bolder than she had since he'd entered her world, she fingered his cock. Liquid from both of them greased his length.

"Can you get it back?"

"I don't know. Hok'ee, the only reason I'm able to tap into your past is because of Cougar. I think he, being an animal, serves as the conduit. Do you understand what I'm saying?"

"I think I do. So, without him making his presence known, that's all there is?"

His emotion had been crystal clear during the conversation with his *girlfriend*. Although the circumstances were far different now, there was no questioning how important this was to him, not that she should be surprised.

"You want to do this?" She touched his cock again, a light

brushing of her fingertips that brought a lump to her throat and tightened her nipples. Even as she willed herself not to, she imagined drawing his organ into her mouth and licking him clean. "Learn what happened?"

"Wouldn't you?" he demanded. Grabbing her wrists with one hand, he forced her arms to the side. "If you had no knowledge of your existence before today, would that be enough?"

"No, of course not." He'd pulled her off balance. So much for allowing herself to believe they were equals. "But if I'm looking at the last day of your life—"

"Then I'll know how I died."

Except he wasn't dead after all. Or rather, he'd come back to life, albeit in altered form.

"All right," she whispered. "But you're going to have to step aside a bit and encourage Cougar to increase his presence."

"Encourage? It's always been a battle between us."

But if they were capable of working in harmony, what were the possibilities? Barely able to contain herself, she nevertheless forced thoughts of the Anasazi to the back of her mind. "I have to be touching you, you and Cougar."

The way he looked at their hands made her wonder if he'd been unaware of what he'd just done. He released her and she straightened. Then, studying her as he worked, he untied the rope she'd come to accept as part of her.

"It'll be easier for you this way," he said. "Now you can touch me when and where you have to."

Just like that, had their relationship changed? Maybe.

"What about Cougar?" she asked. "Is it possible for the two of you to reach a balance? Share the same space?"

Instead of answering, Hok'ee stood and paced to the opening. He stood with his back to her, looking out at the landscape. It was late afternoon, which meant Garrin had to be impatient for her return. She still believed he wouldn't think to come anywhere near here, but that didn't quiet her concern. Garrin carried a pistol and kept a rifle in his tent. If he spotted Hok'ee in cougar form—

Hok'ee threw back his shoulders, drawing her attention to him. He was so comfortable with his nudity. Maybe he'd left the human he'd once been far behind him.

Ryan. He'd once been a motorcycle-riding man with a short, strong name—and a baby who would never be born.

Beyond the mating, male cougars had no involvement with their offspring, and hadn't she read that males have been known to kill their youngsters? In contrast, Hok'ee's reaction to what she'd told him about the abortion had been all human. How hard it must be for Hok'ee to have to turn his head and heart over to an animal. No wonder he and Cougar were in conflict.

More muscle flexing on Hok'ee's part fascinated her. Grateful for the end to weighty considerations, she ran her fingers through her hair. It was tangled and dirty. What man would want to play with that mass? Maybe she'd—

What the hell did she care about her hair?

Dismissing the drying sweat on her naked body, she slipped off the bed and took a couple of steps. Hok'ee had gone back to staring at the world beyond the cave, and she didn't know whether he was aware of what he was looking at. Maybe he was engaged in some kind of conversation with Cougar.

Stifling a laugh, she resigned herself to waiting for him. After hours of being under his control and hands, she didn't know how to handle the change. Much as she appreciated being able to do what she wanted to with her arms, she needed him to be back in charge, and for everything to revolve around sex.

Shifting his weight, he turned in a slow, smooth half circle. With the light behind him, she couldn't make out his features. Yes, his chest was larger than before, his ears longer. His limbs were broader. Unlike when he'd shifted into Cougar earlier, he still stood upright, and she saw no sign of a tail.

"Come here," he said, the words issuing up from someplace deep in his chest. "Quickly. Touch me, before it's too late."

On less than steady legs, she put an end to the distance between them. His flesh had taken on a golden cast because of the thick, short hairs that had sprouted everywhere. Feeling as if she was having an out-of-body experience, she placed a hand on his chest, then pressed until she felt his heartbeat. A predator took shape in her mind, magnificent, deadly, compelling.

Then, responding to the urgency in Hok'ee's voice, she shook off the image and opened herself to her gift.

There, the man on the motorcycle.

14

It was dark, maybe late at night, judging by the lack of traffic. Ryan and his screaming black beast were on a single lane road with evergreens growing close on either side, and seemingly endless hills and turns around him.

He was going so fast that when he sped around a turn, he and his bike were nearly parallel with the road. Much as she wanted to beg him to slow down, she knew it wouldn't do any good. Instead of easing off the gas, he forced yet more speed out of the machine until the engine squealed. Hating and fearing what she had to do, she slipped closer to the hell-bent man until she started sliding into his body.

Ryan's confusion and anger surrounded her. She shared his hammering heart and pulled the same air into her lungs. But unlike Ryan who seemed to be embracing danger, she feared the speed and lonely road.

"What—" Hok'ee started.

"Not now. I have to concentrate."

A long-nailed hand covered the one she'd pressed against

Hok'ee's chest. Cougar! Maybe trying to take over. Then, fighting, she pulled herself back together.

Still exceeding the speed limit and ignoring the instinct for preservation, Ryan wrapped his body around his machine. Anger pounded through him. His rage had grown so strong that confusion had given way to the more powerful emotion. He hated not the woman who'd ended the life of his unborn child, but himself.

Determined to learn why, she reached deep into his mind. Beyond harsh emotion lay Ryan's memories and past, but the man's self-protective barriers got in the way. It wasn't just that he didn't want her to see his truth; he hated facing it himself. Fearing she'd never have a chance again, she continued to probe.

Now she *saw* a boy perched on a wooden chair in a small room with posters on the walls. Although the boy stared at a middle-aged woman sitting behind a cluttered desk, Kai first focused on the posters.

Open Your Heart and Home to a Child in Need, one read.
Each Child Deserves Love.
Foster Parents, The Best Job There Is.

So this room belonged to an agency that dealt with children who couldn't live with their biological parents. Ryan had to be the tense boy on the chair. She couldn't hear what was being said, maybe because the boy's distrust and helplessness was so powerful, she couldn't concentrate on anything else. One thing she did know, although he'd thrown up a *I don't care* façade, beneath the outer shell, he was utterly alone, lost.

The way she'd felt the day her father died.

The image faded. For several seconds she was back on the deadly motorcycle, but then that fell away, and she found herself at some kind of celebration. Sturdy women with long black hair were dressed in bright blouses and long skirts. Exquisite jewelry made from turquoise and silver hung from their necks and wrapped their wrists and waists. Dark-haired men wearing equally bright shirts and jeans sat in a large circle as they beat drums and chanted. Occasionally they looked at the children who moved their moccasin-clad feet in time with the drumming.

Recognizing a Navajo powwow, she wondered if she'd somehow tapped into something that was happening right now elsewhere in the state. But then she spotted the nearby parking lot filled with vehicles from the eighties and nineties, and knew she was still in the past, although maybe not as far back as she'd been with the boy.

Whatever camera lens she was looking through zoomed down and closer until it focused on a bored teenager and a man who appeared to be in his forties. The teen was trying to hide behind baggy, sloppy jeans and an oversized faded shirt. He wore dirty tennis shoes, and his unkempt black hair caught on his shirt collar.

Touching the boy's arm, the older man pointed at a beautifully dressed elderly Navajo woman. With her oversized turquoise and silver necklace, long gray braids, and deeply lined face, she represented not someone in costume for a celebration, but the real deal. From what Kai could tell, that's what the middle-aged man was trying to impress on the teen. All he got in return was a practiced *I can't believe you're making me do this* look.

Stifling the urge to slap the handsome young face, she pushed closer. There was no denying Hok'ee's dark skin, black eyes, and solid bone structure.

"Just a few more minutes," the man said, "that's all I'm asking."

"I don't want to be here," young Hok'ee—or should she say Ryan—retorted. "I told you—"

"That you don't give a damn about your heritage. Yeah, I know. But you're wrong when you say you don't have any roots. There they are. What's so hard about acknowledging them?"

"If the Navajo are so all-fired big on keeping their bloodline going, why did they throw me away?"

"I don't know. Ryan, I can't change what happened to you when you were little. All I can do is give you this, and the roof Carol and I've provided."

More shifting, the scene dissolving, words fading, and the loneliness beneath young Ryan's stony expression slipping away.

Fighting tears, Kai waited for what might come next. She was vaguely aware of the warm, naked body standing next to her and the hand with the beginnings of claws covering hers as it lay on his powerful chest. But though she longed to increase her awareness of Hok'ee, she wasn't done doing what she must.

The speeding motorcycle came back in view. But instead of feeling as if she was riding it with Ryan, she now hovered over the leather-clad form, not touching, no longer tapped into his emotions.

"Something's about to happen," she muttered. "I'm not going to want to be there."

"I'm with you," Hok'ee muttered in his deep-throated way. "I won't leave."

Unless Cougar takes over.

Too much speed, tires hissing, and the muffler hot enough to burn. Ryan clinging to the great beast, staring straight ahead but not slowing for the upcoming turn.

Despite wanting to scream at him not to throw his life away, Kai could do nothing except stare at the turn. The pavement at the road's edge had been attacked by weather and countless other vehicles over the years, causing it to break down. Ryan entered the turn, but this time, instead of marrying himself to the motorcycle, he sat upright, staring.

The wheels, slipping, losing traction! The cycle, tipping, tipping even more. The harsh screech of metal against pavement, and the sound going on and on.

Sparks, a fender, and other motorcycle parts flying in all directions. The too-late smell of rubber as brakes were applied.

And then the cry of a dying man.

"I was Navajo."

Listening to himself, Hok'ee silently cursed the stupid comment. He only had to look at his dusky complexion to surmise that he had Native American blood, but until now he'd dismissed his heritage as immaterial. What mattered was the here and now, specifically learning how to survive in this land of remote canyons he felt compelled to stay in. Once he'd reconciled himself to stealing in order to fill his human belly and have a bed to sleep on, he'd been forced to come face-to-face with something even more difficult to accept than reconciling himself to Cougar's existence—solitude. Yes, there were the other Tocho, but none of them was female.

And so he'd captured a woman in a damn insane attempt to end the lonely nights. But look where that had gotten him.

"You honestly have no memory of your childhood?" Kai asked. "If we knew where and when you entered the foster system—"

"What does it matter?"

"Maybe it doesn't," she said after a short silence. "At least not yet. But you deserve a past. I can't believe you aren't interested in it."

"I can't go back."

"No, you can't. Hok'ee, I saw you die. Doesn't that bother you?"

"The way you said I was driving, I deserved it."

"Your mind wasn't on what you were doing because you couldn't stop thinking about that woman aborting your child."

They were back to sitting on the bed because he'd led her to it. She'd been shaking, so he had been concerned she'd pass out. He'd held her until she'd stopped trembling. Then, although he'd already sensed some of what she was going to say, she'd told him what she'd *seen*. He wasn't sure how he felt knowing the manner of his death; he'd deal with that later.

He still cradled her naked body against him, just him because Cougar had gone back to wherever the predator existed when he wasn't trying to take over. Why should he? After all, Cougar could care less about human emotion.

"There's nothing," he admitted. "I appreciated the pictures you drew for me, but none of that resonates."

"Maybe later. I think, Hok'ee, that I don't believe you were killed outright the moment of the crash. I heard moaning, and for a while you tried to move."

Despite the hot distraction of her body, he clawed into his mind, searching for something, anything. Maybe he was simply feeding off what she'd told him, but was that the sound of metal against pavement? And that smell—rubber?

Crushing her against him, he concentrated. His right thigh started to burn, and his left wrist throbbed. Pain gnawed at his spine, and he felt like there was blood in his mouth. The sensations grew. His wrist more than ached; he had no doubt it was broken, maybe shattered. And his thigh burned because the skin had been scraped away from hip to knee. Agony now chewed at his knees, and he'd scream if he hadn't bitten off his tongue.

"Enough!" he bellowed. He jumped to his feet, knocking Kai to the ground as he did. Instead of helping her stand, he stared down at the pale crumpled form. Who was this woman? Instead of the simple warm cunt he'd been determined to bury himself in, she'd stormed into his life and torn it apart.

That's what he'd do to her, tear and rip, bite and claw. Force her to admit she'd lied about what she said she'd seen.

How damnably insane he'd been to believe she could look into his past! How dare she manipulate him into freeing her!

"It's happening, Hok'ee. Cougar is—"

"What?" Grabbing her hair, he hauled her to her feet.

"You're hurting—"

"Shut up!"

Her sharp gasp hurt his ears, but as he lifted a hand to slap her into silence, he spotted a red mark on her cheek. He'd already hit her, something he had no memory of.

"I'm leaving," he heard himself say. "I'll return when—I don't want you trying to run, because I'll know. Understand?"

"I'll be here."

Here. As he walked away, his feet made a dull slapping sound that reminded him of his heartbeat in the middle of the night. Although he wanted to apologize, he didn't dare look back at her. Neither did he tell her that he'd hunt her down if she tried to escape—or rather Cougar would—because she had to already know that.

Although it wouldn't be dark for a while, the sun was behind a sandstone rim and the shadows muted his surroundings. Cougar was retreating inside him, no longer desperate, fierce, and all-consuming. With his mind clearer, he studied his surroundings. He'd become so accustomed to the shadows that most times he dismissed them. Now they reminded him of what Kai had said about a dense, dark fog surrounding him, or had it enveloped Cougar? More important, what had the fog represented?

No thinking or questioning. He'd put necessary distance between himself and her, and then let Cougar have his way. The beast would hunt, and in the hunting the man would connect with this compelling world. Nothing else would matter.

He'd changed direction so he was heading toward the back of the rim, when he heard a familiar cry. Anaba, in cougar form. Breaking into a trot, he looked forward to finding his friend. They'd either hunt together or, both of them assuming human shape, they'd talk. As for what he'd tell Anaba—

* * *

Anaba was behind the rim and standing in the sun, his tail lashing and fangs exposed.

It's me, Hok'ee, he said in the silent way the Tocho used when they were Cougar. *Study me. You'll see I speak the truth.*

Instead of answering, Anaba lifted his head so he could catch the breeze. His tail stilled, and he closed his mouth. As Hok'ee grew closer, Anaba began changing form. By the time Hok'ee was close enough to speak in a normal tone, his friend had become human.

"You heard my call," Anaba said. "I hoped—"

"That's not why I came. When I first heard you, I tried to tell myself it was nothing I had to concern myself with."

"You left her?" The handsome, hollow-eyed younger man frowned. "Is she dead?"

"No. I would never—"

"But Cougar might."

Nodding reluctantly, he waited for Anaba to continue. After a moment, Anaba dropped cross-legged to the ground, prompting him to do the same. Although like Anaba, he was naked, he gave little thought to the rough surface his buttocks were on. Both men's cocks were limp.

"I left you alone because what takes place between you and the woman is for the two of you," Anaba began. "But I came close enough that I could hear and smell. Tell me, when you were fucking her, were you aware of anything else?"

Normally nothing or no one could approach his home without him knowing. Realizing how vulnerable he'd been caused his muscles to contract. But because he'd never lied to Anaba, he shook his head. "When I'm with her, nothing else matters. I become weak."

"Maybe that's why there are no female Tocho. He who has power over us wants us strong, horny but strong."

He who has power over us. How simple and yet complex the

explanation was. More importantly, would that mysterious and powerful force kill Kai because of what she'd done to him? Better he die a second time. After all, he'd been the one to bring her into his world.

"I didn't want to say what I just did," Anaba continued, "but I felt I had to."

"I should have thought of it. I didn't because . . ." He glanced down at his cock.

"I understand."

"Tell me, have you felt the force today? Perhaps it knows what I've done."

"I can't answer that. Only you can, eventually. Hok'ee, I wanted to stay where I was so I could hear . . ." His eyes nearly closed, Anaba cupped his hands around his cock, drawing Hok'ee's attention to the other man's newborn erection. "I came just from listening to the two of you."

"You're human."

"Sometimes. Hok'ee, I was still sitting there when I sensed something that made me uneasy. After becoming Cougar, I went in search of it."

This, he now understood, was why his friend had wanted them to talk. Much as he longed to tell Anaba what Kai had revealed about his past, that would have to wait. "What did you find?"

"The man who came here with the woman. He has left their camp and the cave they've been exploring."

Alerted by the tension in Anaba's tone, he leaned forward.

"At first I thought he was searching for her, but then . . ."

"Where did he go?"

"White-Falls."

The Tocho had given the name White-Falls to a thin waterfall that began at the top of one of the highest canyon walls. The waterfall had all but dried out this summer, but the small deep pool at the base still provided water for the area's animals, including him and the other Tocho when they were near there. As vital as the water was, that wasn't why his belly had suddenly knotted.

"He made it to the top?"

Anaba nodded. "It took him a long time. He kept looking around, often using his binoculars."

"He didn't see you, did he?"

"A predator knows how to stalk without the prey being aware."

Suddenly understanding, Hok'ee shook his head. "He wasn't looking for Kai, was he?"

"I don't think so. I believe he wanted to see where White-Falls began, but he didn't want her to know what he was doing, which is why he waited until she was gone. Hok'ee, he found it."

There was only one *it*, the complex and virtually intact structure that had been built in a deep crevice partway up the canyon and was within easy walking distance of the creek that became White-Falls. The canyon wall's many angles hid what the Tocho called Ghost House, until someone was nearly on top of it.

Although Tochona was home to a half dozen ancient ruins, only Ghost House remained as it had been at the beginning. It even included a burial pit, complete with the bones of the humans who'd once lived there. Because of Ghost House's location, it was sheltered from most winds and the worst of the seasons. And inside the multi-storied, multi-roomed house lay proof of what The Ancient Ones' lives had been like. He and the other Tocho spent little time there because it belonged to Anasazi ghosts.

"Where is he now?"

"On his way back down. He was inside Ghost House only a few minutes before he hurried out."

"Maybe he sensed the ghosts."

"Maybe." Anaba frowned. "As soon as he came outside, he used his binoculars to look around for a long time. I heard him muttering to himself, and his legs and arms shook. Hok'ee, if he tells others what he's found—"

"Outsiders will come here," he finished. "Maybe hundreds."

"And we'll no longer be safe."

What, he asked himself, would Kai say and do if she saw Ghost House? She'd come to Tochona to explore the area's past, but she hadn't expected to find anything remotely like Ghost House. She'd be as excited as her companion had been, and she would have a hand in bringing in outsiders.

He could keep her with him, not allow her to get anywhere near Ghost House. But even if he did, the man would—

"Hok'ee, I know why he didn't stay up there."

Blinking, Hok'ee focused on Anaba. "Why?"

"Not just because of the ghosts, but because he doesn't want her to know."

"What? They're companions. He—"

"Companions, or competitors?"

One of the problems with not being able to remember his past was that there were holes in his knowledge of what it was like to be human. In addition to using the nearest town as hunting ground for a sex partner, he educated himself about the human species. Anaba had been a Tocho longer than he had, and thus had learned more about those strangers.

"Hok'ee, there's only one way to stop him."

And her. "But if he doesn't return to where he came from, someone will look for him," he said, unable to mention Kai.

"If his body is found far from here, and we move or hide his belongings, the searchers might not come anywhere near Ghost House. In time, Tochona will cease to interest them."

"I pray you're right. When you and I are human, we care for each other. If one of us was killed, the other wouldn't rest until we learned who was responsible and made the killer pay."

Nodding, Anaba released his cock and patted Hok'ee's knee. Occasionally, when solitude and the need for sex became too much for them, they pleasured each other. They just didn't talk about this aspect of their relationship.

"If it looked as if he'd fallen," Anaba said, "there'd be no reason to investigate further."

Putting off the moment he couldn't ignore, he pondered how he might force the man over the top without leaving proof of his involvement. He didn't care how long it took for the man to die, or whether he screamed until death overtook him. Recalling what Kai had told him about his own death, he accepted that he had no more concern for what he'd once been and endured than he did for the stranger.

"Hok'ee, what about her?"

"Kai," he whispered. "That's her name."

15

Hok'ee knew Kai was where he'd left her long before he ducked and slipped through the opening. Outside, the shadows were everywhere, and because night came quickly once the sun set, he'd resigned himself to hours of darkness. True, he could turn on a flashlight or light a candle, but he wasn't sure he wanted to look at the woman who'd turned his world in directions he hadn't expected. A woman for whom he had the power of life or death over.

Heart beating faster than he wanted, he straightened and waited for his eyes to adjust. There she was, sitting on his bed and eating an apple as if his presence was of no concern to her. She'd put her shirt and jeans back on, but her breasts remained unrestrained, making him wonder if she'd bothered with her underpants.

"Is it you, Hok'ee?" she asked. "Or is Cougar about to break out again?"

"Cougar has turned this body over to me," he said, although that might change at any time.

"I heard something. A high-pitched scream. Was that Cougar? He was hunting?"

"Anaba was calling me. I went to him."

"Anaba?"

"My friend."

She frowned, then nodded. "What did this friend want from you?"

"Not want. He had something to tell me," he evaded as he stepped toward her. "You didn't try to leave."

"I should have."

"Why didn't you?"

"Damn it!" Jumping to her feet, she started toward him, only to stop with her head held high and nostrils flared like a deer sensing danger. Looking at her, the blood in his temples pulsed. Only a few minutes ago he'd been awash in self-hate for having approached her in the first place. If he hadn't hauled her into his world, he wouldn't be facing this terrible decision. Now, although he was no closer to committing himself than he'd been during his reluctant walk here, it suddenly didn't matter.

She was woman, sex and energy, breasts he'd cradled and a cunt he'd flooded with his seed. It was enough. Tonight, sex was enough.

Wasn't it?

Although he knew Cougar was responsible for some of what he was feeling, he gave no thought to making certain the beast was under control. In truth, having Cougar pulsing inside him would make tonight easier. He'd fuck, not think, not look into tomorrow, just fuck.

"Don't look at me like that," she ordered. "It makes me uncomfortable."

"Like what?"

"You know what I'm talking about, as if you're a predator

and I'm—shit, tell Cougar to go back to sleep, or whatever he does. Otherwise, I'm walking out of here."

Instead of giving into the impulse to laugh, he stalked toward her. Cougar's muscles flexed, contracted, flexed again. As unsettling as the sensations were, he loved existing between man and animal, the single-minded strength, the simple emotions.

She was beautiful, a doelike creature. Although she stood her ground, he sensed she was a heartbeat from bolting. If she did, Cougar might spring after her. She had to know that; maybe it was why she was trying to dig her toes into the hard ground.

"I have no doubt my coworker is looking for me. He's armed. Did I tell you that he's armed?"

"No, he isn't."

"What?" Her eyes widened. "How do you know what weapons—"

"He isn't looking for you."

Frowning, she shook her head, then went still. "Is that what Anaba had to tell you?"

As his respect for her was growing, he mentally reached out for Cougar. No matter how fiercely Cougar fought for freedom, he vowed not to let the predator loose now. Concentrating, he waited until he'd achieved the man/animal balance again. Then he took another step. Her smell drifted over him.

"You and I are in here," he told her. "What takes place elsewhere doesn't matter."

She stared at the scant distance left between them. "What is this about? You intend to *reward* me for telling you what I did about your past by—by forcing yourself on me?"

"You want me."

"I want civilized, damn it! I deserve to be treated like a woman."

The only woman he had any knowledge of had ended his

unborn child's life and robbed him of his one chance at having a family, of belonging to someone. Was that why he'd driven the motorcycle the way he had, because he'd wanted to join his child?

"You won't fight me," he told her. "I know you won't."

"You don't know anything about me! Hok'ee, you're scaring me." Judging by her suddenly widening eyes, she already regretted her admission.

Fear had a scent far different from sex, and yet both reached deep inside him. Not content to let Hok'ee have these moments, Cougar pushed into the inner space Hok'ee hoped to claim. But even as he resented the intrusion, he fed off Cougar's energy.

Looking at Kai's widely staring eyes made him regret his role in her agitation, but any emotion was better than the nothing that coated most of his days. She was his, his possession, a beating heart after too long of hearing only his own.

"You're getting that look," she muttered. "The cougar look."

Cougar's muscles rippled, leaving no doubt of his frustration with the confined space. Hok'ee wanted his own body, his arms and legs, hands and cock, but not that thin veil called civilization.

Stalk her, close in on her, let her know what was going to happen.

"Get back!" she snapped. "God damn you, don't play your stupid game."

"It's not a game."

Judging her expression, she already knew that. Another wave of fear coursed through her, but although she took a backward step, her fearful expression didn't last. He wanted to try to know what she was experiencing, but it wouldn't happen now, not with blood flowing into his cock, his chest hot and tight.

Melting into Cougar without surrendering human form was

easier than he'd thought, probably because for the first time in this short shared existence, he wanted to be both man and animal. A man stalking the woman he intended to claim.

"Ah, shit," she muttered. "Fucking shit."

"You want to fuck?"

"Not like this, damn it." Not taking her gaze off him, she crossed her hands over her crotch. "I don't know who you are, or what you're capable of."

"Touch me, then you will."

It was the last thing she wanted to do. He only had to catch her strangled breathing to understand that. But did she have any choice? Willing himself to stand his ground, he held out his arms, palms up, so hopefully she'd know he was opening himself to her.

"You're—" she started. "Damn you for putting me through this."'

A man should have a response, right? But there was too much animal in him for that to happen. He'd keep his human form; doing that was vital. As for the rest of him, in truth, he had no interest in the man who'd been given the name Hok'ee.

Her nostrils flared as her gaze skimmed down him. Her hands, still protecting her crotch, pressed against her jeans. Then, her cheeks reddening, she slid her right foot forward. How long, slim, and yet strong her legs were, made to wrap around a man's body. And that soft, ever flowing cunt—just thinking about it made him grunt.

Hearing the raw sound, Kai started. Then, putting everything she had into it, she willed herself to return to the wordless challenge Hok'ee had thrown at her. Although he remained fully human, he seemed larger than before, more intimidating, determined.

He'd had a number of reasons for returning to her, most of which she wasn't sure she wanted to know. Despite his reasons, right now only one thing mattered to him. He reminded her of a prisoner forced behind bars for too long. Now that he was free, he cared about nothing except exploding in the nearest cunt. Only once he'd accomplished that could he begin to think about the rest of his life.

What force, event, thought, or impulse had turned him on? He'd climaxed not that long ago with her willing body wrapped around his. Shouldn't he be satisfied?

He wasn't, though, and from everything she could tell, sex was the only thing that mattered to him. Feeling the pull of his energy gave her the insane courage and energy to slide those last few inches and place her fingertips on his hips. Holding her breath, she stood on her toes, ready for what?

Yes, Cougar, crouching beneath the human skin, but sharing the same lungs and breathing in the same scents. No surprise, because Cougar was all about sex. No matter what it took to achieve the predator's goal, he'd do it. What did he care if the female resisted? Only his needs mattered.

What a sad, hollow, and dangerous way to live.

Even as she moved her fingers upward in hopes of determining whose heart beat the strongest, she acknowledged the impact Cougar was having on her. Despite what she'd just told herself, she loved his simplicity and primitive qualities. He was the most honest living organism she'd ever come across. There was no questioning his needs and goals.

Or how much her needs mirrored his.

Afraid, yes. Challenged, certainly. Hungry, maybe more than she'd ever been.

"Do you know what you're doing?" Hok'ee muttered as she flicked his nipples.

"I hope so."

"I'm not sure—I can't guarantee what's going to happen."

"I know." Still touching him, she shifted her thoughts from

Hok'ee to the other half of him. *I can't give you what you want and need,* she told Cougar. *No one can. But I'll listen. I promise I'll do that.*

"Kai?"

Just like that, she could no longer concentrate on trying to communicate with Cougar, but with the beast so close to the surface, maybe it didn't matter. Maybe he knew.

"I don't understand what I'm doing," she admitted. "A large part of me wants to trust instinct, but one of us has to think and reason."

"Why?"

"That's what you'd like, isn't it?" she threw at him. "Both of us going at it like animals. Sorry, but that's a luxury I don't dare allow myself."

If her words had made an impact on him, she couldn't tell by his expression. "All right, all right," she repeated, stalling because, somehow, she had to pull herself together. "You say Garrin isn't looking for me. What *is* he doing?"

"No."

No? What kind of response was that? Mind spinning, she dropped her hands to her sides. Not touching him made it easier to think, marginally. "Oh, God. You didn't—what did you and Anaba do to him?"

"Nothing."

Was that a silent *yet* she was hearing? "Damn it, I'm trying to make sense of things, but you aren't making it easy. You were willing to admit that you, or Cougar, and your friend, spied on Garrin, but that's as far as it goes? What the hell did you tell me anything for?"

"You asked."

Had she? She wasn't sure. Even more disconcerting, her clothes were suddenly too tight. "He's all right?" she asked, because if she didn't say anything, her ability to reason might shatter.

"For now."

"For now? Why are you threatening him?"

"It isn't a threat."

How many times was this conversation going to spiral off in unexpected directions? Even more important, how long before she didn't care about talking? It was his fault, damn it! The least he could do was put on some clothes.

"He was doing something you don't approve of, wasn't he? Something you have no intention of telling me about. Fine, fine." Stifling the urge to punch him, she nevertheless clenched her fist. "I should have taken off while I had the chance. I just thought, hell, I guess I thought we needed to talk one more time before I did."

"You aren't leaving."

"How are you going to stop me, Hok'ee, or should I say Cougar? By tying me up again?"

Night had slipped in while they were talking, making it nearly impossible for her to read his expression. Just the same, she was positive that was exactly what he intended to do if she took so much as a step toward the opening.

Having his ropes around her would take the decision-making out of her hands. Once more she'd become his his sex toy.

His possession, yes, that's what she'd turn into.

Freedom lost, will gone.

An emotion she couldn't put a name to flowed into her. Without parents to anchor her, freedom and will had become everything to her. Without those things, was she still human? But maybe he didn't care. All that mattered to him was her body.

About to push him as maybe he'd never been pushed, she planted her palms on his chest and shoved. Although he didn't give way, neither did he retaliate. Only half-comprehending what she was doing, she slid around him and started for the opening. The night called to her, promising cool isolation and necessary time alone with her thoughts. She needed solitude as she'd never needed anything in life.

"Kai, don't."

Don't respond. And whatever you do, don't speak his name or look back at him.

Night, she silently repeated. Heed the night's call.

Close, so close, cool air on her cheeks and throat, and the wilderness waiting. Hotly alive, she nevertheless kept her pace measured. She was in the entrance now with Hok'ee behind her, and maybe the rest of her life ahead of her.

Then his arms snaked around her waist, and he lifted her off her feet. Fighting but not sure whether she was fighting him or herself, she dug her nails into his forearms and tried to kick back.

Growling low and long, he hauled her back into his space, his world. Angry and excited, she twisted in his grip. Still growling, he tightened his hold so her spine was smashed against his chest. She gave thought to thrusting her buttocks at him and hopefully striking his cock, but before she could, he threw her from him. Her hands hit the bed first, followed by her breasts. She was bent at the waist, her feet still on the floor. Pushing his legs against the back of hers, he easily prevented her from slipping free.

Leaning over her, he planted his hands over her shoulder blades and held her until her struggles quieted. He'd done this to her before, and she'd survived. Maybe not emotionally, but at least with her heart still beating.

A beating heart, yes, that's what she'd been thinking about before he'd overwhelmed her. She'd been trying to determine whether man or Cougar was in control. She still didn't know the answer.

Hot pain at the back of her head brought tears to her eyes. Once again he'd taken hold of her hair and was pulling her upright with his handle. When he had her in position, he released her, but then grabbed her shirt and yanked it over her head.

"Damn you!" Twisting as best she could, she glared at him, but the night was his friend. The only thing she knew was that his legs still anchored hers to the bed—and she was naked from the waist up.

Another shove between her shoulder blades sent her into the bed again, this time facedown with her arms out, as if she were doing a belly flop. Feeling his weight shift, she turned her head to the side. Ah, air!

Then his fingers closed around her left wrist and pulled her arm behind her. "Damn you, no!" Feeling the rope on her forearm, she cursed him once more. Before she fully comprehended what he was about, he'd lashed her hands, one over the other, so they rested on the small of her back.

Captured, again. Helpless once more.

"That's so you won't hurt yourself," he explained, and brought her upright.

"How considerate of you. Overbearing and unfair, but considerate."

Was that a chuckle? If so, could she take that as proof that Hok'ee was still in charge of the body behind her?

His breath trickled over her neck and down her spine. Remnants of her earlier anger pooled in her belly but did little to distract her from the sensation. When he released her arms, she remained in place. Despite her jeans, his legs continued to heat hers. Between the moist air on her back and the pressure on her calves, she swore she was losing her mind. Her breasts felt heavy, her belly tight.

When he changed position so he was at her side, she turned in that direction. He was little more than dark muscle and height, strength and fire. She didn't need to ask why he'd overpowered her—the answer lay in his presence. Cougar demanded his own energy and space. He'd claimed his share of her in the only way that resonated with the predator.

And it didn't matter whether she wanted to be claimed.

A human hand took hold of her bound wrists and lifted, forcing her to lean forward. Another human hand circled the breast closest to the man and drew it from her body. Unable to remain motionless after all, she repeatedly shifted her weight from one leg to the other. Someone other than herself was responsible for her jerky rocking, someone who knew how to handle the energy inside her.

"I didn't know what I was going to do with you," he said. "All the way back I kept asking myself the question, and not just because Anaba had put it to me."

Something in his tone spoke to her, but when she tried to look up at him, her hair fell forward, nearly blinding her. Damn it, why hadn't she hacked it off years ago? Just because her mother had worn hers the same way? After a moment, he released her breast and repositioned her hair so it rested on the back of her neck. She didn't hate it so much.

"I couldn't just let you walk away; that might be the only thing I did know."

"Why not?" Speaking with her head down forced her to swallow so she wouldn't drool.

"Because you'd return to him."

"Him? Garrin, you mean?"

When he didn't respond, she knew she'd guessed right, but surely Hok'ee wasn't jealous of Garrin. Despite the heady distraction of Hok'ee's presence, she mentally sent feelers from her body into Hok'ee's, or rather, she went in search of Cougar.

He was there, of course, his strength sliding through human veins.

Come to me, please. Let me into your thoughts. I know they're there, and that you're more than an animal.

Cougar's strength grew with each second, and yet it was different from before. Yes, he was a predator, but for the first time, something else was being revealed via the animal form.

What are you trying to tell me? Whatever it is, you can trust me with it. Cougar, I might be the only living organism capable of understanding you. I think you know that.

For a moment she believed Cougar was going to respond. Then she sensed a withdrawing.

No! Don't do that to both of us, she begged Cougar. *There's no need for you to be afraid, to—*

"He's gone," Hok'ee said softly.

"Why?"

"I don't know. I never do."

16

Touched by the loneliness behind his words, Kai swallowed around an unexpected lump. Maybe he understood what she was going through because once more he helped her straighten. "Does Cougar ever talk to you?" she asked.

"Not in words, if that's what you mean."

"It isn't. Can you understand what he's thinking?"

"Sometimes I believe I can. It might just be my attempts to reach what can't be reached. He's an animal after all."

But was that the only thing Cougar was? She might have spoken if not for the night. It had taken over everything while she wasn't paying attention, and now she and Hok'ee were locked in a sightless world.

He wasn't touching her, not that it made any difference, because he continued to dominate her existence. With Hok'ee so all-powerful, she had no choice but to release Cougar from her mind. This man existed in a vacuum he had no control over. Not only did he not have a past, his future was empty—except for her.

That's why he'd lashed her wrists together again, to keep her with him. As for why he'd removed her shirt—

Stumbling a bit in the attempt, she sank to her knees, facing him. There, her cheek on his thigh, rubbing it because she had no other way of touching him. He ran his hand into her hair as he'd done before, and she wondered if she'd ever cut her hair again. If he wanted it long and loose, she'd give him that.

Straightening, she turned her head so she could nuzzle the powerful thigh with her nose. When he drew in a sharp breath, she felt rewarded.

Sticking out her tongue, she licked where she'd nuzzled, or rather she hoped it was the same spot. Her tongue told her she'd reached the inside of his thigh where the skin resembled silk, and the hairs were wonderfully fine. He shifted his weight, taking her thoughts back a few minutes to when she'd done the same thing.

Not having use of her hands was an erotic experience. She was both captive and, hopefully, captor. As long as he kept moving restlessly, she could believe she had him off balance. Maybe nearly as off balance as she felt.

Reaching and licking threatened to wear out her tongue and put pressure on her jaw, but even when she winced, she continued to lay damp trails on the satin flesh. His hand remained in her hair, and while she couldn't hear enough of his breathing to judge his restraint, his taut thigh muscles told her what she needed to know. So she'd gotten through to him. She might have, so far, left a certain part of his anatomy alone, but the point had been made. All he had to do was wait, anticipate.

Service him.

The thought made her a little uneasy. Leaning back took her away from him, but the increased distance did little to help her regain her equilibrium. Not being able to see him had something to do with it of course, but even more unsettling was her reaction to having knelt before him. Agreeing to suck a man's cock was one thing, but it would be dangerously easy for him to force her to that thing, service him.

Could she? Did she truly want to open her mouth and settle it over his cock, arch her neck and back to make the alignment perfect, to risk gagging and turn all the power over to him.

She could bite. Yes, that's it. If he forced the invasion, she'd close her teeth around him, and—

No, she'd never do that. And he knew it. Damn it, he must!

Sitting in the dark, an image crystallized in her mind. He'd thrown a strap around her neck, a strap that became a leash and made it simple for him to control her as an owner controls his dog. He'd tighten his hold, and then let her know she'd do what he wanted, how and when he wanted. He'd pull her toward his widespread legs, pulling up or down until he was satisfied with the positioning. Once she'd complied by sucking him deep, he'd demonstrate what he wanted by tugging and releasing, tugging and releasing. Short on breath, she'd struggle to obey.

Not just obey, not just comply. She, his pet, would suck and suck because doing so set her flesh on fire. It wouldn't matter that her cunt remained untouched. She'd feel his arousal throughout her. Faster and faster she'd work, her cheeks bulging, eyes tearing, breasts shaking, her world revolving around the hot meat. His pleasure her only goal, she'd lick and bathe and worship.

Closer he'd come, release and relief nipping at his nerve endings, his breathing sounding as if he was dying. Now her cheeks burned, her thighs ached from supporting her body, and her pussy—

Reaching out blindly, she opened her mouth wide. Her first attempt resulted in his cock sliding along her left cheek. She rocked back, then forward. This time his rod pressed against her upper teeth, prompting her to try once more.

Huge. Massive. Thick and long. Hard and velvet at the same

time. Tasting of him, and this unspoiled land. Flattening her tongue and, when she continued to welcome him in, jabbing the back of her throat. Fighting not to gag, she backed off a half inch, but closed her lips around his meat to keep him in her.

His fingers tugged at her hair, forcing her to arch her neck. The strain along the sides of her neck and mouth made her work at concentrating on him. Her arms were useless, wonderfully useless. Letting need guide her, she took back the half inch of him she'd given up. Even as his cock touched her throat, she began another withdrawal, only this time she kept the movement deliberate. Bit by bit she found a rhythm, a dance. Her saliva coated him, easing her journeys.

If he was still responsible for her arched neck, she wasn't aware of it. Her body became a well-oiled machine. Deep she took him, followed by measured retreat, followed by letting him invade her again. His cock dominated, not just her mouth, but her consciousness. She lived for his quick and harsh breathing, and the loud, sloppy sounds she was making.

This was primitive and primal, woman feeding off man, pushing his sexual limits, part worshipping, part leading the dance. She loved to hear him grunt and groan, to know as deep down as it went that he had no thoughts beyond her. He might have roped her again, but what did that matter? She was in charge.

Of everything except her own body.

Lips slack now, she commanded her tongue to cup as much of him as possible. That done, she advanced and retreated until she lost count and the back of her neck burned. She sounded like a starving animal wolfing down its first meal in weeks, and she lost touch with ounce after ounce and inch after inch of her body. Where were her arms and legs, her breasts? Only her cunt, her hot running cunt remained.

That, and the two of them groaning and snarling.

"Enough!" he rasped. Planting a hand on her forehead, he

forced her off him. Not content with his freedom, he kept pushing until she tipped sideways. Without use of her hands, she
landed awkwardly on the floor with her right shoulder under
her.

"Damn it, what was that—"

Before she could finish, he'd straddled her. Teeth clenched,
she waited for his next move.

"You liked that, didn't you?" he demanded. "Taking me to
the edge."

"You liked it, too. Don't tell me you didn't."

"You don't know what I'm feeling. You never can."

His tone had changed during the last two sentences. It was
almost as if someone else was speaking. Heat seared her. Cougar!

"I wasn't making fun of you," she tried. As uncomfortable
as being on her side with her arms behind her was, she didn't
try to move. "I'd never do that."

"That's not what I said."

"Then what—you didn't like me doing that, taking you to
the edge?"

His silence gave her the answer she needed, or rather it sup-
plied her with a partial one.

"I wanted to give you pleasure, Hok'ee. Can't you understand that?" She deliberately called him by name in an attempt
to determine how much of Cougar remained at the forefront.
"It wasn't that complicated. At least I didn't intend it that way."

"Not complicated?"

He was right. Everything between them was multi-layered.
Darn it, she was becoming more and more uncomfortable, but
even if his legs weren't on either side of her head, how could
she sit up? "What do you want me to say?" she asked.

"Maybe nothing." With that, he stepped back. Then he reached
down and hauled her to her feet.

She felt small in his grasp, even smaller than before. Her
mouth dried at the thought that Cougar might be responsible.

At the same time, being surrounded by this complex creature pulled her back into herself. She'd become more than a little turned on while he was in her mouth. The hot buzzing hadn't died when he'd shoved her away. Far from it, the sensation was still there, insisting on being acknowledged.

What was it about being under Hok'ee's control that turned her so damnably hungry? The thrill of danger maybe?

After turning her from him, he took hold of her tethered wrists and forced her arms up. She offered no resistance as he returned her to the bed, not stopping until her knees pressed against it. A quick, strong push, and she fell forward. This time the bed hit her at mid-thigh, which meant she was deeply bent over with her breasts smashed on what passed for a mattress, her ass high in the air. By keeping her arms up, he had no trouble anchoring her in place. Unfortunately, or maybe not, she couldn't see him.

"It's a little different now, isn't it?" he asked. "Tables turned."

"They've been turned since the beginning," she ground out. "If this is your idea of fair—"

"I'm not interested in fair."

Then what, she wanted to ask, but she already knew. No matter how much he'd learned about her, and she about him, his goal hadn't changed. Cougar's goal remained the same. He wanted, hell, he demanded control because he didn't know any other way.

"You were pushing it," he said in that newly deep tone.

"Pushing? I was trying to please you."

"Why?"

The question struck her as profoundly sad. She didn't know how to begin to answer someone with no memory of kindness. "I wish things were different for you," was all she could think to say. Once again a hot river of need ran through her, making concentrating on anything else nearly impossible. It was so dark, maybe he couldn't see her prominently displayed ass, but that didn't mean he wasn't aware of it. In truth, knowing he had easy and total access to that part of her anatomy made her feel even more sexual than she had a few minutes before. He wouldn't have hauled her over here and positioned her like this if he hadn't intended to take advantage of the merchandise, would he?

And she couldn't do a darn thing to stop him, couldn't do anything except wait and anticipate.

Her arms were starting to burn again, and there was too much blood in her head. A lot of her weight rested on her breasts, and her stretched thighs protested. The sensations stacked one on top of the other to settle into a single unit. Her body, waiting for his.

"A predator sometimes plays with his prey, you know," he said.

"Yes."

"For hours, if that's what the predator decides. Doing what he wants, concerned with nothing except his entertainment."

"Yes."

"Dominating. Immobilizing. Pitting strength against weakness."

His words fed and expanded what she was experiencing. He might have said something like that before; maybe she'd only thought those thoughts where he was concerned.

"How long before the prey stops trying to get free, and accepts what she has no control over? How long?" he demanded.

"I don't know."

"Are you there yet, Kai? Maybe you still remember freedom. But maybe, like me, you've forgotten everything about your past. Having a life."

Do you care anything about me as a human being? "Right now that doesn't matter."

"What does?"

"You know, damn it!"

"Do I?" he muttered. Before she could decide what, if anything, to say in response, he lightly slapped her right ass cheek. They'd been down this road before. She should have things under control.

Wrong.

Moaning, she struggled, not to escape, but to present even more of her buttocks to him. He rewarded her pathetic efforts by slapping her left cheek. Then it was back to the right, followed by a quick return to the left. Again, again, and yet again, his callused hand connected. What had begun as a teasing contact became sharper. She imagined her skin turning dark pink, then red.

"Ow! That hurts."

"That's what I intended." Slap, slap, slap.

"Stop it!" She tried to shift to the side, but of course he had her exactly where he wanted her. "I'm not—I don't like—"

"That's not the point." Slap, slap.

Then what is the point, she wanted to demand, though maybe she didn't. Whatever the answer, she couldn't concentrate for the ever escalating sensations. The pressure on her arms didn't seem as intense as it had been, thank goodness, but she was still a lifetime away from being able to straighten. Flames licked over her buttocks, up her spine, down to her crack.

That's where her focus now centered, her crack, and what was beneath and within it. He hadn't touched her sex, but he didn't have to because that part of her anatomy felt—everything. Responded to everything.

All right, not pain. Something extraordinary and overwhelming. Wonderful!

"I'm your world, your only existence," he continued. "Everything you experience comes from me, understand?"

"Yes!" Fight him. Lie there and take it. Either way, the outcome would be the same.

"I'm playing with you, Kai." Slap. Slap. "Do you understand?"

That deep and not-quite-human tone again. Her nerves shooting off like rockets. And most of all, her cunt river-flowing. "Yes."

"And you like it. Love it!"

Ah, what was that, an exclamation mark accompanied by the sharpest blow yet? And her response, her cunt about to explode. "Yes!" she screamed. "I love it!"

Suddenly he was no longer holding her arms up. She'd started to let them drop when she felt him separate her ass cheeks. Hard male meat slid into the space he'd created, glided along the narrow valley.

"I'm not going to stop, Kai. You know that, don't you?"

"Yes."

"And you want the same thing."

There it was, his cock resting against the entrance to her pussy, and his energy flowing from him into her until she thought she'd come from this simple and yet unbelievably complex touch. What was it she'd just accused him of, not caring about who and what she was beyond his possession? What the hell did it matter?

"Answer me. You want me to fuck you."

"Yes. Yes!"

"Fast, hard, no quarter given."

"None wanted. Damn it, Cougar, none wanted!" Hearing what she'd just said, she froze. Then he roughly rubbed the flesh he'd been tenderizing and she couldn't think of anything else.

He was growling, not grunting, but growling. And yet his hands belonged to a human, and the cock—pushing into her now—was Hok'ee's.

There, an inner voice whispered. *Deed done.*

Only he'd just begun, hadn't he? Or rather, they'd just started to fuck. She was a repository for his cum, a step above masturbating for him, because except for providing the requisite pussy, she brought nothing to the *event*.

But she took everything, took his breadth and length, the harsh, quick thrusts. She started to slide along the bed, but he clamped his hands around her hip bones and anchored her in place. Secure and secured, she rocked with him. The bedding abraded her breasts and cheek, even the front of her thighs. No pain, she acknowledged, no wanting anything different. In truth, the friction added to the heat boiling through her.

Her pussy reacted and recorded, sensed him and sent hot messages throughout her body. Had everything melted together? She'd become a hundred-plus pounds of cunt, and precious little else.

She wanted to laugh at the damn insane thought. Instead, she closed her teeth around the top blanket. She started chewing on it, tearing and grinding, growling the way he'd done.

Was there no end to the pounding her body was taking? He could go on and on, holding back his climax until he'd shredded her much as she was doing to the fabric?

The roller-coaster ride that signaled her impending climax had begun its uphill pull when suddenly he stopped. He remained deep and hard inside her, and she sensed a shift in the alignment. Maybe he'd bent his knees, either that or spread his legs so he was coming at her straight-on instead of at a slight angle as before. His hold on her hips tightened as he pushed even farther into her channel. He was everything and everywhere, and she the ultimate prisoner.

Far from wanting to fight, she pushed back in silent welcome. He responded by releasing her, only to rake her reddened buttocks with sturdy nails.

"Oh shit, shit!" she bellowed. The blanket forgotten, she struggled to suck in oxygen. She'd only half-accomplished her goal when he once more anchored her hips and reared back. Then forward.

Hit! Slammed. Hammered.

A river caught her. Tumbling like a small helpless creature, she sensed endless water rushing over her. She was being sucked into a tunnel where water churned and foamed, a place of darkness and sound, and no air. Suddenly the river caught fire, and she blazed with it.

Her pussy spasmed, then relaxed, only to tighten again. There he was, riding the river and her climax with her. She had him, had him! His cock was her pussy's prisoner, and she'd never let him go.

The darkness grew. She still couldn't breathe. Couldn't remember what she'd been trying to do. Heard nothing. Felt everything.

"Oh, shit, shit. Ah!"

Limp, useless, and worthless was only the half of it, Hok'ee admitted. Still, he found the strength and will to pull what was left of his cock out of her core. Although his legs trembled, he remained on his feet as he untied her hands. Looping an arm around her waist, he drew her upright and toward him. Her sweaty back rested against his equally sweaty chest, and he wasn't sure which of them shook the most.

Muttering something he didn't catch, she slid away from him. Then she all but dove onto the bed. He sensed more than saw her curl onto her side and could only guess that she was looking up at him, or trying to.

What could he say, that he'd just fucked her and yet it hadn't really been him, not wholly. Would she understand Cougar's role in what had taken place? Even more important, could she accept that he been unable to control Cougar?

Maybe, he acknowledged. Then his knees sent a desperate message to his brain, and he joined her on the bed in the split second before he would have collapsed.

After a few minutes of almost companionable silence, she shifted about. It took all his self-control not to pull her against him. He was utterly exhausted, at least his body was. In contrast, his mind worked in double time. Unfortunately, or maybe fortunately, little of what he was thinking made sense, and he couldn't hold on to any of those random thoughts long enough to work with them.

He'd spent the night with a handful of women since his death and damnable *rebirth*, primarily because it hadn't been worth the effort to come up with an excuse for leaving. But this was the first time a woman had shared his bed with him. As for the ones that had come before he'd run a motorcycle off the side of the road—

No, he wasn't going to think about that. It served no purpose, and changed nothing. Neither did he want to replay what she'd told him about the last day of his life, or any other day, he amended. Learning that he was at least partly Navajo hadn't been that much of a shock. After all, he was on what had once been Navajo land.

Not just the Navajo. What about those who came long before them, the ancients responsible for what you've made into your home?

Pulled out of his lethargy by the question, he fought to keep his reaction from Kai, whose breathing was lengthening. He'd *heard* things from Cougar before, but the concepts had been animal-simple. Cougar needed to sleep or hunt, or fuck.

They're called Anasazi, The Ancient Ones, he told the other half of his existence. *I've read about them.*

I know. I was there when you were reading that book—and long before.

The *and long before* caught his attention, but his body was on its way to sleep, and he couldn't and didn't want to fight it. Tomorrow he'd insist Cougar tell him what he was talking about, and why, on this night with Kai, Cougar had revealed himself as more than a beast of prey.

Tomorrow.

Tonight was for wondering about the remarkable woman next to him, and then falling asleep next to her.

17

The water was colder than she'd expected. Still, Kai dampened the cloth Hok'ee had given her and ran it over her legs. She'd slept like the proverbial dead and had woken hungry enough to eat a horse. Horse had been in short supply, but Hok'ee had cooked pancakes on a portable gas stove. Suspecting he'd acquired the camp stove via other than legal means, she hadn't asked about it. She would have liked to have some butter with her pancakes, but the syrup had been delicious, either that or anything edible would have sufficed.

Now she was cleaning up while Hok'ee watched. Going by the amount of sunlight coming into the cave, it was nine or ten in the morning. Having never worn a watch, she'd become accustomed to getting her time orientation from her car dashboard, clocks at home, or her cell phone. Now she had none of those things, just a silent man with his dark eyes steady on her naked body.

She wished they'd had sex this morning. At the same time, she wasn't sure she was up for a repeat of yesterday's intensity. He'd said little since they'd woken up. Granted, she hadn't been any more of a conversationalist, but there was no doubt of who was in command of their relationship. Him.

What was going to happen now? A return to ropes? And if he insisted on that, how long before Garrin called in the troops to look for her?

Garrin, that's who she should be thinking about. More than thinking, she needed to impress upon Hok'ee how much of a danger her coworker and those who'd be here in a few days presented.

But if/when she did, they'd have to deal with the real world.

For just a little longer, she wanted her existence to revolve around the half man, half predator she'd fucked. To think of nothing and no one else.

"My turn," Hok'ee said, sliding off the bed where he'd been reclining. He strode naked and tall toward her, drying her throat and causing moisture to bloom in another part of her anatomy. When he reached her, he held out his hand. For a moment she believed he wanted her to place her hand in his. Then she realized he only wanted the cloth. Feeling oddly abandoned, she handed it to him. Needing something to do, she turned her back on him and walked over to where he'd placed her clothes. He didn't tell her not to, so she dressed, even putting on her boots and retrieving her cell phone, camera, and pistol.

Now what?

Looking at him for the first time since she'd left his side, she found him staring at her. The lighting in here was far from the best, which was good because she couldn't read his expression.

Say something, she mentally commanded herself. Ask him where we go from here. Instead, she watched him scrub his legs. His hair was damp, making her think he'd started at the top and worked his way down. Why hadn't she seen him handle his cock?

Speaking of his cock, it was someplace between flaccid and erect, maybe waiting for a signal or move on her part to help finish the job. And then what? More sweaty sex, followed by another one of what her dad had called a spit bath, followed by yet more sex?

Was that going to be her existence? Or would she walk out of here and return to the world she'd left?

"Come here," he said.

Startled by the unexpected command, if that's what it was, she squared around so she faced him head-on. If she'd ever been more conflicted, she couldn't remember. She wanted him and his body with every fiber and nerve of her being. At the same time, she hated that he had the power to change her from everything she'd ever been. She wanted, needed, to be the woman she'd always believed she was. To have the life that maybe didn't mean anything to him.

"Come here."

"What do you want, Hok'ee? Or is Cougar talking?"

"Cougar is quiet this morning."

Which meant she'd only be dealing with the man. How much distance lay between them? Ten feet, maybe? It seemed like a thousand miles and less than two inches at the same time. "What do you want?"

"You."

How simple everything was for him. With no life beyond the need to keep his body going, he could indulge his body's desires. She, on the other hand—

"Are you fighting me?"

"I don't know. Will it come to that?"

She took his silence to mean he wasn't sure how to answer. But much as she regretted complicating things, it was necessary.

"We can't go on like this," she said, because one of them had to speak. Besides, if she didn't do something other than stare at that magnificently fit body, nothing else would matter. "The people I'm working with will look for me. I have a job, a career, commitments. You remember those, don't you, commitments?"

"All I know is what you've told me."

Was that what he wanted, not her body so much as the light she could shed on his past? She could do that—couldn't she?—grant him time and concentration. All it took was Cougar's co-operation.

Her boots felt strange on her feet as she stepped toward Hok'ee. "If you want me to—" she started.

Before she could finish, a sharp, distant sound stopped her. An instant later the sound was repeated.

"Rifle," she and Hok'ee said as one.

Even as he pushed past her on his way to the opening, she had no doubt who was responsible: Garrin. From everything she and Garrin had been able to determine, there wasn't anyone else around for miles—except for Hok'ee and the other Tocho, that is.

"It's my coworker, it has to be," she said to Hok'ee's back. "He's shooting to see if I'll fire back or follow the sound to him. I have—"

"No. He's shooting at something."

That hadn't occurred to her. Surely he wouldn't fire at another human. But what if it was at something, like a cougar?

Her mouth dry, she joined Hok'ee. Sunlight caressed his shoulders and back. It touched his hair with reddish highlights she longed to stroke. Even with her boots on, he was nearly a foot taller.

He didn't seem aware of her presence as he stood with his head cocked to the side, his eyes roaming the horizon. Tearing her attention off him, she made note of the starkly beautiful cliffs ahead. The canyon walls were predominantly a light, rich brown, interspersed with grays and golds, but here and there was what her father, and others associated with Canyon De Chelly, called desert varnish. Much darker than the rest of the walls, the varnish ran down the stones, reminding her of water stains. The varnish was what remained of flowing oxide-laden water.

Who were the first humans to see this extraordinary sight?

Then a second shot echoed off the cliffs, and she forgot everything else. Not looking at her, and not seeming to be aware that he was naked and barefoot, Hok'ee started running in the direction the sounds had come from.

Stop, she wanted to scream. Be careful!

But if another Tocho had been shot—

Heart thudding, she bolted after Hok'ee. Thanks to his longer legs and faster pace, he was rapidly disappearing from sight. She forced herself to set a slower pace that would allow her to keep going for a long time. She could only pray Hok'ee wouldn't run into Garrin.

Of course it might not be Garrin. Just because they hadn't seen anyone else didn't mean there weren't other hikers around. Whoever was responsible for firing would, of course, be shocked if he saw a naked and formidable-looking man charging him. If that person decided to shoot first and ask questions later—

Abandoning her plan not to push herself to the limit, she started running full out. Before long, however, her right calf threatened to cramp and her lungs started screaming for relief. Fighting panic, she slowed a little. Much as she wanted to put her hands over her ears so she wouldn't hear another shot, she didn't. It was like when her father had died. No matter how much she'd hated what she'd had to do, she had no choice.

Garrin was an academic, a little more ambitious than she felt comfortable with, but hardly a physical or violent man. She couldn't comprehend him firing at anything unless he believed his life was at risk, but he might if a cougar got too close.

"It isn't a true cougar," she said aloud as if Garrin could hear. Then because she didn't have the wind for more, she switched to an internal monologue. If only she could have told Garrin about the Tocho.

Like he would have believed her.

Fortunately, there was a break in the canyon walls ahead of her, which meant she didn't have to try to climb them. As she passed through the narrow opening, the steep sides rose up to engulf and diminish her. How incredibly naïve and arrogant she'd been to believe she had any right to force this incredible land to give up its secrets. No wonder those secrets had gone undiscovered for so long; the land protected them well.

She felt relieved once she was beyond the walls, but then the land flattened into a broad valley, and she realized how vulnerable she was. Vulnerable? As far as she knew, no one had any reason to harm her. Just the same, she stopped so she could scan her surroundings. She could see much farther than she'd been able to before, but the bright sunlight created heat waves that distorted distances. Between that and the monochromatic light brown ground, it was nearly impossible to make out details. What she wouldn't give for a predator's keen eyesight.

Why hadn't she called out to Hok'ee? If he knew where she was, maybe he'd join her and tell her what he'd found. But there was still the matter of who was carrying that rifle.

Mentally shaking her head at the turns her life had taken, she started walking again. She couldn't see Hok'ee's footprints, of course, and could only hope her interpretation of the direction the sounds had come from was correct. At least there hadn't been a repeat of the shots.

If something happened to him—no, she wasn't going to go there! This wasn't her father all over again, damn it! However, despite her vow to keep things simple and in the moment, she'd be a fool not to face possibilities. Hok'ee lived in a world beyond her comprehension. The rules were different there, the concept of kill or be killed more than a mental exercise. For all she knew, he had no memory of laws and rules, and knew little of society's conventions. Feeling no guilt, he stole to supply himself with the few things he needed.

Most telling, at times Cougar took over. And *civilized* human beings feared predators.

That's what Hok'ee had feared had happened, wasn't it? He'd left her because he was afraid someone had shot one of his kind. At the thought, she swore she could feel Hok'ee's tension. He needed to know, and yet that was the last thing he wanted to do.

This is his world, his life, she told herself as she started jogging. Unlike yours with your petty concerns about gas prices and burned dinners, he lives with the knowledge that every day brings risks to his life. The possibility of death.

She didn't need that. Didn't want it.

18

Anaba.

Disbelief rippled through Hok'ee. It took everything he had not to throw up his hands and blot out the sight of his closest friend. He'd spin around and go back where he'd come from. He'd fuck the woman who'd complicated his existence, and let Tochona claim Anaba.

But because Anaba would never abandon him, he couldn't do any less.

His muscles popped and expanded. He sensed the change to his bones and felt the increased blood flow throughout his veins. Earlier he'd fought Cougar's emergence because he hadn't wanted to terrify Kai. Now he vowed to remain human, at least until he'd discovered whether Anaba was dead or alive. Then he'd do what he had to. Become a killer.

In cougar form, Anaba lay stretched out on the dusty earth. The lean predator looked as if he'd been dropped while running. One moment he'd been filled with strength and energy. The next, someone had destroyed him.

Caring nothing about his nudity, Hok'ee took one leaden

step after another. His keening senses constantly tested his surroundings. Anaba's killer had been here; he could smell the faint yet harsh scent. But he'd left.

Knowing that the wielder of that deadly rifle had left Anaba to bleed to death sent Cougar-fury charging through him. He understood and embraced killing as long as it had a purpose, but this made no sense.

Even though it was the last thing he wanted to do, Hok'ee sank to his knees and placed his hand on Anaba's furred chest. It didn't move.

"My friend," he whispered. "Don't leave me, please."

Although he waited, not breathing, for the better part of a minute, his hand remained motionless. Anaba's body was still warm, his jaws parted to reveal teeth perfect for tearing flesh. His claws still contained deadly purpose.

Scooting back a bit, Hok'ee let his hand slide off the inert chest. Picking up a foreleg, he rested it on his thighs. A claw raked his skin but only momentarily pulled him out of disbelief. Tears burned his eyes. Loneliness dug at his heart. Along with that came a growing need to be doing something.

Not just something, he acknowledged as he stroked the great but useless paw. Anaba's death would be avenged, by him.

Eyes closed, he took himself far from where he was. In his mind he became a breeze moving from one place to another in search of a murderer. He drifted over the treetops, swooped down to examine every possible hiding place. Time didn't matter. Eventually he'd find his enemy and right a terrible wrong.

Cougar would kill, Cougar with his angry strength.

"Hok'ee?"

The voice came from a distance. Although he knew Kai was calling out to him, he put off having to acknowledge her. Instead, he found a reason to continue watching Cougar's image stalk the puny man who'd believed he had a right to end a life. In his mind, he was careful to make sure the man couldn't see him. At the same time, he allowed his essence to spread out until it touched the man. Seeing the look of alarm in those ugly eyes gave him a reason to smile briefly.

"Hok'ee."

Kai, much closer now. Opening his eyes, he reluctantly acknowledged her presence. She stood no more than a dozen feet away. If it had been anyone else, he would have already sprung to his feet.

"Oh, God. Oh, God. I'm so sorry," she whispered.

Her words stroked his heart. Without a word from him, she'd known what he was going through, at least part of it. He wanted to say something, but what? If he wasn't careful, she'd know how wounded he was, and he'd never allowed that to happen, not even when he'd learned that a woman he'd thought he loved had put an end to his unborn child.

The small blip of memory and accompanying heartbreak distracted him, but then Kai came closer and he let go of the past. He couldn't bring himself to release Anaba's paw.

"Is he—dead?"

"Yes."

Wrapping her arms around her middle, she closed her eyes. Her cheeks were flushed. In contrast, her lips were bloodless. When she opened her eyes, he saw raw agony that perhaps exceeded what he felt. "He is—he was a Tocho, wasn't he?" she asked in a barely audible whisper.

"Yes. What's wrong? The way you look—"

"Nothing," she said and clamped her hand over her mouth. "It's just—I was so afraid of what I'd find. To know it's as bad as I feared . . . What do you want to do? Can . . . can I help with the burying?"

The idea of placing Anaba beneath the earth appalled him, but neither did he want the carrions to pick over his friend's body. No Tocho had died since he'd come to live here, so he didn't know how deaths among his pride were handled. He could seek out another shape-shifter, only not now. Not until he'd done what he needed to.

"Hok'ee? Is there anything I can—"

"No," he said and stood up. His knees ached from pressing against pebbles, and he was aware of his nudity. His awareness of Kai grew with every breath he took. If he wasn't careful, she'd distract him from his deadly task. "You don't belong here."

"Then where do I belong?" she shot back. "I'm sorry. This isn't about me, is it?"

Did she want him to answer, or was she trying to convince herself of something?

"You're sure we're safe?" she asked after a moment. "The killer isn't around?"

She knew enough about Cougar that she trusted the predator's senses. Maybe she also understood how close Cougar was to taking over.

"He's gone," he told her. "Two bullets, and a life ended."

"I'm so sorry," she repeated. "I know losing someone you love is so incredibly hard."

"Yes, it is."

Eyes bright with unshed tears, she nodded. Then she held out her hand, and he took it without knowing he was going to.

He had an erection. Despite that, he felt nothing. He might have had sex with Kai last night, but it was a distant and vague memory because suddenly the only thing that mattered was Cougar's insistent voice inside him. *Vengeance,* Cougar kept saying. *Justice.*

"You're changing again," Kai said softly. "Your hand, look at it."

Although he didn't need to, he glanced at what was turning from fingers into claws. His throat tightened. Much longer, and he'd be incapable of speech.

"I know what's happening," she said. "At least I believe I

do. You, or should I say Cougar, is determined to find whoever was responsible."

"I have to."

"Do you?" Her grip tightened. "Hok'ee, you're talking about facing someone with a deadly weapon. Look what happened to your friend. How far away was the killer when he fired? You might not have the chance to get close enough for these"—she indicated his claw/hand—"to do what they're designed for."

The changing had stopped, leaving him someplace between animal and human, still capable of understanding her but limited in his ability to respond.

"I can't let you do it," she went on. "I just can't. No more needless deaths, damn it. No more!"

He might have found a way to push her to explain herself if he hadn't sensed a change in Anaba's body. The younger cougar hadn't moved, at least not in ways he was familiar with. Instead, Anaba's coloration became less distinct, as if a fog had blunted the details.

Kai must have noticed it, too, because she released his hand and stepped back. He gave a half thought to forcing her to his side again. Not only was Anaba becoming colorless, the body was losing definition. Already the tail and limbs were disappearing.

"What—" Kai started. "Oh, my God."

With an effort that left him weak, Hok'ee forced Cougar to return to the quiet place he usually inhabited. He leaned down to touch Anaba's fur. Whatever his fingers came in contact with had little substance. "He's leaving."

"Leaving? Where . . ."

Kai dropped to her knees next to Anaba. Her features drained of blood, she blew on her hands as if to warm them, then took hold of what remained of Anaba's head and lifted it. She did so easily. Hok'ee joined her on the ground. Rocking slightly, she rested Anaba's head on her lap and stroked it while making soft muttering sounds. Maybe she was talking to Anaba, or at least trying to. Because he'd been the object of her rare ability to communicate without words, he didn't interfere.

Anaba was becoming smoke. Hok'ee understood the loss of a creature's life force at death, but this was beyond his comprehension. And yet he'd rather see Anaba float off in the wind than rot in the ground. In less than a minute after the change had begun, nothing remained of his closest friend.

"I saw . . ." Kai whispered at length. "I know where he went."

"Where?"

"To some ruins built into the side of a canyon. I don't know where they were; I've never seen them." She sounded in awe. "Only they weren't ruins. They—Hok'ee, it was new. The stone structure I was standing near was absolutely amazing. The workmanship—"

Ghost House. "Anaba was in it?"

When she didn't immediately answer, he gave her his full attention. Her eyes were enormous, and her whole body shook. He'd never wanted anything more than he wanted her, yet he was afraid to touch her.

"Not in," she said at length, and started stroking the ground where Anaba's body had lain. "Floating over it. He was looking down at what was going on and . . ."

"What was happening?"

"Life," she whispered. "Ordinary life. Hok'ee, maybe I'm losing my mind." She picked up a handful of dirt, only to let it sift to the ground. "But I saw and heard and even smelled things—people were everywhere. Talking, laughing even. Several women were squatting around a fire pit. I wish I'd paid more attention but—I think they were smoking meat, each of them tending to their own meat but enjoying each other's company."

"That's what you smelled?"

She nodded. "Children—I heard their laughter. It was the

most delightful sound. Then a couple of men entered the open area in front of the house—it was large enough to hold several families—and the children ran over to them. Everyone was glad to see the men. They were carrying something, a cut-up deer carcass I think, although it might have been an antelope."

"What did Anaba do?" he asked, though maybe he should have remained silent and let her continue. But once more Cougar was insistent, and Hok'ee needed to learn as much as he could while he was capable of concentrating.

"He—Hok'ee, so much was going on that I couldn't focus on him—but, yes, he continued to float. And then . . ."

She didn't want to go on, and he wasn't sure he wanted to hear, but he had no choice. When she started scooping up more dirt, he stopped her by closing his fingers around her wrist. "What happened?"

"The people—it *had* to be the Anasazi—were no longer where I could see them. I heard their voices, inside the house It had become night. Either that, or the fog made it appear like that."

"Fog?"

"Thick, black. The same as what I *saw* around Cougar earlier. It was more like the kind of smoke that comes from burning rubber, terribly dark, only without the smell."

She still wasn't looking at him so maybe she wasn't aware of his battle to remain human.

"The fog, or whatever it was, surrounded Anaba as I saw it do to Cougar. Then it sucked him up and away. It was as if—all right, this is going to sound insane—but you need to know. It was as if after Anaba's body faded from here, he tried to join the Anasazi. But then that *thing* caught up with him and prevented him from making the connection."

Hok'ee's muscles expanded, straining against the prison of his skin. His lung capacity was increasing, and his eyesight was already Cougar-keen. At first he thought Anaba was calling to him. Then he realized the draw came from the *thing, the deep dark.* "What is it?" he asked, rushing the words before his throat closed down.

She started rocking again. Her wrist felt fragile in his grip. Afraid he might hurt her, he let her go. The moment he did, he wanted her back, not under his control but so he'd have something to cling to, a way to battle Cougar.

"You expect me to know . . ."

"If not you, who?"

"Give me time. Let me concentrate." Her voice trailed off. Then: "Chindi."

Kai waited for Hok'ee to say something. When he didn't, she struggled to pull herself free of whatever was swirling through her mind, and blinked him into focus. He was changing, half human, half Cougar, beautiful and fierce and terrifying all at the same time. Even as his features morphed into those of a killer, she ached to join him. They'd roam this remarkable land together, hunt with a single purpose, kill as one.

And when they fucked, it would be with rough abandon.

Close to laughing over the insane notion, she stood and backed away. So little of the man remained that she barely remembered what he looked like, and although some of Hok'ee's heart still beat inside Cougar, she'd be a fool not to acknowledge the danger.

Damn it, did he have to change right now? Why couldn't he have waited until she'd told him what she'd just learned?

"Hok'ee, I think I understand why you became Cougar after the night the man you used to be died on a motorcycle," she said. Hopefully, he could hear and comprehend what she was saying. Hopefully, what she was about to say made sense to her as well.

"Chindi were and maybe still are vital to traditional Navajo beliefs. The tribe believed, absolutely, that an evil force was released at death. That force or ghost had—has great power. It can kill, but that isn't all. I wish you already knew this!" she snapped, angry at him. "You would if you'd accepted your heritage."

Nothing of Hok'ee remained in the large, intimidating beast standing a few feet from her. Yes, she'd faced Cougar before, but that didn't blunt his impact. If anything, he was even more awesome now that she understood how he'd come into existence.

Fighting the need to back away farther, she returned Cougar's intense gaze. His eyes were ancient and wise. Maybe that meant Cougar understood more that Hok'ee did.

"Can you hear me? Do my words make any sense to you? I hope so, because I have to try to get through to you. Chindi? Does the word mean anything to you?"

Except for his slowly lashing tail, Cougar was motionless. His beautiful and deadly eyes threatened to suck her into their depths.

"Maybe I'm crazy to be thinking this, but I'm going to say it anyway. When you died, a Chindi force was released. Not just a ghost spirit but a malevolent Skinwalker. That's why you're now half human and half cougar. Maybe, back when you were Ryan, you did something to enrage the Skinwalkers. Maybe— maybe it was denying your heritage."

He was still staring at her, thank goodness. "Once they had hold of you, they decided to make you pay for not acknowledging that you were Navajo. What could be worse than being forced to exist the way you are now, belonging nowhere and accepted only by other Tocho."

Her speech had given her a headache. She could only pray that Cougar's continued silent stillness meant she'd gotten through to him. "Maybe I'm wrong about why you're being punished, but I don't think so. It had to be something that means a great deal to Skinwalkers. The *scene* I saw from your past when your foster parent tried to interest you in your heritage—why else was that revealed to me? You'd turned your back on your Navajo blood."

Cougar's tail lashed furiously. Her head screaming, she continued. "Maybe it was the same for Anaba, and the other Tocho. You're all being made to pay for the same thing."

Movement rippled along Cougar's spine. She tried to tell herself a breeze was responsible. Then the ripple repeated. "What is it? Is this your way of telling me you agree?"

Cougar's lips curled back to expose not just his fangs, but his gums as well. At first she believed he was trying to answer, but then something about his intensity changed her mind, that and his pricked-forward ears. He was listening to something.

Damn it, she'd forgotten about the rifle that had killed Anaba, and whoever had fired it. Like she didn't know.

Shielding her eyes, she slowly turned in a circle. She'd paid little attention to where she was going when she'd been following Hok'ee. Now, spotting several familiar landmarks, she realized they weren't far from where she and Garrin had set up camp. Garrin had shot what he'd believed was a wild animal. If he saw Cougar now—

"You can't overpower him," she insisted. "He'll bring you down before you get close."

The heavy tail lashed. If anything, Cougar exposed even more of his fangs. Most frightening, he lowered his body so his belly nearly scraped the ground in a stalking stance.

"No! Damn it, can't I get through to you? Your claws and fangs are nothing against a rifle."

Surely Cougar heard. He might have even understood, but he'd become a predator. He obviously had no intention of backing down. Shielding her eyes again, she looked in the same direction Cougar was focusing on. Much as she wanted to deny it, she couldn't. A man was coming toward them, albeit a long way away.

"It's him. My coworker." She couldn't say why she was whispering now. "He's armed. He'll shoot the moment he believes he has a decent shot. I know he will."

It belatedly dawned on her that if she could make out Garrin's scrawny form, Garrin would have no trouble seeing Cougar—or her.

Calling herself fourteen kinds of a fool, she hurried to Cougar's side. Ignoring the warning in his powerful body, she touched his shoulder. The instant she did, the world she was in disappeared. She'd been pulled back in time and was once more within a few feet of the Anasazi house.

Then the stone walls evaporated.

19

Cougar growled, the low sound coming from the depth of his being. His tail continued swishing, and the hairs on his back remained on alert. His attention locked on Garrin.

This was pure predator. Maybe touching him had transported her back in time to where Anaba's essence had been taken, but maybe the connection between Cougar and Anaba had been responsible.

Would there ever be anything like that between her and Hok'ee?

"Go. For God's sake, leave. I couldn't handle it if he killed you. No more deaths, no more!"

A faint shout tore her attention from Cougar. Her heart threatened to burst from her chest as she forced herself to focus. Garrin had lifted his rifle to his shoulder. He was close enough that she should have heard what he'd shouted, but maybe the wind was blowing in the wrong direction.

"Run!" she repeated. She slapped Cougar's side. "Now!"

A sound like death shattered her world. The echo seemed to last forever.

Cougar screamed. Under her trembling hand, his body tensed.

"No, damn it, no! Hok'ee! Don't let Cougar take over. Run. Please, please, run!"

She was trying to decide what else she might say, what she'd have to do to get through to the man beneath the beast when Cougar spun in a half circle. Beautiful as always, he leaped forward. One, two, three strides and he was racing full out away from Garrin. *Thank you.*

"Kai!" Garrin called out. "Kai!"

Despite the mix of urgency, disbelief, and anger in Garrin's voice, she couldn't take her eyes off Cougar. Even as he faded into the distance she remembered his touch and the hot glide of his cock inside her. She hadn't been alive until he'd walked into her life, and now he was gone.

Her pussy clenched. For a moment she nearly gave into the need to climax. Then because she had no choice, she faced Garrin. As soon as she did, reality surrounded her. Judging by his flushed cheeks and neck, to say nothing of how close he was, he must have continued running toward her while Cougar distracted her. His sweat smell nauseated her. She longed to wrestle the rifle out of his grip and beat him to death with it.

"What the hell was that?" Garrin gasped. "That cougar, damn it, I know I killed it. The one I saw just now, it couldn't be the same beast I shot."

Not bothering to respond to his curse, she glared. "Why the hell *did* you shoot?" she demanded. She felt as primal as Cougar had looked.

"Why?" Garrin still held the rifle as if he had every intention of using it as he tried to wipe his forehead on his forearm. "Are you kidding? That was a cougar."

"I know it."

"You—you were right beside—right beside. If you weren't so close I would have—how is that possible? Why didn't it kill you?"

"You think everything has to be about killing or being killed?"

Looking dumbfounded, he stared in the direction Cougar had gone. Then he looked down at where Anaba had lain. "It was going to attack," he muttered. "I did the only thing I could."

More likely Garrin had panicked at the sight of Anaba in cougar form. "Did you?" she snapped. "We're suppose to make as small an impact on this area as possible." The longer she was forced to look at him, the less she respected him. "That, in part, is why you and I were sent here ahead of the others. We were trusted to—"

"Don't spew that bureaucratic crap at me, Kai! I've been part of academia a lot longer than you have."

"And I've spent more time in the wilderness than you have. I understand animals, remember. Communicate with them. That's what I was doing."

"What the—I don't believe you."

"Then I feel sorry for you because it's the truth." *Part of the truth.*

When she'd first met Garrin, she'd concluded that he was a perfect fit for his job. A devote believer in "publish or perish," he'd had several wordy articles published in professional journals, and was working on a book comparing modern archeological techniques with the early years, as if anyone cared. His office was crammed with books, papers, and trade magazines. From what she'd been told, students dreaded going into his office because he droned on and on about what they were convinced was the only thing he cared about, the archeological field.

She was beginning to suspect she'd been wrong about Garrin. There was a lot more to him.

"Cougar attacks are rare," she pointed out, when the last thing she wanted to do was continue the conversation. "And they usually happen when the animals believe they or their turf is being threatened. Even though there's no body, you say you killed one. Couldn't you have just walked away?"

"Walked away? You have no idea what I've been through. Not—not knowing where in the hell you'd taken off to, or what might have happened to you."

Garrin swore? She'd never suspected. Determined not to let herself be backed into a corner, she asked what he meant by what he'd been through.

"That's none of your business," he snapped.

"What? Garrin, there—"

"You're hardly one to be asking me questions." His lips thinned. "Where were you last night? And don't tell me you got lost. With all these landmarks, a blind man could find his way to camp."

They'd been so polite to each other since coming out here, too polite in fact. Now Garrin had obviously taken off his gloves and was itching for a fight, but why? Either that, or he was trying to turn the conversation in another direction. Perhaps most important, why wasn't he demanding a remotely believable explanation of why she and Cougar had stood side-by-side, or continuing to insist he had killed Anaba? If the tables were turned, that's what would be on her mind, not dodging questions about what she'd been up to.

Unless she had something to hide.

"I'm sorry if I worried you," she said deliberately noncommittally. "Something became more important than where I slept."

It didn't surprise her when his gaze narrowed and he set his jaw. What was that something? his expression plainly asked.

"I need to change clothes. I don't know what you're going to do, but I'm heading for camp." Adding action to her words, she started in that direction. She'd barely begun when he grabbed her arm. Memories of Hok'ee's easy and complete control over her threatened to distract her.

"Let me go," she ordered, although she could probably break free.

"Not yet. Two things we're going to settle first."

"Oh." Pasting on a *I don't give a damn* look, she stared at his fingers on her.

"You're damn right. If you think I'm going to let you get away with not documenting your activities, you're wrong."

I could say the same about you. "I don't owe you—"

"The hell you don't." His hold tightened. "You're not keeping anything from me."

So that's what this animosity was about? He believed she'd uncovered or come across something important. As for why he'd think that . . . "Why would I do that?"

"Maybe so you can grab the glory for yourself."

"What? I'm not after glory. All I care about is communicating with—"

"With that cougar?" he finished for her. "Kai, I killed one. I know I did."

"Then where is it?"

Releasing her arm, Garrin shook his head. He looked to be at such a loss for words that she nearly felt sorry for him. Then her mind snagged on the image of Anaba's lifeless body, and the grief in Hok'ee's eyes.

"Bright sunlight distorts things," she offered. "You must have been a long distance from it. If you didn't actually stand over it and—"

"I know what I saw. What I did."

She could have demanded to know why he'd fired at one of nature's creatures, but they'd only go around and around in this conversation he must be as weary of as she was. Talking to Garrin was the last thing she wanted to do, especially since she had no idea where Cougar was, what he was doing, and when Hok'ee would reappear.

This was insane. Her whole life was.

"All I know is there's nothing here." She indicated the ground. "Not even blood."

Garrin recoiled, then leaned over and studied the earth. Her only explanation, which she wasn't about to share with him, was that a Skinwalker, if that's who had been responsible, had taken back everything of what had once been Anaba.

"What about the animal you were *talking* to?"

Garrin had whispered more than spoken. The poor man—he really was losing it. And she had to take advantage of his confusion. "It ran off when it saw you."

"Just like that?"

"Just like that."

"This *conversation* you were having? What was it about?"

"We didn't get very far, unfortunately."

He opened his mouth, but instead of saying anything, he licked his lips. The way he was studying her, she sensed he wished she was anywhere except here. Something had definitely changed about the man, not that she couldn't say the same about herself. Deeply weary, she started toward their camp. Garrin had been right about one thing. Thanks to the impressive and unique canyons, a person would have to work at getting lost.

Going by what her senses were telling her, he was following her. She tried but failed to dismiss the fact that he carried a weapon, and that he'd used it.

Hok'ee would protect her.

Hok'ee had turned her life on end, taught her things she hadn't known about her body and heart. She'd worn his ropes, and if he'd come to her with fresh bonds, she'd let him place them on her. She'd handed him pieces of his past, and he'd given her his body as his gift. If that wasn't proof that something rare . . . Rare? Except for having learned what turned her on, what did he know about her, and did he care?

Right now that didn't matter. What did was that he'd protect her.

Return for her.

How would that happen, she pondered when she should have been thinking about the man behind her. Maybe Hok'ee would wait until she was asleep. He'd slip into her small tent and place his big hand over her mouth to keep her from crying out. The moment she knew it was him, she'd stop struggling.

They wouldn't need to talk; their bodies would say everything that needed to be said. Even with remnants of Cougar clinging to the man, she'd take what she could get. She'd welcome him by opening her legs and guiding his cock home. There'd be no foreplay, and no thoughts beyond sex. He'd hit her hard and fast, and she'd hit back with the same wild frenzy. She'd drink from him and then drink some more, until she'd exhausted him. Then, shaking and done in herself, she'd curl up next to his warmth and fall asleep.

In the morning—

Why did there have to be a morning? She wanted sex and then more sex, to climax until her mind shattered and her pussy became too tender to touch. He'd give her a break, maybe finger-combing her hair and bruising her mouth with his rougher one. But then, watching her expression, he'd run his fingers over the length and breadth of her sex until the inner fire blazed. Maybe he'd finger fuck her this time.

Whenever she reached for his cock, he'd pull her hands off him and straddle her. His weight would rest on her thighs. Although only inches separated her thighs, he'd plunder her easily. At first she'd offer no resistance as one climax after another signaled his expertise with her body. Then once again, her heated tissues would scream for rest, and she'd press her legs together.

This time, however, there'd be no rest or recuperation. One moment she'd be under him. The next, he'd plant a knee between her thighs and force them wide. With a forearm pressing against her swollen breasts, he'd demonstrate his total mastery of her. No matter that she tried to roll away, no matter that she raked his forearm with her nails or tried to lift her head so she could bite, his hand would remain on and against and often in her cunt.

Capturing her clit, he'd drag it in one direction and then the other while she cursed and begged. Then, changing tactics, he'd release the hot nub, abandon it while he played with her sex lips. Whatever he wanted to do to them, it would happen. Pulling, tickling, rolling his finger pads over them would cause her to beg for relief. She'd split in two—half of her desperate to escape the assault on her sanity, while the rest rejoiced in being the center of his attention.

Simply keeping her highly stimulated wouldn't be enough for him. From a secret place, he'd produce a pair of metal clips which he fastened to her sex lips. Then he'd haul her to her feet and command her to stand so he could see what he'd created. When he ordered her to place her hands behind her head, she'd obey without a whimper of protest.

Gathering the courage to look down at herself would take longer. She might still be working on it if he didn't press against the back of her neck and force her chin onto her chest.

Gleaming gold chain dangled from the clips and nearly reached her knees. The clips themselves were large and exquisite. Her labia was buried beneath the ornamentation, trapped and throbbing.

"Walk," he'd order.

"Please, I can't."

A slap to her right buttock would get her moving, and she'd step after him with her legs splayed, the chain swinging with each step. Every tug and jerk would force a moan. Tears would spring to her eyes, while tears of another kind leaked out of her. Everything was about sex, about her being reduced to his plaything.

"Walk faster."

"Master, please, I—"

"That's right, I am your master." The words said, he'd take hold of the chain and haul her behind him. She'd waddle, knees bent outward, hands still on the back of her head, her juices pooling on the gold clips.

"This"—he'd shake the chain, causing her to moan in pleasure/pain—"is the connection between us. Maybe not the only one, but the one I choose for tonight. You want it, don't you, Kai? Want everything I do to you, no matter how painful or demeaning."

Demeaned? Did she really feel that way? It was hard to concentrate with sensations she'd never experienced or expected to experience swamping her. She was drowning in sex, and him.

"You aren't answering me, Kai." He'd shake the chain, then stop and haul her next to him. "You want this, don't you?"

She'd been staring at him while hobbling after him, but she'd forced herself look again at what he'd done to her. Spring mechanisms had kept the restraints in place. She could have reached down there and released the pressure on the springs. As soon as she did, she would have been be free.

Or would she have?

"I need you, Hok'ee."

"Just as I need you. You're beautiful like this, I want you to know that. Exquisite in your captivity. Magnificent wearing my proof of ownership."

Hok'ee was a man of ropes and strength. How had he turned into a master of bondage? Maybe the change was in her, and not him. He'd become what she wanted.

Risking his disapproval, she lowered an arm so she could slide her hand between her legs. The chain was taut, her labia stretched to its limit. The scent of wanting rolled through her. The clamps were heavy and solid, the small flat surfaces against her flesh slick with her arousal. "You own me," she whispered.

"For now."

A warning note in his voice pulled her out of the spell she'd wrapped around herself and back to reality. As the self-imposed fantasy faded, she realized her hand was indeed between her legs. If not for her jeans, she would have been touching herself. Garrin was behind her, hopefully unaware of what she was doing. She didn't dare face him until she'd found a way to cool her flaming cheeks and throat.

Hok'ee, are you aware of what just happened? Are you responsible?

And is that all you want from me? It is the only thing that matters to you?

"Where were you last night?" Garrin asked.

Determined not to face him, she stopped and made a show of looking off into the distance. "I told you—"

"That something came up. It's also not nearly enough."

"I'm answerable to Dr. Carter, not you. I don't owe you an explanation."

"Don't you? You were gone all night."

Alerted by his tone, she faced him. Except for a certain residual energy, everything about her fantasy had faded. Earlier, Garrin's behavior had set off warning bells. Now they returned. "I apologize for that. If it had been practical, I would have returned." Liar. "But I wasn't going to risk breaking my neck walking around in the dark."

"There wouldn't have been a risk if you'd returned before it too late. Damn it, you know your responsibilities."

"Why don't you spell them out?"

He looked as if he considered her less than bright. "You know the parameters of the grant as well as I do. We're to do a thorough evacuation and evaluation of—"

"That's your responsibility. Mine is less clearly defined. I'm allowed a lot more leeway," she interrupted, then was sorry she had.

"Not the kind of leeway you took yesterday. You took off without giving me more than the minimum of information about where you were going. And you certainly weren't back by the time I returned."

"Returned? Where did you go?"

He hesitated, then: "I was looking for you, what do you think?"

"Why would you do that?" Hands on her hips, she squared on him. "Unless you didn't believe me."

He set his shoulders. She didn't for a moment believe that his shifting of the rifle from one arm to the other was an unconscious gesture. Nature's creatures, even predators, lived lives defined by the need for caution. Those who lived did so because they took nothing for granted. Maybe Cougar was responsible for her increased awareness; maybe her own instinct was at work. Whichever it was, she had no doubt that Dr. Garrin Gentry wasn't the mild-mannered professor she'd taken him to be.

"Are you threatening me?" She indicated the rifle.

"What?" He looked flustered.

"It's a question I have to ask." Was Cougar nearby? Would he come to her defense if Garrin tried anything? "I'll tell you what I'm thinking," she went on. "Then I hope you'll let me know whether I'm onto something."

"Go on." He held the rifle in the crook of his left arm, his right hand only inches from the trigger.

"You didn't object to my leaving yesterday because you wanted to be alone. You weren't looking for me. You had your own agenda."

"And what would that agenda be?"

"I've seen the way you've studied our surroundings, and the things you've said about how there might be more significant sites in the area than that one kiva. I wasn't the only one interested in exploring Toch—Sani."

Garrin clenched and unclenched his teeth. At the same time, he rocked back and forth slightly. He kept his gaze on her, barely blinking. Perhaps most telling, his nostrils flared and stayed that way.

"You're guessing, Kai. Fishing."

"You're not denying it."

"I don't owe you anything. Do I have to remind you, I'm the senior—"

"And I'm an independent contractor. You aren't my boss."

He sputtered but didn't say anything. As the silence stretched out, she admitted they weren't getting anywhere this way. At least things were out in the open, to some degree. Garrin *had* been searching. As for whether he'd found anything—

He hadn't seen her and Hok'ee. Otherwise, he would have already thrown that at her. What did she mean, throw? If Garrin knew where and how she'd spent the night, he'd want nothing to do with her—if he could wrap his mind around the truth.

"I really would like to know if you found anything," she said, keeping her tone as neutral as possible. "You were hardly frantic with concern for me, which makes me think you had other things on your mind." She took a deep breath. "Of course if you'd seen a cougar—"

"I more than saw one, damn it. Look, just because I didn't break into tears when I spotted you doesn't mean I wasn't worried."

"Were you?"

For too long he didn't react, and his belated nod lacked conviction. "I tried calling you. Either you didn't bother to answer, or you didn't want to get in touch with me."

She wouldn't have known about his call, if there'd been one, because Hok'ee had taken her cell phone.

Which, she reminded herself, wasn't the point. Although the lack of disclosure from either her or Garrin bothered her, the truth was that she was finding it hard to focus on the conversation. She'd shaken loose of most of her crazy fantasy about clamps and chains. Now if she could just rid herself of the sensations that had accompanied that fantasy. Want it or not, her labia continued to burn.

"I killed that damn cougar. I know I did."

Determined not to let more get past her, she brought Garrin back into focus. He needed a shave, and dust clung to whatever he used to hold his sparse hair in place. His shoulders were narrow for a man of his height, which she took to be just a hair under six feet. In contrast to his well-fed middle, his legs were scrawny.

Next to Hok'ee, he wouldn't stand a chance.

"I don't know how to respond to that," she said. "I saw what I saw, or rather didn't, which was a dead predator."

"What were you doing standing on that very spot, huh? Answer me that?"

There was no winning this argument, no story creation that would dispense with his questions and suspicions. "I'm not going to try," she handed him, "because no matter what I say, you'll take exception to it. My suggestion: we have most of the day ahead of us, and a job we're both earning decent salaries to accomplish. As soon as I get some fresh water, I'm going to get to work. What about you?"

"Don't worry about me, Kai. I know exactly what I need to do."

20

She was with *him*. Standing close to the man who'd killed Anaba. Talking to him.

From where he crouched, Cougar couldn't hear what the two were saying. He considered slipping closer but didn't, because he wasn't certain human words would make sense. Besides, the man kept looking around nervously. And he carried his rifle.

Cougar revealed his fangs in a smile without warmth behind it. It was right for the man to be afraid, and to wonder where danger might come from.

Did he know he was being watched by a creature that wanted him dead? More than want, Cougar *would* avenge Anaba's death.

In his mind, he slipped down to where the man stood. Because he'd been created with the instinct for survival, he knew what it took to remain hidden. He also understood the danger the rifle represented. However, a sudden attack would knock the weapon out of the enemy's arms. Then he'd take his time.

The cold smile died, replaced by the image of the coward as

he tried to run. The man would scream and cry. Nonsensical words would bubble out of him, along with saliva and great gasping breaths. Cougar would allow him to run, for a while. He'd hold back just enough so that the foolish human would dare believe he might live. Then, pushed on by thoughts of Anaba, Cougar would close the distance between him and his prey. Shrieking in rage and justification, he'd expel his hot breath against the back of the man's tender neck.

The stench of the man's loosened bowels would fill the air. He'd collapse onto his knees. Scrambling around, he might clamp his hands over his throat in a useless attempt to protect it.

Understand my vengeance, Cougar would tell him. The words finished, he'd bury his fangs in the man's hands and pull them off his throat. A single bite, and bones would break and blood begin to flood. The man would cry or scream, it didn't matter which. After letting him do so for a few moments, Cougar would silence him by ripping out his throat.

The woman would see.

Shaking his head, Cougar struggled to concentrate. The woman had a name, a smell, a voice. He knew her body, or rather, the man Hok'ee knew it. Hok'ee would never forgive him if he harmed the—if he harmed Kai.

Kai. A woman. Soft, yet strong. Brave. With knowledge about him he hadn't believed possible.

What was it that had happened when she'd touched his fur and then reached through it to his muscles? She'd taken them both far into the past where everything had begun. With her by his side, he'd returned to the time and place of his birth. Together they'd watched a people Cougar had loved but who no longer existed. Together they'd watched those people build and cook, and they'd both rejoiced when the men returned with fresh meat.

Kai hadn't known such a journey was possible until he, unwittingly, had shown her the way. And because they'd taken it together, they would be united for as long as they both lived. Maybe there'd be more than one step into history.

Did Hok'ee understand that? Would he share her?

In terms of work accomplished, the day had been a bust. True, she'd talked to Dr. Carter, who'd reiterated that she indeed was at liberty to let instinct and intuition define what she did. She'd come close to telling him about the ruins she'd spent last night in but hadn't, because she didn't want to risk mentioning Hok'ee. Maybe later, if she could find a way to separate the discovery from everything Hok'ee represented.

At least in the afternoon she'd found a fairly decent example of the wattle and daub architecture the Basket Makers were known for. The partial pit house wall she and Garrin had uncovered near the original kiva strongly represented the meshwork of poles and reeds held together with thick layers of adobe-like mud, but it wasn't as if archeologists hadn't already written extensively about the process. Or rather, she acknowledged, they'd written about the steps and finished product. What had always been missing was how the pit house builders had felt while they were working on it.

There she was going on again, she admitted as she stretched out in her tent after dinner. Ever since learning of Hok'ee's existence, she'd longed to dive deeper and more fully into the past. Had the Anasazi sung as they went about their work, and if so, what had their songs been about? What stories had parents and grandparents told the children? What legends and beliefs had been passed down through the generations?

So much lost.

Unless Hok'ee and Cougar . . .

Running. Strength in her muscles, and the wind cooling her temples. Surrounded by massive stone walls that whispered ancient stories.

She was naked; even her feet were bare. Her heart felt massive and powerful, her lungs capable of endlessly providing the oxygen her body demanded. She was running from something, and yet she wasn't. The answer to what was happening would soon matter, but it didn't right now because rejoicing in what her body was capable of had become everything.

She was no longer a modern woman. She had no ties to anything civilization offered and demanded. Instead, fueled by her newly enlarged heart, she embraced the primal. Survival was assured to those who heard this land's song, and made it their own. That's what she'd done somehow. She'd opened herself to listen and learn, and had been rewarded with perfect muscles and bone. Maybe her intellect had kept pace; she couldn't be sure because she no longer thought as she always had. Instead of words spun into a cohesive whole, she reacted to what her senses told her.

Run here, listen to that sound, study the movement next to that bush, taste the air and know whether it promises rain.

Joyfully hugging herself, she silently thanked the Anasazi for showing her the way into this world she'd never known existed. Then before she could throw out a prayer, she sensed a change. Her nerves told her she wasn't alone, warned her to treat the newcomer as any animal would, with caution. Stopping, she looked in all directions while brushing sweat off her streaming body. She was alive with the joy of life; the simple words said it all.

There. Watching her. Waiting.

Staring back at the dark form, she accepted that the newcomer was both man and animal. Although his form was human, he was one with the land, and that made him more.

What do you want, she silently asked. How long have you been following me?

"Forever," the man/creature responded. "I've always been here."

"Impossible."

"How do you know?"

She didn't, and that was the hell and thrill of it. As a man, the newcomer was everything she'd ever wanted. He was well over six feet tall, with sculpted muscles and sun-toasted flesh. Thick golden brown hair framed a broad forehead, impossibly deep-set eyes, and high cheekbones. Like her, he was naked, his erection huge.

Her own sex responded by loosening and then tightening. Her breasts became heavy with hard, sensitive nipples. Unwilling to deny the truth, she fingered the aching points.

"Look what you've done to me," she said.

"I've made you into what I need."

She was trying to form a response when the man shifted, changed. There, the animal coming through. Not just animal but a big cat, a predator. All raw power.

"What happened to him?" she asked, trembling.

"The man, you mean?" Cougar replied. "He's still here, just beneath the surface."

"I want him back."

"What you get is me."

She'd known the predator was going to leap before he did. Instead of trying to flee, she widened her stance and set her legs. He struck her in the chest, knocking her off her feet. She landed on her ass, arms back to break her fall. Instantly furious, she scrambled onto her hands and knees, then buried her nails in the form looming over her. Her fingers found only fur.

He leaned so close that his breath heated her lashes.

"What is this about?" she demanded. "I haven't done anything—"

"You belong to me."

Was that true? She couldn't think, let alone decide.

"You belong to me, and him," the cougar added.

"Him? Hok'ee, you mean. Show him to me. Let him come through."

"Not tonight."

Movement, the powerful form pushing against her side until she gave way. Before she could think what to do, Cougar lay her on her back and straddled her. She'd been here before, or a place and emotion close to this one.

Reaching up, she stroked her captor's front legs. He loomed over her, around her, everywhere. She smelled only him, his animal heat. She tried to open her legs, only to stop with her thighs pressing against his rear paws.

"You can't want this," she told him. Bending her knees, she ground them into his belly. "Not just this when you can have more."

"I take what I want. You can't stop me."

"Maybe I don't want to try."

She stared at those great killing teeth so close. Then his tongue emerged, pink and thick. She didn't move. He repeatedly licked her cheek and the side of her neck until the abrasions made her whimper.

"I'll take you," Cougar said. "But not as Hok'ee did."

"Animal to animal, you mean? But I'm not one."

"I don't care."

Another harsh lick sent hot shivers down her body. She was waiting for the sensation to end when he lifted himself off her. A paw capable of ripping out a heart rolled her onto her belly.

The ground carried a million memories. It had been trod on since the beginning of time and would be here long after she ceased to exist. But right now she and the earth were the same, either that or she was drawing wisdom from those countless memories. Dirt and rocks absorbed the sun's heat and accepted a winter night's cold. It asked for nothing, yet provided roots with the nourishment plants needed for life.

She wanted life, wanted Hok'ee. But he wasn't here, or

rather his physical form wasn't. Maybe he'd sent Cougar in his stead; maybe Cougar had fought him for supremacy.

Didn't matter. Only life did. Life at its most elemental.

Planting her hands under her, she lifted her upper body. Cougar lathed the back of her neck, compelling her to set her elbows to keep from falling. Her neck felt as if it had been stuck by a finger of lightning.

Another rough touch from the great creature stole her breath. He hadn't used his tongue this time. Instead, he'd placed his fangs around her neck.

She froze. The lightning strike that lived within her grew in intensity until it was everywhere and everything. She was on fire, afire, so alive there wasn't room for anything else. Sharp points pressed against her tendons and veins.

"I'm yours," she said, not moving.

"I know."

When the pressure increased, she tucked her knees under her and lifted her lower half off the ground. After a moment, Cougar released her. Eyes drifting closed, she let her head drop. She needed neither encouragement or warning to spread her legs. The tongue that had taken her down into animal trailed over the base of her spine. More flames coiled through her, making her pant. Her mouth opened, and she drooled. Lowering her upper body a little, she offered her ass fully. Harsh, wet kisses tracked from her spine to her ass. Sucking in air, she tried to reach behind her so she could separate her rear cheeks, but had to stop because she couldn't keep her balance.

A female ready for servicing—that's what she'd become.

His tongue created the space she'd been unable to by pushing into the dark valley. When his tip found her puckered opening, she sobbed and rested her upper body on her elbows. Her eyes stayed closed as he washed and stroked.

She wanted to remain still, wanted nothing except those primitive caresses. At the same time, her growing need for re-

lease kept her on the move. She managed to confine her move-
ments to erratic muscle clenches. The raw rasp of his breathing
made her wonder if he was laughing at her. As long as he fed the
lightning, what did she care?

As easily as a hot knife slicing through butter, his tongue re-
peatedly slipped along her crack. Whether he approached from
the top, or so low that his tongue tip bathed her cunt didn't mat-
ter. It was all good, all overwhelming.

He must have moved behind her and lowered his head
nearly to the ground, because after a momentary respite, he
began lathing her sex lips. She rewarded him with a constant
flow and deep moans she had no way of controlling.

When had she started shaking?

Her mind swirled. His tongue became her world. She shiv-
ered when he bathed her buttocks, and whimpered each time he
licked up her offering. In a disjointed and unimportant way, she
built an image in her mind.

She, a naked and submissive female, huddled beneath the
powerful predator body. His dominant form dwarfed her. He could
end her life in a second, but reckless and uncaring, she continued
to offer herself to him. More than simply offer, she repeatedly
thrust herself at him. If she could find a way to trap his tongue
between her ass cheeks, she would have.

The heat, wet heat. And his tongue scorching her cunt, soft-
ening and preparing it.

Oh, yes, her cunt! Sounds rattling in his throat, he pushed
into her one wet inch at a time. More lightning threatened to fry
her nerves, yet still she stood her ground, all soft and swollen
and receptive. It wasn't the cock she'd been silently begging for,
but this was good! Incredible. Forceful and tender by turn,
going deep and full, spreading and preparing her. Tickling some-
times. Resting her forehead on the ground, she gnawed on grass.

A cougar's tongue penetrating her hole. Unlike anything she'd ever experienced. Pushing her to the edge of everything, only to withdraw slightly, holding her suspended.

When that happened, when her cunt muscles started to spasm, she lifted her head and then her upper body. Her arms burned. Her head became even heavier, forcing her to let it hang. He waited her out, still buried in her but no longer testing her limits, just resting and waiting and reminding her of his all-encompassing presence.

"Please, please," she whimpered.

Instead of heeding her, he drew back and left her wet and throbbing. Crazed, she longed to pummel him and make him bleed. Even more, she needed him!

But she wasn't going to beg, she wasn't! She'd crouch here like the bitch she'd become, ready for servicing. But she wouldn't plead, and she wouldn't thrust her ass at him anymore, somehow.

She jumped, shrieked. Only when the cry died did she realize he'd bitten her left buttock. Not a real bite, nothing designed to draw blood or wound, but a primal act nonetheless. A predator's claim.

He bit her again, on the right cheek this time, fangs raking over her skin and making her shiver.

"Oh God. God!"

After that, the punishment came too fast for her to have any chance of staying on top of it. One cheek and then the other stung with each nip. She had to do something—scramble to her feet and clamp her hands over her buttocks. Attack, pummel, punish her punisher. But she didn't. Instead, her head remained low and her hair dragged over the ground she'd fallen in love with.

She took what he dished out.

Drowned in sensation.

Spittle bubbled at the corner of her mouth, prompting her to try to lick it up, but some escaped to track a line to her chin. Any other time she would have been embarrassed, but such emotions belonged to the woman she'd been a lifetime ago. This primitive thing she'd become crouched, ready and frantic to be fucked.

The bites weren't painful, and she didn't think he'd broken the skin, but they might leave bruises. Maybe she wouldn't cover them up. Maybe she'd leave the blood-dark marks exposed as a badge of some kind of honor, the ultimate hickey.

More spittle filled her mouth, prompting her to spit it out. Just then something powerful wrapped around the joint between pelvis and thighs, and drew her back. She knew the feel of Cougar's paws, the thick, harsh pads and exquisitely curving claws. Going still again, she tried to imagine how he'd accomplished what he had. He might have had to squat on his haunches in order to free his front legs, but maybe Hok'ee had begun to make his presence felt again.

Who was behind her, animal or man?

It didn't matter. She'd take her mate's cock. Hok'ee or Cougar, she'd take it.

Almost as if she'd willed it, something touched her pussy. She was no longer being pulled toward who or whatever was behind her, but her body resonated with the memory. Something heavy settled on her spine and buttocks. Panting open-mouthed, eyes closed so she could concentrate on the video being played in her mind, she clutched her gathering climax to her.

The cock remained against her swollen nether lips. Her lips were so sensitive. Still she couldn't determine whether the cock belonged to Hok'ee or the other half of his being. Maybe it didn't matter.

And maybe the two had fused into one.

Slow pressure parted her sex. He, whichever one it was, had entered her. She welcomed him with awkward muscle contractions. She was an animal now, a female creature in heat. She'd swallow the offering until the man/beast had no more to give and she was full.

Full? Not there yet but getting closer with each second, and her cunt soft and swollen and welcoming. She lived for and through her cunt, had no other existence. Yes, her breasts ached with their own heat and every inch of skin felt abraded, but those things were secondary to her pussy.

The man/creature behind her wanted to fuck. Hell, he'd begun the act. And she, female/creature that she'd become, joined him. She panted and gasped. Her pussy took the gift of a cock, took it deep and deeper still. Her buttocks stung, her head pounded. Something poked her left knee, and her locked elbows burned with fatigue.

Everything was sensation.

Disbelief and acceptance.

When her penetrator shoved, she set herself to accept his thrusts. Somehow her head was up and her eyes open. She couldn't see anything except colors, endless colors. A moment ago she'd been aware of her aches and weakness. Now she embraced rhythm. When he pushed, she held steady. Then he pulled back, propelling her to close her sex muscles around him.

The two of them kept going, temperatures rising, her body rocking under his strength. She'd forgotten how to breathe, not that it mattered. Her heart slammed against her ribs. Maybe he, whoever he was, had grabbed her around the groin again, maybe she only imagined it. Either way, she rode him. Rode and climbed and cried.

"Damn, damn, damn you," she hissed.

"No, damn you."

Good. They'd fight, throw words and curses at each other. As long as his bulk stretched her, she didn't care. Bleating like some lost fawn, she advanced and retreated. Everything was on fire, muscles screaming and nerves shouting.

Climax! Hammer-blow hard. Shaking her. Going on and on. Fading only to rise again when his hot cum spewed. She sucked his offering into her, deep and deeper still, her pussy drinking from it, filling herself with what he had no use for.

Not knowing who or what she was.

21

Morning came too soon. Kai was more than exhausted. Her body ached, and her mind wasn't good for much except wondering why the hell there wasn't any more coffee. She ate her granola bar and washed it down with water, standing up because her ass felt as if it had been rubbed with sandpaper. She should have checked, but because she suspected she'd find bite marks, she didn't.

It had to have been a dream, right? The most vivid dream of her life.

"What are you up to?" she asked when she noted that Garrin was putting on his boots. He'd been outside when she'd crawled out of her tent, but had only grunted in response to her groggy hello. He hadn't said much after that, not that she was a great conversationalist, either. Just the same, she needed to know whether he planned to look over her shoulder.

"If you must know, I intend to examine something I found in a little more detail." He shrugged a bit too elaborately. "And regardless of what did or didn't happen yesterday, I'm taking my rifle. I strongly suggest you do the same. A pistol isn't enough."

"I appreciate the advice." No matter what had taken place yesterday, she needed to remain as civil as possible around Garrin.

"Appreciate? But will you take it?"

"It depends on what I decide to do. Like you, I want to re-examine something."

"And that something is?"

"At this point I'd prefer not to say." She kept both her voice and gaze steady. "I think its time we acknowledge that you and I have separate agendas."

"That we do. And I could care less about yours, as long as you give me the space I need."

"I haven't infringed on your territory, if that's what you're talking about," she shot back, instantly wide awake. "Do you want to talk about it now? Professional competition, I mean?"

"Is that how you see it, professional competition? If so, then there's nothing to talk about. We came into this with clearly de-fined roles. I'm the archeologist, while you're—" He shrugged. "You have your own field. What I'm saying is, given your ab-sence yesterday, I trust you intend to be on-task and responsi-ble today. There's entirely too much at stake, to say nothing of the monetary investment, for either of us to be anything but the consummate professional."

He was starting to pontificate. Instead of pointing out that she was a professional—something she hadn't been yesterday or last night—she kept her expression as neutral as possible.

She indicated his backpack. "I take it I'm not going to see you for a while. I also thought we agreed to keep each other ap-prised of our whereabouts."

"You didn't. Why should I?"

Garrin was being childish, something she'd never expected of the man. "Point taken."

His shrug was obviously designed to downplay her response. Also, obviously he wasn't interested in being any more forthcoming about his agenda than she was. She wished she didn't care what he did, but she couldn't dismiss the possibility that Garrin and Hok'ee's paths might cross. The rifle he'd killed Anaba with was strapped to his backpack.

Hoping she was keeping her reaction to herself, she shrugged and reached for her own boots. "We've gotten on each other's nerves," she came up with. "I suppose it's inevitable given the nature of what we're doing and the fact that we're the only ones doing it—our isolation. I hope that will change."

He licked his lips. "The business with the cougars yesterday—I'm still trying to, how do they say it these days, wrap my mind around it. Bottom line, I know what I saw. You can't change my mind. If only I'd thought to take pictures." Another lick of his lips. "There's so much pressure—I'm sure I don't have to spell that out."

In that regard, he was being sincere; she had no doubt of it. If the situation had been reversed, she'd be begging Garrin to explain the unexplainable. Standing, she held out her hand. A moment later, he shook it. His palm felt clammy. "Be careful," she told him, when what she wanted to do was beg him not to fire at another cougar.

"I need to say the same of you."

"I intend to."

By the time she'd laced her boots, Garrin had taken off. Standing alone, she took in her surroundings. It was so peaceful, and lonely.

Where was Hok'ee? And had he regained human form? Maybe it was better if he didn't; it'd be easier on her nerves if she didn't see him today. Easier than coming face-to-face with a cougar?

She *had* to pick up the threads of her life, and do the job she'd been hired to accomplish. If nothing else, Garrin was right about that. The time she'd spent as Hok'ee's prisoner and sex partner had been the ultimate in erotic insanity, but it had nothing to do with the real world. She had a goal to reach, responsibilities to meet, expectations to fulfill. Most of all, she needed to regain her sense of self, her sanity.

Dad, I don't know if I want you around right now. If you have any idea what I've been doing—God, I'd give anything to have you to talk to!

Spent by her emotional outburst, she crawled back into her tent where she'd stashed her backpack. Instead of wandering off unprepared as she'd done the day before yesterday, she'd take the pack today. She'd keep it light—water, something for lunch, her cell phone, the promised but dreaded rifle.

And her digital camera. The moment she picked it up, she knew what she was going to do. Hok'ee might disagree. Hell, he might even try to stop her from taking pictures of where he lived. But she couldn't pretend she hadn't seen what she had any more than she could lie away their wild sex.

"It's over, at least it will be before all this ends," she muttered. "I'm talking about your way of life, Hok'ee. You and the other Tocho. This place will be known by one name, Sani. Tochona will cease to exist." Silenced by the lump in her throat, she waited until it had loosened. "I don't know what Garrin found, but neither you nor I can stop people from coming here. Everything is changing. Everything."

Unnerved by the way her words closed in around her, she exited her tent. But even as she filled her pack, she faced yet more reality. She'd been given glimpses into the past, not just the world of the Navajo, but of a time long before the tribe came here. Cougar and Anaba had been responsible for that mind-expanding look into ancient history.

She needed more.

Hok'ee stood and stretched. Remnants of Cougar clung to his muscles, but before long he'd feel fully human. He gave thought to putting on some clothes, but he'd rather stay where he was and watch Kai approach. As Cougar, he'd paced her while she made her way to his home. He wanted to believe she was returning to him, but because he'd seen what she'd included in her pack, he knew it wasn't that simple.

Cougar had seen little more than strange objects, but as Hok'ee, he'd been able to make sense of her selection. He didn't understand why she was armed, or maybe the truth was, he didn't want to think about that. In contrast, there was no mistaking why she'd brought along her camera.

She intended to photograph what she had no right to.

The way she frequently looked around, he guessed she'd sensed Cougar's presence, but Cougar hadn't wanted anything to do with her. Or maybe, Hok'ee amended, Cougar had been afraid to get too close.

That couldn't be. Cougar feared nothing.

But Cougar had never encountered a human capable of reaching into his mind.

Shaking his head did nothing to clear his confusion. He, Hok'ee, wanted her here, and yet he didn't. Even at this distance, his fingers remembered her soft skin, and his ears held memories of her excited cries as she climaxed.

Cougar had traveled at a higher elevation than Kai, which had made it easy to watch her. Whenever she'd looked in his direction, he'd dropped to the ground, trusting that his body would blend into his surroundings. In preparation for reaching the ruins, she'd left the valley floor and started up the gentle slope leading to it. He was still above her, but she'd come close enough that his time of being able to hide was coming to an end.

Earlier he'd been full of himself. He'd believed victory lay in making the strange yet compelling woman his prisoner. He was no longer sure.

If Anaba was still alive, he'd have someone to talk to.

"You're here," Kai said, her voice echoing. "I know you are. Please, we have to talk."

The shirt she wore was a different color from the one she'd had on yesterday, and she'd changed from jeans to sturdy shorts. Even though the hem came nearly to her knees and she wore socks, he had no trouble remembering what her legs looked like. Unlike before when it had been loose for the wind to play with, she'd contained her hair within a single braid. He could still control her with it.

Only half-believing what he was doing, he stepped out of the shadows. He'd had an erection when he'd shifted out of cougar form, and looking at her had sent more blood to his cock. Enough of Cougar remained with him that he felt no embarrassment.

"You're all right?" she asked after a short silence, during which she stood with her hands on her hips while her eyes took in everything about him. "What about the other Tocho? Have you seen them? They know—about Anaba?"

"They know."

"Where are they?"

She wanted to look around but was forcing herself not to show any sign of nervousness. Sensing her mood increased his awareness of the difference between them.

"You're not going to tell me, are you?" she asked. "Why not—because they're waiting to ambush me?"

"Your kind killed Anaba, not the other way around."

"My kind? You're human, too, Hok'ee."

"Am I?"

Instead of attempting an answer, she shrugged out of her pack and lay it on the ground. Not taking her eyes off him, she dug into it and pulled out her camera. "Do you know what this is?"

"Yes." His groin ached. He didn't dare decrease the distance between them, and hoped she wouldn't try to take advantage of his weakness.

"And why I brought it with me?"

"That's what you want to talk about?" he challenged. "The pictures you hope to take."

"Hope? Are you going to try to stop me?"

As the words spread through him, he struggled to accept that that was why she'd come here today. She hadn't been looking for him after all. Or maybe her plan had been to use him in order to get what she wanted.

Too much of Cougar clung to his edges. Cougar trusted nothing human and never would, not even a human he'd had sex with.

But that was good, wasn't it? Cougar had instinct Hok'ee would never be able to match.

"I had a dream last night," she said, stopping his thoughts. "About you—and Cougar. How is he?"

"You care?"

To his surprise, she pressed a palm to her forehead. "I don't know if I want to. The truth? I want you to be who I initially thought you were, a man." Lowering her hand, she tucked it in her back pocket. She still had hold of the camera. "I don't want things this complex between us."

"What do you want?"

"Sex." She gave an embarrassed laugh. "Tell me something, you deliberately didn't get dressed—am I right?"

By way of answer, he stroked his erection. It was as if fucking her had never happened; he craved her as a starving man craves food. At the same time, a part of him wished Cougar would rip her heart from her chest. Everything would be so much simpler without her.

"We're not going to get anywhere, are we?" She sounded weary. "Every time I try to get you to open up, you hide behind silence. Everything's about you, your life, your agenda. I feel lost in it."

"Do you?"

"Yes, damn it! What if I touched you? Would Cougar let me know what's going to happen between us?"

"Maybe, if he knows."

"You don't have to worry, because I'm not interested." She blinked several times, but her eyes still glittered. "It's been real, Hok'ee, maybe the most real thing I've ever experienced. But I've had the night to think things through, at least the part of the night when I wasn't dreaming about . . ."

She kept pushing a button on the camera, but he wasn't sure whether she was aware of it. He didn't think she was taking pictures.

"Did you have a career?" she asked. "A job you were passionate about, meaningful work?"

"I don't know." He should walk up to her and pull off her clothes, lay her down and bury his hard, hot length in her soft tissues. They wouldn't talk.

"I'm sorry, wrong question to ask. I have a skill, a talent I'm passionate about. I've been able to do some exciting things because of it, but nothing has come close to what I believe is possible here. This"—she held up the camera—"is a small part of what I want to accomplish. I have to photograph where you live, I *have* to."

"What do you mean, a small part?"

She started, and he wondered if she'd become accustomed to his silence. "Where I saw Anaba go after he died. Wherever it is, the place is incredible. And the Anasazi. They were there. I can reach them; at least I have to try. But I don't know if I can find it on my own. I need your help."

I won't give it, he nearly said. But her gift would allow her to reach through the mist of Cougar and Anaba's memories to this land's original residents, The Ancient Ones. Even he knew how incredible that was.

Looking at her, he became aware of something he hadn't noted before. Her shoulders were broad for a woman. In contrast, her neck was short. Her bony knees were scraped because of what he'd done to her. The town women he'd turned to when his need for sex became too strong wore makeup and dressed to accent their femininity. In contrast, Kai's features lacked artificial definition, and her clothes were asexual.

This was what she was, not some nameless creature he'd selfishly captured. And yet in many respects she remained a stranger.

"You're staring at me, Hok'ee. What are you thinking?"

"The things you want from me—it won't happen quickly, will it?"

She didn't seem to know what to do with his question. In truth, he wasn't sure why he'd asked it.

"I can stay here as long as I need to, if that's what you're talking about." She again pressed her palm to her temple. "There are limitations to the current grant I'm working under but—that's not what this is about, is it?"

When he'd first spotted her, he hadn't thought beyond being given a reason to go on living. He'd wanted to fuck, to control and to fuck.

So much had changed since then. And yet all he really wanted was to fuck. To not care about anything else.

She jabbed her fingers at him. "Answer me, Hok'ee, damn it!"

"I don't care about your career." He stepped toward her. "Or about the Anasazi."

Mouth open, she studied him, starting with the top of his head and sliding down. She paused briefly at his cock. "Why not?"

"That's your concern, Kai, not mine," he lied. "Remember, I died. Then something, a Chindi or Skinwalker, turned me into what I am. This is me." He all but slapped his cock. "The only thing that matters."

"No. It can't be. When Anaba—when Garrin killed him, you mourned. And hearing about the child you could have—"

"Shut up!" Pain ripped through him, and he lost awareness of his cock's demands.

He'd erased all but the final few feet between them while they were throwing words at each other. Close enough that he could smell her, he acknowledged how easy it would be to let her scent engulf him. The pain would end. He'd no longer care about what she called her gift or her goals. He wouldn't give a damn whether she ever learned about Ghost House. Maybe most of all, he'd stop wishing he'd never met her.

He wanted to run her down again, wanted her to try to flee so he'd have a reason to make her his prisoner. This time he'd keep her gagged, and it wouldn't matter whether it was fucking or rape.

Her arms dangled at her sides now, one empty, the other holding the camera. As soon as the outside world saw what she'd photographed, they'd descend on Tochona. He and the other Tocho would have to go elsewhere. But where?

Reaching out, he snatched the camera away. Eyes glittering, she came at him with her nails extended. He stopped her by clamping his fingers around her throat. She buried her nails in the back of his hand.

"It's back to this, is it, Hok'ee? Everything physical. Animal."

"I am animal."

"No, you aren't, damn it!" She dug deeper.

"What do you care? You didn't come looking for me. It's Cougar you're after."

Her eyes went big and deep and threatened to suck him into a place he didn't want to go. Then her eyes started to glitter again. "That's what you think?" she whispered.

Even with everything he had to think about, he couldn't ignore the pain she was inflicting on his hand. Although he had to force himself to do it, he released her. When she didn't return the favor, he shook himself free.

"Where's Anaba's killer?" he demanded.

"I don't know. He wouldn't tell me. Does it matter?"

"Maybe, maybe not." Truth was, he didn't want the man to have anything to do with today. "Does he know where you are?"

"No. I had no intention of letting—"

"You're certain he didn't follow you?"

"I think you know the answer to that. After all, you've been watching me all morning."

"Not me, Cougar."

"Cougar," she whispered. "All the time I was walking today, I thought about what I'd have to do to convince you to let Cougar take over so he could help me reach the past, but why should you? After all, as you said, what matters to me isn't important to you. You're selfish. That's why you captured me, so you'd have what you wanted—a female body to fuck."

If he wrapped his arms around her, would she be able to look into his past and tell him what he'd been doing with himself before everything had been ripped away? He'd hold her and hold her, and eventually he'd have all the answers? But if he used her that way, she'd have a right to use him, or rather Cougar.

"What's it going to be?" she asked, sounding tired. "Will you at least let me take this"—she indicated the camera—"into the ruins."

"They aren't ruins. They're my home."

She closed her eyes. Moments later, she swayed. Thinking to

steady her, he took her arm only to have her jerk free. "I don't want you to touch me. You did last night—in my dream. Only it wasn't you. Cougar fucked me."

At her words, Cougar flexed his muscles. If he wasn't careful, the other half of his being would break free—and maybe turn her fantasy into reality.

"You let him?" he asked.

"It was a dream! I had no control over—do you dream, Hok'ee?"

He didn't want to go on talking to her. In the heart of his hearts, he wished he could walk out of her life, but if he did, he'd always regret it.

"What about last night?" Her voice was small. "Did you even think about me?"

Last night had been Cougar's time, so he didn't know how to answer. "I can't let you take your pictures," he said.

She took a backward step, then stood her ground. "Why not?"

"Skinwalker."

He thought she was going to press her forehead again. Instead, she covered her mouth and spoke around her fingers. "What about Skinwalker?"

"Don't you remember what you told me about the fog, only it wasn't fog. If you're right, and I think you are, Skinwalker brought me here, me and the other Tocho. This land belongs to the spirits."

Confusion spread over her features, then she nodded. "Maybe. And maybe I'll have to ask Skinwalker."

Much as he needed to ask how she hoped to accomplish that, he couldn't concentrate on the question. He must have once loved a woman, otherwise he wouldn't have reacted the way he had when one had denied him fatherhood, but his mind held only one memory, of the time he'd spend with Kai. He drew her hand from her mouth, only to bring it near his so he could breathe onto it. She relaxed a little, and her expression softened.

"It's so complex, isn't it?" she whispered. "Between us."

Although he wanted to tell her it didn't have to be, he remained silent; she was right. Much of it was his fault. If he'd initially approached her the way a civilized man would, they might have gotten to know each other. But he wasn't civilized, and he had so little of himself to give her.

"Is there more you can tell me?" he asked. "About the man I used to be."

"You're sure about this?"

"I don't know. Can you?"

"I can try."

But would it make any difference? He couldn't go back to that person any more than he could expect her to join him in his world.

Let her go. Walk away.

Instead, he drew her close, pulled her arms behind her, and leaned over her. She tried to turn to the side, then, sighing, looked up at him.

"What is this? A return to the way things were between us? I do whatever you make me do?"

"You like it." He bent her back farther, spreading his legs to assure he wouldn't lose his balance. "The cougar in me turns you on."

"It can't just be sex between us. There has to be more, something substantial."

"Why?" he shot back, her body sending him messages that threatened to swamp him.

"You can't be satisfied with—"

He silenced her, pressing his lips against hers with enough force that her head snapped back. Unwilling to break the contact, he kept after her. She again tried to turn away, and this time he stopped her by sucking her lower lip between his teeth and holding on. Her breath hissed against his cheeks and nose. When she stopped struggling, he nibbled on her lip, sucking in her sweet essence, tasting her soft and delicate tissues, thinking about doing this to another part of her anatomy.

Moment by moment, she relaxed. Her arms were limp, but he kept them behind her because he loved the feel of control it gave him. Maybe she loved the same thing.

That was what would keep them together, their separate and yet compatible needs? He'd determine the amount of freedom he'd allow her, and she'd live within those confines? He'd define their relationship, particularly the timing and content of their sex life. She might ask and sometimes beg, but he'd always be in charge.

Yes, he could control her, rule her! Keep her with him.

Shifting position, he captured both of her wrists in one hand. Then he bowed her even more and ran his teeth over the tight expanse of her throat.

"Oh God. God!" she blurted. "Damn you for—oh, damn you."

He'd silence her, or even better, turn her words into pleading. He'd strip off her clothing and—

Bam!

22

Kai ran as she'd never believed she could run. But although her feet flew, and her lungs felt capable of endlessly supplying enough oxygen, her speed was nothing compared to Hok'ee's. Within a minute of starting, he was so far ahead she knew he couldn't hear if she cried out.

Because of the great stone walls, the rifle shot had echoed, making it impossible for her to be certain whether she was going in the right direction. But Hok'ee had shown no hesitation as he took off. Because he'd headed due east, so had she. Between having to keep an eye on her footing and coming to terms with what they'd heard, she had little opportunity to think ahead to what they might find. If only she'd been able to convince Garrin not to take his rifle.

One thing she did know, maybe the only thing that mattered, was that she didn't want Garrin to have shot another cougar. She wasn't sure Hok'ee could handle the death of another Tocho, but would it be any easier for her?

Her shins started to ache, and she was getting blisters. If she stopped to deal with either condition, she wasn't sure she'd be able to get going again. And so because nothing was more important than being there for Hok'ee, she fought the pain in her shins and heels.

What was she thinking? She couldn't possibly know the right things to say if the worst had happened. Although it still hurt when she thought about it, her experience with death was so different from Hok'ee's.

Vengeance. That's what he'd turn to.

Hok'ee had headed for the top of the canyon, and although she'd been grateful for the animal trail that allowed her to climb at a steady, gradual pace, when she reached the top, she felt exposed. On the other hand, the view was spectacular. She could see for miles. Granted, it was difficult to make out the crevices she knew she'd encounter on the rim, but it was like being on the top of the world.

This was where eagles landed, she told herself even though she wasn't sure they really did. Certainly the ancients must have posted guards here, and hopefully they'd appreciated the scenery. With nothing to slow the wind, she was glad for the braid that kept her hair out of her eyes. If she remained out in the open for long, she'd wind up with a sunburn, but with her senses telling her she was still following Hok'ee footsteps, she concentrated on covering as much territory as possible.

Soon, all too soon, she'd know the story behind the rifle blast.

A sound she hadn't heard before, and at odds with the wind, captured her attention. Slowing, she took inventory of where she was. To her surprise, she realized she'd been heading back toward her and Garrin's camp, albeit at a much higher elevation than before. She was also within feet of a ledge.

Confused, she stopped and shielded her eyes from the sun. She hadn't reached a steep drop-off after all. Yes, she risked a long fall into nothing if she continued going in a straight line, but to the left was a slope leading down to what—she had no idea.

The moment she reached the slope, she knew without a doubt that Hok'ee had gone this way, only it hadn't been Hok'ee. Cougar had taken those steps.

When had he shifted, and why?

The why came all too easily. He needed to be a predator.

Hand to her throat, she started walking again. The slope was so steep she had to angle her body back, which made it difficult to see where she was going, though her footing was secure. When she glanced down, she discovered she was no longer on an animal trail. Instead, steps had been carved into the rock. The narrow, widely spaced stairs were worn down from years of exposure to the elements.

Who had done the work, when, and why?

Overwhelmed by the multitude of questions, and not enough answers, she nevertheless shook them off so she could concentrate on what she needed to. Cougar's essence clung to the steps. Yes, he was animal, and yet what she sensed was more than that. Telling herself she'd tapped into Hok'ee was the simple explanation, except she couldn't quite make herself believe it was that simple.

Opening up her mind even more, she slipped into an untested space and time. She was seeing with Cougar's eyes, only there was something different about the predator she'd come to accept as Hok'ee's other half. This Cougar was older, centuries older. Even more incredible, he was no longer in the here and now. As a consequence, neither was she.

She'd slipped back in time; there was no other explanation. Just as she'd done following Anaba's death. The physical world was crisper somehow, the sky bluer, the sun warmer.

Several men, naked and toasted nearly the color of their surroundings, crouched maybe a hundred feet ahead of her. Their hair was long and tangled, their hands wrapped around stones they pounded against the ground. There was no doubt that they were chiseling out more stairs.

There was something almost transparent about them, making her wonder whether they existed only in her mind. Sweat glistened on their backs. They were talking to each other. At least she assumed that's what the frequent clicks and grunts were. Within reach of each man was what she recognized as an atlatl, which was a two-foot long throwing stick, along with a handful of darts.

Anasazi.

She couldn't take another step, couldn't remember how to breathe. The more intently she studied the ghost-men, the more her awe grew. The atlatls left no doubt that she was looking at what archeologists had labeled the early Basket Makers, the original Anasazi who'd yet to develop bows and arrows.

Cougar, maybe with the help of Anaba's spirit or a Ghost-walker, had taken her back to the beginning.

Dad. Oh, God, Dad! Are you, can you—

Bam!

Even as she started, the Anasazi workmen evaporated. What a moment ago had been a not-yet-completed stairway aged, and a faint haze muted the sky. The rifle shot had come from somewhere below.

Wishing she was doing anything else, Kai half-stepped, half-jumped from one stair to the next. She could only pray she wasn't being watched.

Garrin had no reason to cause her harm. Or did he? If something had happened to frighten or disturb him, who knew what he was capable of. She'd have to use the greatest possible care when it came to approaching him. She'd speak softly and calmly while assuring him—

A sudden chill forced her to admit that she'd been focusing

on Garrin because she didn't want to think about the ramifications of that horrible sound, but she had to. If Hok'ee had been wounded or killed—

No!

Sweat had collected in her armpits and at the base of her spine by the time she reached the last step, yet she was cold. Getting used to being on level ground took a moment. Then she looked around. She hadn't reached the valley floor after all but was on a natural shelf the elements had carved into the canyon wall. The shelf was maybe a hundred feet wide. It was about twice as deep, but what made her dizzy with disbelief was the great stone house at the far end of the shelf.

Two stories high and maybe fifty feet wide, it had three doorways and several smaller square openings that must have once served as windows. The roof looked to be flat, or nearly so, the workmanship incredible. Short stairs led up to each doorway, seemingly waiting for her to step inside. Instead, she stared open-mouthed.

What she was looking at had to be thousands of years old, and yet from what she could tell, the elements had barely touched it. The wind she'd been dealing with no longer toyed with her hair here, and the canyon wall shielded her from much of the sun. Either by accident or design, the house had been constructed in a natural weather pocket.

Minutes passed as she struggled to comprehend not just what she'd come across but that she'd caught glimpses of it yesterday when she'd followed Anaba's spirit into the *afterworld*. She was in the presence of something breath-stealing, the rarest of rare finds, and she half-believed that a Chindi had a hand in keeping the structure safe, not just from the seasons, but from humans as well.

No wonder Anaba had wanted to come here after his death.

Tears blurred her vision. She'd pulled her camera out of her pocket but couldn't bring herself to start taking pictures. What right did she have? This—this gift from the Anasazi deserved all the reverence she could accord it.

Maybe by walking away, leaving it to the ages and Skinwalker.

But she couldn't do that. The rifle shot had come from near, if not right, here.

Her right calf threatened to cramp, proof of how long she'd been on her toes. It took all the will at her command, but she made herself look at something other than the ancient house. She'd been wrong when she'd thought the ledge was only about two hundred feet wide, because instead of coming to an end at the right, it continued on, albeit at a downward angle as if the ledge was being pinched.

It was quiet, too quiet. Why hadn't she noticed that before now? Barely able to hear for her heart's thudding, she forced herself to start walking in that direction. Her destination brought her closer to what she couldn't truthfully call a ruin. It loomed over her now, stark and impenetrable, making a mockery of any thoughts she'd ever had of her importance.

Dad, nothing in Canyon De Chelly touches this.

The ground under her feet now angled down a little. She didn't try to shake off the feeling that she was walking into the great unknown. A large number of massive, flat boulders ahead of her made her think of monster-sized headstones. Whatever they were, they appeared to be naturally occurring, and not man-made. What made the hairs at the back of her neck stand up was the question of what was behind the stones. Most could easily provide shelter for several humans or predators, and the shadows running out from them were darker than she felt comfortable with.

Stopping, she concentrated. There was still no hint of a breeze, but it wasn't as quiet as she'd previously thought. Unfortunately, she'd have to get closer to the headstones before she could be sure what she was hearing. She just wished it didn't sound like someone was whispering. It took longer than she cared to admit, but finally she forced herself to cover a few more feet. She was nearly to the first of the boulder slabs, and feeling dwarfed.

Whispering? No, that didn't accurately describe the sounds. More like breathing? Scared and yet calm, she took another three steps and stopped with a hand on the closest boulder slab. It was warm, densely warm, as if the heat went clear through to the center. Something or someone could be behind it and she wouldn't know until she'd walked around it. And with in excess of twenty of the strange forms, she could be within feet of an army and not see it.

An army of humans or predators?

Gathering what might be a fatal calm around her, she listened. The longer she did, the more convinced she became that she was indeed hearing lungs at work.

Anasazi?

Of course not, couldn't be.

Why not? Hadn't she already seen ancient workmen?

"Stay there . . . I swear—I'll shoot."

Garrin's voice, faint, coming from somewhere deep in the gravestones. He was too far away for her to be sure, but she thought he sounded not frightened exactly, but disbelieving.

Her impulse to call out to Garrin lasted maybe two seconds. Then, feeling utterly alone, she slipped around the stone she'd been touching. Nothing was behind it, thank goodness, but she couldn't say the same for the others.

She hadn't seen anything dead, no beautiful but bloodied cougar form stretched out on the ground. She just wished she could believe that meant the bullets hadn't found a predator's body.

Cougar's body.

Strange, she'd gone several minutes without thinking about Hok'ee. Now that he and his other half reentered her mind, she had to struggle to think of anything else. He was here; she had no doubt. What she didn't know was what form he'd taken.

It's me, she tried to tell him. *Do you feel my presence? Maybe you knew I'd follow.*

I know.

A spear of life jumped through her. She had to fight not just her nerves, but her entire body to keep from crying out. The strength of his unspoken words and unseen body frightened her. She didn't want him to be this strong or for her pussy to instantly demand to be filled with him. Only an absolute fool would let sex get in the way of self-preservation, a fool or a woman who'd bonded with a man/animal.

Are you all right? she asked. *Please tell me you haven't been wounded.*

"Get back!" Garrin bellowed. "I'll shoot, I swear—"

"Garrin!" she called out. "It's me. What is—"

"Where are you?" Garrin demanded. "My God. Ah, shit, get back."

Straining to locate where Garrin's voice was coming from, she begged Hok'ee to understand why she couldn't mentally stay with him. "Who are you talking to?" she asked her coworker.

"Cougars. Everywhere. Ah, shit!"

23

His voice bounced off the surrounding stone, and she was now all but certain of his location. She couldn't remember ever hearing such fear from a grown man, which meant that as long as he had a weapon, he was dangerous. Sexual energy beat throughout her. Just the same, she managed to push the sensation to the back of her mind. One cautious step at a time, she approached. Her muscles had never felt so finely tuned, her senses so keen. Hok'ee would be proud of the wild animal she'd become.

"I'm coming." She spoke quietly and calmly, a reasoned adult chasing off a child's nightmare. At the same time, her fingers curled inward, much as Cougar's claws did, and her muscles felt capable of meeting whatever task she needed them to do. "I'm nearly there. I need you to remain calm, to put down your rifle, and—"

"No! They're going to kill me."

Garrin was in no condition to listen to reason. All she could do was pray he'd recognize her for what she was—and that he'd comprehend she wasn't afraid of the cougars.

As for her own rifle—damn, it was back where she'd been when she and Hok'ee had heard the first shot.

Do the others know who I am? she asked Cougar.

They know.

But will they accept me, she needed to know. Unfortunately there wasn't time to wait for the answer because she'd just spotted Garrin. He was standing with his back pressed against one of the gravestones. Because she was behind him, slightly to the side, and he was looking straight ahead, he hadn't spotted her, which meant she had to take great care in approaching him. Always before, Garrin had struck her as a committed professional, driven really. Now she smelled his abject fear. He was overwhelmed, lost and confused. If he hadn't killed Anaba, she would have felt sorry for him. Instead, she acknowledged that he was getting exactly what he deserved.

Still she didn't want to see him dead, especially by Cougar's fangs and claws.

"How many cougars are there?" She spoke slowly, softly, a casual question one friend asks another. "I don't see them."

Garrin fairly jumped but didn't turn around. She caught a whiff of urine, proof of how totally unhinged he was.

"I'm going to join you," she continued in the same measured tone. "That way I'll be able to see what you're talking about."

She thought he might order her not to put herself in danger. His silence served as further proof of how far he'd slid from the man she'd thought he was. There was a feral quality to him, a trapped animal looking for a way out of hell. Like a cur dog, he'd attack anyone or thing he perceived as a threat.

Are you responsible? she asked Cougar. *You've done this to him?*

He deserves it, and more.

She was in no position to argue the point with him, and although it disturbed her to realize how little concern Cougar had for Garrin's mental health, that too was something she'd deal with later.

"This place is incredible," she said when she was within six feet of Garrin. "Absolutely unbelievable."

"They're going to kill me."

They? she nearly said. Then she saw them.

Four cougars, each crouched near a different headstone, their attention zeroed as one on Garrin. They were far enough apart that she couldn't look at all of them at the same time, and the shadows made it difficult for her to form a clear impression. Hok'ee was one of them, she had no doubt of that. But they were all large and sleek and deadly, and she couldn't be certain which one was the man/animal she'd been fucking.

There was something horrible and yet exquisite about them. Any other time she'd be as terrified as Garrin was, but even then she would acknowledge their perfection. She wanted to run her fingers over their coats, look deep into their eyes, share the air with them.

Their patience was disconcerting. She'd always assumed that a cougar about to attack would be hugging the ground, their muscles taut, tails lashing, and mouths open. Instead, all four were relaxed. No, not relaxed so much as waiting Garrin out. They'd wear him down physically, mentally, and emotionally, wound his mind instead of his body.

What did she think she could do, order them to leave Garrin alone? This was about avenging Anaba's death.

Rocking back on her heels, she abandoned her thought of touching Garrin, letting him know that these weren't ordinary cougars and thus he didn't really need to fear them. Yes, she could tell him that the beasts had once been humans, but had been re-created by Skinwalker.

"This is why you were willing to let me leave this morning, isn't it?" she said, indicating the great house behind her. "Why you wanted me gone. You'd found this place. You wanted to keep your knowledge to yourself."

If Garrin hadn't let out a noisy breath, she wouldn't have been certain he'd heard.

"We have to talk about this. I don't know how you thought you could get away with such secrecy. It's unbelievable, the find of a lifetime. Garrin, I'm concerned about you. First you try to tell me that you shot and killed a cougar yesterday, and now—"

"Shut the fuck up."

Garrin might never know this, but she'd accomplished what she'd hoped to. She'd gotten his attention.

"You're right. This is hardly the time to talk about professional and ethical considerations. I just want you to know I have every intention of calling Dr. Carter as soon as possible. He needs to know about your behavior."

Garrin twitched but didn't glance at her. He looked tense enough to shatter. Again, she felt sorry for him. She also didn't trust him.

He's dangerous, Cougar. Any sudden move on your part and he'll shoot.

We know.

That's why you're waiting? Of course it is. You don't want what happened to Anaba to happen to anyone else.

When Cougar didn't respond, she nearly asked why he and the others didn't simply walk away. Then she remembered Anaba's ruined body and knew why. She didn't waste her breath trying to convince Cougar not to let the need for vengeance take over. He and the others lived according to rules she couldn't comprehend.

She'd had sex with an animal, not a physical and demanding man, an animal. And no matter that her blood now ran cold, she still wanted to mate with that predator.

Barely aware of what she was doing, Kai joined Garrin. She stood beside him, not touching the profusely sweating man.

She started with the cougar to the far left, studying his form, letting his body speak to hers. The creature was everything a fierce predator should be. Health and raw self-confidence poured out of him. It didn't matter whether he was Cougar or not, she'd welcome him into her body and howl her climax.

But he wasn't Cougar. Her body knew.

She had the same reaction to the next cougar, and the third. Even before she focused on the beast standing to the far right, her muscles loosened and her pussy softened. Maybe she'd subconsciously known the truth and had put off this moment so it could build within her.

I need you. Want you, she mind-spoke.

I know you do.

He hadn't said it, but she was certain Cougar felt the same way. Staring through the shadows at him, she noted the luminicent eyes, the rich coat, and potent body. He was larger than the others, not by much but enough that she felt his size in her bones. No wonder her cunt had given way to Hok'ee's cock. No wonder she'd dreamed of fucking the animal half of him.

For the first time in her life, she wanted to be something other than a human female. Cougar deserved a mate, a fierce and fearless equal. Together they'd hunt and kill, eat and fuck. Her belly would swell, and she'd give birth to small, helpless cubs. They'd raise their offspring together. As the cubs suckled from her full breasts, Cougar would track down rabbits and deer, and bring his kill to her so she could nourish their children.

"What are they doing here?" Garrin whimpered. "I've never heard of cougars acting like this."

"Revenge," she said. "For what happened yesterday."

"You said I didn't kill—there wasn't a body."

The conversation exhausted her. It also served as a reminder that she was a woman and not a predator. "I'm not going to try to explain things. And, Garrin, I don't know if I can save you."

"You—save . . ."

Cougar's gaze hadn't left her. She had no doubt he understood everything that was being said. The same might be true for his companions. As a member of the human race, her overriding concern should be for her coworker. However, it wasn't that simple. It never would be again.

"What do you want, Cougar?" she asked. In the wake of what was happening, trying to keep anything from Garrin didn't matter. "All of you, what do you want?"

An eye for an eye.

The response, coming from four minds, shocked her, and yet she wasn't surprised. She wondered if they understood that a part of her agreed. Garrin had taken a life. He should pay.

"You can't be talking to them," Garrin blubbered. He jabbed her in the side with his elbow, forcing her to look at him. He still clutched the rifle with white-knuckled fingers. Sweat beaded his upper lip and ran down his temples.

"You don't understand." That said, she shook her head. Even if she was willing to reveal the truth, this wasn't the time. "Let me do what I have to. It's the only chance you have."

When Garrin didn't reply, she accepted the stark truth. This man who not long ago had proclaimed himself the undisputed head of everything that happened at Sani had just turned his survival over to her. He might still have the only weapon, but even in his agitated state, he knew that wasn't enough.

"Don't move," she warned. "And whatever you do, do not fire."

Without a wind to cool things, the temperature here was warmer than she preferred. Either that, or her body was responding to the man behind the predator. Whichever it was, she didn't dare let herself be distracted. Talking to Garrin had helped remind her of who and what she'd been up until the last few days. She couldn't live with herself if she turned her back on that woman.

"You need to leave," she told Cougar. She could have mind-talked but this way, hopefully, everyone would hear the same thing. "All of you." She looked at each cougar in turn. "No matter what you believe about your right to kill a killer, if you do, you'll be hunted down."

"Kai?"

Not bothering to acknowledge Garrin's pitiful voice, she stepped away from him and started toward Cougar. Pure energy emanated from him and wrapped around her. The bonds were as tight as any rope. This was going to be even harder than she'd thought.

"If you were in human form, I think the four of you would know what I'm talking about," she continued. "As cougars, you're predators. You kill because that's your nature. In some respects, humans are the same."

There hadn't been enough distance between her and Cougar; she hadn't had time to prepare for his impact. Or maybe the truth was, she'd always react like this to him. Stepping into dangerous territory, she stopped just out of Cougar's reach. As a young teen, she'd fallen absolutely and totally in lust with a high school senior who lived in the neighborhood. He'd played football, and she'd stare as he ran down the street most mornings. Wearing nothing except shorts and shoes, his incredible body had glistened. He'd barely been aware of her existence of course, and that had probably been her saving grace, not that she'd seen it that way.

The only thing she'd known, the only thing she'd been able to think about for maybe three months was that the world's sexiest man had turned her mind and body on end. She couldn't sleep, couldn't think about anything except him. Her days revolved around seeing him. Her nights pulsed with fantasies of hot embraces—as a virgin, she'd lacked specifics of what came after that.

Then she'd seen him walking arm in arm with an *older* woman, and she'd absolutely known she was going to die. She'd cried until she had no tears left, then cried some more.

She was no longer that naïve and love-struck teen, but the emotions and sensations hadn't given way to maturity after all. The only difference was that today, she lusted after a predator.

"Listen to me," she said when she longed to drop to her hands and knees and present herself to Cougar as she'd done in last night's dream. "If you kill Garrin, whoever finds his body is going to know how he died. Even if you haul him away from . . ."

We call it Ghost House.

Ghost House. "Even if you leave his body somewhere else, someone will eventually find his remains. You have no idea how large a search there'd be—Cougar, I'd have to help. Otherwise, I'll be accused of killing him."

We did, not you.

"Which is why whoever conducts the search won't rest until they've eliminated the threat. That's what everyone will see you as, a threat."

What if there's no body?

Although she wasn't sure which of the predators had asked the question, she continued to address Cougar. The link between them was too strong for it to be any other way. "Didn't you hear me, I'd be expected to tell them everything I know."

Don't tell them anything.

"Even if I was willing to lie, what could I say that they'd believe? Whoever comes here—and once they find this"—she nodded at Ghost House—"people are going to come from everywhere. There'll be archeologists, anthropologists, state and federal officials—Cougar, there's never been anything remotely like this." Overwhelmed, she fell silent.

Behind her, Garrin muttered something. It sounded as if he was saying the same thing over and over again. Even if he was capable of grasping everything he was seeing and hearing, she couldn't begin to put her mind to how she might explain. If she couldn't convince Garrin of the reality of Chindi and Skinwalker—and she didn't know how to begin—how could she find the necessary words for everyone else? They'd think she was crazy.

Stop them. Don't let anyone come.

"I can't do that," she snapped, still not caring who was *speaking* to her. "No one can. It's a free country. People have . . ."

It didn't matter, not now. Reality was this moment.

"Please, believe me. I could tell people I don't know what happened to Garrin, but they'd still search for him, maybe bring in search dogs. What if one of those dogs spotted a *cougar?*"

She half-expected one of the Tocho to insist they'd tear the dog apart. When no one did, she wondered if she was starting to get through to them. "Those people will be armed. When, not if, but when they catch sight of one of you, they're going to shoot. They might not stop until all of you are dead. Maybe someone will survive, but what kind of life will that be?"

Had she ever been more tired, more torn between conflicting emotions? Against everything she'd always believed about herself, she'd do whatever she could to spare the lives of those Skinwalker had condemned to a shattered existence. But even with commitment pulsing through her, the only thing she really wanted to do was have sex. It didn't matter whether it was with Cougar or Hok'ee.

"This isn't happening." Garrin's voice carried unexpected strength. "It isn't, can't be."

"Shut up. Just, please, be quiet," she snapped.

You want him to live?

"I don't know," she told Cougar. "Maybe that makes me some kind of monster in your eyes, but I honestly don't know."

"What are you talking about?" Garrin demanded. "What do you mean, a monster?"

Are you going to answer him?

"No," she told Cougar. That was it, wasn't it? Garrin's survival or death was out of her hands now. She'd done everything she could, hadn't she?

Newly calm, she wiped her palms on her shorts. Although she didn't completely trust her legs, she approached the man/beast who dominated her world. Her hand didn't shake as she touched Cougar between his eyes.

Garrin hissed, then whimpered. In a way, his sound fed her own emotions. When had she first voluntarily touched Hok'ee? It had to have been after he'd given her back use of her hands, but her memory was foggy. Maybe he remembered, but maybe Cougar wasn't concerned with such things.

"It's overwhelming," she whispered. "Everything is."

When Cougar didn't respond, she dropped her hand to her side. Instantly she felt lost and alone, yet more alive than she'd ever been. The jock she'd had her first crush on—what had he looked like, and had she ever heard his voice?

She didn't remember. Neither could she pull up any memories of the men she'd known before Hok'ee had taken over her world. He was her everything. He and the others of his kind, and the man whimpering behind her. And Ghost House.

Only there was no future for her and Hok'ee.

"Go." The word tore at her throat. "Take the rest of the Tocho and find someplace safe to live. Otherwise . . ."

What about you?

Hok'ee was still there, he had to be. Certainly Cougar didn't care about her emotions. Or did he?

Dizzy, she swayed toward Cougar. As she did, she reached out with both hands to catch herself. Maybe Cougar was trying to give her something to rest against when he leaned into her. Maybe she'd never know, because the instant she touched him, Garrin screamed.

A moment later, a rifle blast deafened her. Every molecule of her being needed to scream, but when she spun and faced Garrin, she did so silently. As silent as the cougars.

Judging by the way he was holding the rifle, Garrin had fired into the air. Pushing her aside, Cougar stalking toward Garrin. His fellow Tocho did the same.

"No!" she cried. It didn't matter who she was trying to reach. The cougars' weapons consisted of fangs and claws. They'd been created to kill, and their bodies were honed to do that one thing. Muscles rippled across their backs and down their legs.

But Garrin's weapon was capable of destroying all of them.

Horrified, she gaped as Garrin aimed at one approaching cougar, and then the other. Although his legs trembled and he breathed as if he was having a heart attack, he held the rifle steady. The cougars slunk toward him one slow and measured step at a time, communicating wordlessly. She prayed one hadn't volunteered to give up his life so the others could live. And kill.

They were going to attack, to rip and tear—unless Garrin shot first. Violent death would surround her, again.

"No." Her voice was calm again, in control. "Stop it, Garrin. Put that thing down."

"Are you crazy! Oh, shit. Shit."

"Cougar. Don't make it like this, please. Wasn't Anaba enough?"

Stay out of this.

"I can't."

"Stop doing that!" Garrin insisted. "Talking like those beasts—oh, shit!"

He was going to fire again. The primal need for action and self-preservation was written all over his face. Acting instinctively, she headed for Garrin at a dead run. A single swipe from Cougar's paw could have stopped her, but she was past him so fast maybe he didn't see her in time.

Head lowered, she threw herself at Garrin. The top of her

head struck him in his gut and sent both of them flying backward. Garrin landed on his back, his breath whooshing out of him. Feeling a strength she'd never known was possible, she yanked the rifle out of his hands and flung it behind her. Then she straddled him. It took every bit of self-control she had not to pummel his face.

"You idiot, you God damn idiot!" she bellowed.

"No, no, no!" Garrin dug his nails into her forearms. At the same time, he bent his left knee and struck her between her legs.

Suddenly she couldn't breathe. Pain screamed through her. Releasing her forearms, he reached for her throat.

As his fingers tightened, something grabbed her by the shoulders and yanked her off Garrin. The same something half-lifted and tossed her to the side. Through the hair that had fallen into her eyes, she saw a naked man drop to his knees beside Garrin. The man began pummeling Garrin's face. When Garrin tried to hide behind his hands, the man grabbed his wrists and yanked Garrin's arms over his head. He started to kneel on Garrin's throat.

"No!" Kai cried. "Hok'ee, you'll kill him."

"He tried to kill me. And you."

Garrin didn't know you were human, she stupidly wanted to tell Hok'ee, but it didn't matter, did it?

"Hok'ee! Listen to me, damn it. Do you remember what I said when you were in cougar form?" His knee was only an inch from Garrin's throat, prompting her to rush her words. "That if anything happened to him, your way of life would be forever changed."

Still pinning Garrin's arms to the ground, Hok'ee looked over his shoulder at her. He was human again, and yet Cougar had left enough of himself in the man that she felt not intimidated but awed. Hok'ee's original life might have been taken from him, but look what he'd been handed in return. He now walked in two worlds.

"They'd have to find me." Hok'ee said. After giving Garrin a withering glare, he settled onto his haunches but continued to pin the other man to the ground.

"And they might not," she agreed. "But do you want to have to live like a fugitive?"

"Is it any worse than this?"

"Only you can answer that."

Garrin kept looking from Hok'ee to her, then back. He trembled so his teeth clattered, and she thought he'd wet himself again. Not long ago she'd believed she could work in partnership with Garrin. Now he seemed pitiful. Wrecked.

In telling contrast, intellect deepened Hok'ee's gaze. Yes, he was still part predator, but the halves of his existence had meshed into a whole she might never fully comprehend. After all those years of being surrounded by educated and reasoned men, one ruled by the drive for self-preservation took her to a part of herself she'd only briefly glimpsed.

Behind the woman with the college degree was one who could see into the hearts of animals. Because Hok'ee had brought her into his world, she now understood that her connection with living creatures was much more than a way to deepen knowledge of those creatures.

It was a blessing, a rich treasure.

One that would forever set her apart.

"Get him off me," Garrin blubbered. "Oh, God, please help me."

Disgust written on his face, Hok'ee released Garrin's wrists, and not so much stood as glided into a standing position.

A low, sharp growl pulled her attention off Hok'ee. One of the three remaining Tocho now stood near Garrin's head. When a blubbering Garrin tried to sit up, the cougar swatted him down, tearing his shirt in a couple of places in the process. Sobbing like a terrified child, Garrin buried his head in his arms.

"He doesn't belong here," Hok'ee said. The three cougars growled as one, and Kai took their response as agreement.

"I can make a call." She tapped her pocket where her cell phone lay. "To the head of the university this man works for. Tell Dr. Carter he's had a breakdown. They'll send someone, probably several people, to pick him up. Get him out of here."

She thought Hok'ee would agree, so wasn't prepared when he shook his head. "I won't let you kill him," she insisted. "I thought I made that clear."

"You did. I don't want anyone else coming here now, seeing Ghost House."

That would happen, eventually. But Hok'ee was right. Today was much too soon. "Then what—"

Lifting his head, Hok'ee let loose with a series of clipped grunts and grumbles. The three Tocho responded in the same vein. The more time she spent around them, the more their intellect impressed her. Maybe they were capable of coexisting with humans, if they wanted.

"They're going to take him to your camp," Hok'ee explained. "Tell your doctor to have him picked up there."

She was about to point out that Garrin might not emotionally survive being hauled off by three predators when, almost as one, the cougars became men. Naked, they weren't shy about letting her see everything they had to offer. They were all relatively young, with the oldest not yet thirty. In addition, they were physically fit, with black hair and toasted skin—Navajo.

She'd been right then? Skinwalker had sentenced them to *life* as Tocho as punishment for having rejected their heritage? Then why were they healthy and strong men? More possibilities held her attention. Maybe Skinwalker was only interested in those who could have benefited and enhanced the Navajo race if they'd embraced their bloodline. As for their being male— that could be pure cruelty on the Skinwalker's part. Not only were the Tocho loners, there were no members of the opposite sex. Then she'd arrived, or rather, Hok'ee had pulled her into his world.

Feeling overwhelmed by everything she'd just considered, she watched the trio disappear into one of Ghost House's openings. She glanced at Garrin, only to shake her head at his wild-eyed stare. She'd seen looks like that on strung-out drug addicts and street people who talked to themselves. Garrin might regain his sanity; she hoped he eventually would. Right now, however, she couldn't imagine anyone believing him if he rattled on about shape-shifting or dead cougars who disappeared, let alone his insistence that he'd seen her talking to one of the predators.

The Tocho men emerged dressed in clothing she suspected had once belonged to hikers. "They're ready," Hok'ee said. "Do you want to make your call now, or wait until you're back at your camp?"

He hadn't said it, but she understood the message behind his words. He wasn't going to leave here.

Not rushing her reaction or thoughts, she headed toward where the men had gone for their clothes. This close to Ghost House, she felt overwhelmed by it. Not only did it loom over her, she swore she could sense the effort it had taken to create the amazing structure. Seeing Anasazi ruins with her father had been one thing. She'd been impressed by the workmanship that remained, but countless years had sanded away a great deal. The ruins had been, in essence, dead.

In contrast, Ghost House, despite its name, served as a vibrant tribute to those who'd built it. There'd been almost no sanding away of the outer surface, and the details were amazing. She spotted notches in the stone made by whatever tools the Anasazi had used during construction. If she touched those notches, would she *see* the long-dead workmen?

Only if she was in contact with Cougar at the same time.

He was behind her, silent in that way of his, alive in ways she was just learning to comprehend.

Alive.

Tears burned her eyes and sealed her throat. Standing with her back to the man who'd changed her world, she asked herself if he'd ever understand her tears, or care enough to ask.

Determined not to drown in the grief she'd hoped she'd put behind her, she lightly touched the wall. "How did Garrin find this?" she whispered. "All these years, and no one has. If I hadn't been following you—"

"Maybe we'll never know." Hok'ee rested a hand on her shoulder. "Shortly before he died, Anaba told me that Garrin had been here."

Anaba. Hearing Hok'ee friend's name gave her something to think about. Although it didn't entirely distract her from the warmth on her shoulder, she called up the memory of the incredible glimpses into the ancient world she'd seen right after Anaba's body had faded to nothing. Maybe what remained of Anaba was responsible for her being here.

Maybe his essence remained.

"I'm not going to leave," she told Hok'ee. "This place—I have to stay."

24

Using a low battery as her excuse, she kept the call to Dr. Carter as brief as possible. Garrin had suffered some kind of mental breakdown and needed immediate medical attention. Fortunately, a group of hikers had offered to take him out on the ATV she and Garrin had used to get here. She'd decided to stay where Garrin had had his breakdown. No, she was fine. She could remain here until the university group showed up. In fact, she intended to use her solitude to connect with as much of the area's wildlife as possible. Two, three days, it didn't matter. It wasn't as if she'd never been in remote areas.

"This is really what you want to do?" Hok'ee asked when she'd finished her conversation.

"Yes." Determined to make her point, she again touched the stone wall. "My dad devoted much of his working life to places like this. I want to follow in his footsteps."

She'd had her back to Hok'ee because it was safer, but when he took hold of her shoulders and turned her around, she didn't fight. Having his hands on her took her back to those early hours with him. At the beginning of their relationship, everything had been about him. He'd controlled, not just her body, but her sexual responses. He'd taken her deep into herself, where she'd found not strength of will, but a primal slut. She wasn't ashamed of what he'd pulled out of her; regret changed nothing.

What bothered her so much was that the only thing he'd wanted from her had been her body. Horny and without access to the women he'd had access to before his death, he'd stalked his victim, her.

"I want you to leave me alone," she said. "What I said to Dr. Carter was the truth. I need time to myself." Even if that meant she'd be depriving herself of her conduit to history.

She thought he might hand her proof of how little strength was in her words. If he flamed her flesh as they both knew he could, she'd melt before him, melt and surrender. Draw him into her center and scream in primitive release while his cum seared her.

But eventually sanity would return, and she'd hate him for it.

"Tell me why you want me gone," he said as his fingers slid down her arms. Reaching her hands, he squeezed, then let her go. "Is it because of Cougar?"

"Cougar?"

"He's too wild, a killer."

"He's what nature made him. I'd never blame—"

"Then what?"

They'd slipped through the entryway while talking, and in this place where the shadows never left, past and present flowed together. She still needed space around her as much as she needed her soul back and yet even if Hok'ee wasn't here, she wouldn't be truly alone. The Tocho had called the structure Ghost House because Anasazi ghosts remained.

"Do you feel them?" Hok'ee asked. "Maybe they're speaking to you."

"No." Not yet, she almost added but didn't because she'd

need Cougar for that. "Maybe they're not making that much of an impact because it isn't the first time I've been in Anasazi ruins."

When he didn't respond, she tried to tell herself he was being considerate of her emotions. Then he returned to the opening and stood for several moments with his back to her. She had to clench her fingers to keep from touching him.

"They're having to carry him," he said. "They tried to get him to walk, but his legs keep collapsing."

She didn't care about Garrin. He belonged to a world she wasn't sure she still had anything in common with.

But if not that, where did she belong? With the Tocho?

Hok'ee was one of them.

And what existed between them wasn't enough.

"You have a right to more than I've given you," she whispered, unsure where the emotion and words were coming from. "Someday, if you want, I'll go back into your past. Maybe we'll learn who your parents were, whether you had siblings."

His shoulders straightened, and he stood rocklike. Studying him, her mind filled with the image of a toddler standing alone in a small Navajo hogan with a dirt floor. The boy had been crying, but his tears had dried. His small body had a stoic quality about it, as if that hadn't been the first time he'd been abandoned.

"Maybe you don't want to know about your family," she managed. "Sometimes the past needs to stay dead."

"What makes you say that?"

Oh, God, had he ever been this magnificent? Lonely strength rolled through him.

"Something I just—I'm not sure it's real. I wasn't touching you or Cougar, so I can't be certain."

"You don't want to tell me, do you?"

Measuring the distance between them, she shook her head. "What's going to happen now?" she asked, trying not to tremble or care. "You and the others must have talked about what you'd do if or when Ghost House was discovered, it and the other places."

"We can't leave. We don't belong anywhere else."

"But—"

"We'll learn to adapt, Kai, to remain hidden."

"What kind of a life would that be? Have you tried going anywhere else? You don't know what it'd be like if you don't—"

"I go to town sometimes, but then Cougar needs out and I have no choice but to return."

She'd been trapped once, unable to escape a nightmare. But in time the nightmare had faded enough that she'd been able to pull her life together and go on. Some days were easier than others. She wanted to ask Hok'ee to learn from her example, but his situation was different because for as long as he lived, he'd share his existence with Cougar.

And maybe Cougar couldn't live anywhere else.

"Just walk out of here now," she told him when every fiber in her cried out for his arms around her—arms that turned everything into sex.

He studied her for too long. His eyes drilled into her, and she wondered if he was searching for the holes and wounds she'd worked to keep to herself. Even as she threw up her defenses, she silently thanked him for caring—or pretending he did.

"I wish it had been different between us," she wound up saying. "If you hadn't captured me—it didn't occur to you that I might hate you for what you were doing."

"Do you hate me?"

"Go, damn it, just go!"

Believing he was going to comply, she concentrated on holding herself together until she could no longer see him. Instead, he came even closer. "I've changed my mind. You can't stay in here after all."

"Can't?"

"We call it Ghost House for a reason. With everything you've been through, you deserve sunlight and warmth, simplicity."

Sunlight and warmth. How wonderful that sounded. And yet—

"Don't do this to yourself, Kai." Holding out his hand, he continued his scrutiny. "You're an incredibly strong woman, stronger than I was, but it's time to stop pushing yourself so hard."

"Me, stronger than you?"

He gave her a rueful look. "I took the easy way out when I chose death by motorcycle."

"It wasn't like that. You were wrapped in knots and not thinking about—"

"Don't." He pulled her toward him.

"Don't?" The interior was much cooler than outside, but his chest continued to carry the sun's warmth.

"Everything has been about me. Me taking you because I was a damn selfish bastard. Me forcing you into my world, getting you to fill in some of the blanks, endangering your life."

"Endangering?" she parroted so she'd have something other than his body to think about.

"Garrin could have killed you."

"You think—he was afraid of the Tocho, not me."

"And rapidly losing his mind. Why did you do it, Kai? Instead of letting us take the risks, you walked up to an armed and dangerous man."

She wanted to hand him an explanation, but the truth was, the only thing she remembered was her desperate determination not to let anything happen to him.

"Why?" he repeated.

His hand was gentle around hers, comforting and protective. It hadn't been like that for her in so long. "I don't know."

"I don't believe you."

About to tell him he was wrong, she stood with his naked body inches away. "I couldn't handle any more deaths."

"More? You were willing to risk your own life in an attempt to stop that from happening again?"

He sounded so confused she wished she could explain things, but she was being surrounded by something dark and cold. For a moment she wondered if a Skinwalker had found her.

"You're shaking, and you're turning white," he said.

Not waiting for a response, he lifted her in his arms and carried her outside. Still holding her, he turned so the sun warmed her back.

"Talk to me, Kai, please."

"I—I want you to leave."

"No, you don't. And even if you do, I'm not going anywhere."

Hadn't he just promised to give her the space she needed? But if she was alone, the dark force might grow in strength. She'd felt like this before, trembled before hellish images, but she'd always found a way to outrun them.

Maybe the time of running had come to an end.

"Is this backlash for everything I put you through?" he asked. "It's the last thing I wanted. I just—hell, I'm not sure I'll ever understand why I did the things I did."

"I do. You're part predator."

A deep sigh lifted his chest. "Yeah," he said. "I am. But right now I'm trying like hell not to be. I just wish my body would listen."

He wasn't the only one incapable of separating the physical from the emotional, as witnessed by her tightening nipples, and an undeniable softening in her pussy.

"I want you to talk about what just happened to you. If you need to curse me, I hope you do. But maybe this isn't about me."

She couldn't talk, not with the darkness lapping at her edges and exhaustion tearing down her defenses. She'd been strong; she had! Put the nightmare behind her. Why was it coming back now?

Leaning over, he assisted her in sitting on the ground. Then he sat cross-legged across from her, his erection bridging much of the space between them. Much as she wanted to touch him, she didn't.

"I'm not good at this sort of thing," he said. "Hell knows I haven't had much experience getting people to confide in me, because I haven't done the same in return. Then you with your sight came along, and suddenly there's nothing I can't keep from you. I'd like that to work both ways."

Not long ago she'd ordered him to walk away from her. Now she knew that wasn't going to happen.

"Maybe I'm wrong," he continued, "but I believe things came to a head for you when I asked why you risked your life the way you did. Talk to me. Why, really, were you willing to put yourself between me and a bullet?"

The darkness pushed against her. She could fight it with silence, but it would only return. "I told you. I couldn't take any more deaths."

"Anaba's had that much of an impact on you?"

Although it made her dizzy to do so, she shook her head. To keep from touching him, she tucked her hands under her armpits. "My—my mother died when I was a toddler."

He looked at her, just looked. His gaze was gentle, and if there was anything behind it, she couldn't tell. "I—I'm sorry I brought that up," she whispered. "You don't know anything about your parents. At least I have pictures of my mother, the receiving blanket she knitted."

"Her death impacted your entire life." He rested a hand on her knee.

"I—I'm not sure." Did he have any idea how much his touch meant? "I have no memories of her, so can I really miss something I never had? My father was an incredible parent. I never felt I was a burden in any way."

"It was just the two of you?"

Darkness again, nibbling at her, stealing the sun's gift of warmth. She could no longer feel Hok'ee's hand. "Yes."

"What is it? Kai, can you hear me?"

His voice came from someplace far away. Leaning forward, he placed both hands on her knees.

"Of course," she whispered. "I just . . ."

"Just what? You were starting to get your color back. But now it's gone again. This is about your father? Something happened to him?"

She could answer; it wasn't as if she hadn't done this before. "He's dead."

"How old was he?"

"Forty—forty-seven, why?"

When he didn't answer, she forced herself to concentrate on him. His cock still said everything that needed to be said about sexuality, but his focus was on whatever he hoped to read in her eyes. "Too young. How did it happen?"

No! Everything between them had about him, his needs and fractured existence. She'd even seen herself as his white knight, the woman with the special talent who would recreate his past. She had no interest in opening herself up to him, none at all.

Except she just had.

"An accident." She swallowed. "In Canyon De Chelly."

"What kind of accident?"

She didn't think she could speak until he pried her hands off her thighs and placed them on his knees. Along with bone and skin, she found his essence. Naked and exposed, they'd fucked like frenzied animals. In the wake of that, could answering his question be any harder?

"A quad. Not that different from the one I came to Tochona

on. Four fat tires capable of tackling nearly every terrain there is. Sturdy construction, a semi comfortable seat. He was alone. Near Massacre Cave Overlook. I'd—I was in Black Rock Canyon. There were—I'd been spending time there, waiting for some coyote kits to be born. Their mother let me touch them. I was so excited, I kept trying to call Dad. He didn't answer."

She vaguely recalled that Hok'ee had simply asked what had happened to her father. Always before when people questioned her about her father's death, she'd told them as little as possible. Even the senior park ranger didn't know all the details. Now, however, the floodgates wouldn't close.

In a voice that was both emotionless and deep, she told Hok'ee how, unable to shake her unease, she'd left Black Rock Canyon and ridden her own quad to Massacre, so-called because it had been the site of a tragic battle between Navajo and Spanish horsemen.

"They call it a cave, but it's more of a ledge. Hundreds of feet above the valley floor, with boulders the Navajo had tried to hide behind while the Spanish shot at them. Dad had gone to the top because he'd seen smoke. When—I saw signs of people having camped there, but they were gone by the time I arrived. Only Dad . . ."

"He was at the top?"

"No. Partway down. His quad—somehow the damn thing tipped over. He fell."

"It was just you when you found him?"

Could Hok'ee see into her heart and mind? Was he reliving the worst day of her life with her?

"Finding him wasn't hard. The moment I saw the tracks at the edge—it took me so long to climb down to him."

"Take your time. I'm here for as long as you need."

She was going to cry. For the first time since that horrid afternoon. Desperate not to let the tears begin, she pulled her hands free and tried to scoot away. But he came after her and positioned her so she was between his widespread legs, her back resting against his chest. Silent tears ran down her cheeks.

"He was still alive, barely. Broken, so broken. I—I told him I'd take care of him, but we both knew it was too late. I held him until . . ."

"Did the two of you talk?"

"Not much. We said we loved each other. Then—after he stopped breathing, I held him until the rescuers arrived. I—when I knew they were getting close, I climbed back up to the top."

Hok'ee pressed his lips against the back of her head. "Because you didn't want them to sense what had been private between you and your father, right?"

Not wanting to be smothered by more sympathy than she could handle, she'd told the rescuers that her father had been dead when she found him. He'd been the most important person in her life, parent and best friend. He was suppose to be indestructible, this man who encouraged her gift and protected her from the skeptical, and opportunists.

"It hurt so much," she said because it was too late to keep anything back. "Dad was always so careful. He knew how to handle his quad. Maybe—maybe the campers pushed him."

"Was there an investigation?"

Damn Hok'ee for being so perceptive! At the same time, she was grateful for the hard question. "Not much of one. Maybe, if I hadn't lied and said he was already dead—I was—I could barely think."

Hok'ee didn't say anything, and she was exhausted, spent. Still crying her silent tears, she turned her head so she could see him out of the corner of her eye. His eyes glistened.

"Don't feel sorry for me," she managed.

"There's a difference between pity and empathy. Accept what I'm giving you."

What he'd given her was the most unbelievable sex she'd ever experienced. He'd opened her to possibilities for her psychic ability she'd never imagined. And, although she was still coming to grips with this, her sorrow over her father's death had lifted a little.

Still looking at him, she took his right hand and placed it over her breast. She wasn't sure what had prompted the gesture, maybe equal parts sex and companionship. The breeze began to dry her tears.

"I mean it about the empathy," he said. "You weren't thinking straight when your father died or was killed. Your emotions were everything; don't beat yourself up believing it should have been anything else."

"I can't help—"

"Yes, you can. There's nothing you can do to change what happened, just as I can't change climbing on a motorcycle and getting myself killed."

United. In ways she'd never expected.

"I wish I'd known your dad," he went on. "I think I would have liked him."

"I know you would. He loved the out-of-doors. He never wanted to live in a city. Just having to visit one drove him crazy."

"That, I understand."

Of course, he did. In fact she now believed Hok'ee—or Ryan—would have wound up at a place like this, even if Skinwalker hadn't been responsible.

"Kai?"

"What?"

"On top of losing your mother at an early age, your dad's violent death was all you could handle. You didn't have anyone you felt you could talk to, did you?"

"No."

"Today when you thought the same might happen, you acted. You put your life in jeopardy because . . ."

"Because of you."

He had a wonderful sigh, long, low, and steady. It also revealed a great deal. Now she understood why he'd put the other Tocho in charge of getting Garrin as far away from here as possible. It wasn't because he wanted to keep Ghost House a secret; that time was coming to an end. The truth was, he wanted the two of them to be alone.

"You're a wise man," she told him. "Much wiser than I'd expected."

"My acting like a predator threw you off?"

"I didn't complain. I never would."

"Does that mean you don't want me to leave after all?"

She answered, not with words but action. Feeling as weightless as Hok'ee acted when Cougar was strong inside him, she pulled out of his arms and slid around. On hands and knees, she met his unwavering gaze. Then when there was nothing more for their eyes to say, she dropped down to lick the base of his cock.

His sigh was less measured than the last. His belly tightened to reveal washboard abs, and she was lost. Hissing like the big cat she wished she was, she threw herself at him. He collapsed under her, wrapping his arms and legs around her at the same time.

"Got you," he said, challenge deepening his voice. "Not letting go."

"Who's on top?" Not giving him time to answer, she raked her teeth over his exposed throat. Then she ground her belly against him. "Who the hell is on top, Cougar?"

One moment it was her. The next, she was looking up at him while his legs straddled her hips and his hands made short work of her shirt buttons.

They clutched and clenched, bit and kissed. The kiss continued until she lifted her hips off the ground and pressed her groin against his cock. Pushing her down, he tackled her shorts.

Then, somehow she was on top again, fighting her way out of her boots, shorts, and panties. That done, she set her sights on his throat, but before she could reach it, he caught her chin in a broad palm.

"Easy this time, okay?" he asked. "I want this to be between you and me."

In other words, he didn't want Cougar to be involved. The predator brought a thrilling and chilling element to their sex. But she was woman; she needed man.

"Easy?" she repeated. "I don't know if I have it in me."

"Let me," he muttered and pulled her down on top of him. She still wore her blouse, but it barely clung to her shoulders. Under his guidance, she layered her body over his with her legs inside his and his cock sheltered along her pussy.

He started kissing her again, touching her cheeks, nose, eyelids, chin, even her ears. Shiver after shiver rolled through her, making it difficult to remember what he'd said about taking things easy. If he touched her buttocks, she might be gone, but he simply ran his fingers along her backbone. Pushing her shirt up to her shoulder blades, he repeatedly touched the base of her spine, the contact light and quick, ending before she went flying off into space.

The sun was warm on her backside. Greater warmth came from him. Thinking to thank him, she curled into him so her heat-slickened labia glided over his cock. He rewarded her with another sharp sigh. Heeding instinct, she slid down him and half-sat up. Reaching between them, she guided his cock into her.

"Already?" he mouthed.

"Already."

Housing him deep while holding his much stronger body

down filled her with a sense of power she'd challenge any female cougar to match. Hok'ee was her mate. Her nerves and bones knew that and nothing else.

Settling against him, she licked his chest and throat. As she did, she repeatedly tightened her sex muscles around the invasion. Somehow he remained still under her, but she sensed his battle. He needed to fuck her, not play the passive recipient fuck.

"Do it," she said, her mouth on his throat. "Let Cougar out."

Still silent but no longer still, he rolled her onto her side. They lay body to body, fused together and waiting. Lifting his upper leg, he pinned her under him. "Not Cougar. This is all me."

Yes, being fucked and fucking back. Him pile-driving into her until his muscles trembled and sweat sheeted him. Heedless of the ground under her, she answered his strength with her own. His features blurred. He no longer sighed; each grunt rasped her nerves.

Her climax slammed her, knocked her nearly senseless, robbed her of hearing and sight. Bleating helplessly, she dove into sensation. He was there somewhere and locked in his own release. But she needed to be selfish. To feed off what her body was capable of and ride spasm after spasm until, slowly, so slowly, her world straightened. She was drenched and exhausted, her cunt still short-circuiting.

Breathe. Again. Measured this time. Bring air into your body.

"Shit," she whimpered. "Holy shit."

"You're done?"

"Done and dead. You?"

"For now, yes. For the rest of my life, far from it."

"What are you saying?" she managed.

"That I want this to go on. For us to . . ."

"To mate?"

"More than that. We're both carrying around some emotional baggage. I haven't done much of a job handling mine on my own, and I don't want you to have to go on dealing with your dad's death alone."

"Neither do I," she admitted.

"Can you handle what I'm saying?" he asked. "Living the way I do, can you see yourself being part of it?"

"I already am," she told him. "Just as you've become part of me."

Turn the page
for a sizzling preview
of Julia Templeton's SINJIN!

On sale now!

1
_____

London, England

Sinjin and his brothers had barely crossed the threshold into Madame Darion's Pleasure Palace when they were welcomed by a bevy of whores in the large, smoke-filled room. Men of all ages lounged on gaudy red velvet settees and worn chairs, accompanied by alluring women who willingly offered what their wives or mistresses would not.

"Sinjin, you are everything a man should be."

Sinjin looked up from the pair of immense breasts belonging to Paris, a French whore who had straddled him mere seconds before.

Paris rotated her hips in a way that had Sinjin clenching his teeth. "And you are everything a woman should be, my dear." He lightly bit the slope of one luscious creamy-white globe.

Her rouged lips curved in a coy smile. "I imagine you say that to all your women, my lord."

"All my women?" He placed a hand over his heart, doing his best to look hurt. "Paris, you wound me."

"Everyone knows your reputation, my lord. What is the nickname for you and your brothers—the Rakehells of Rochester? You are a wicked one, Sin."

He mentally groaned at the mention of the nickname that had been whispered throughout ballrooms and brothels from Rochester to London of late. True, he and his brothers had a fierce appetite for women, but to label them all as rakehells was a bit extreme. "You should not be listening to idle gossip, Paris."

"Do you mean to tell me the rumors aren't true?" She actually sounded disappointed.

"Not a word," he replied.

Her lips quirked. "Somehow I doubt that."

Sensing that someone watched him, he glanced to the right to find a full-lipped brunette dressed in a daring gown made of cream lace staring at him with a wanton smile. Tall and long-legged, she sat on a settee in a most arousing way, showing him in one glance what she had to offer.

Paris's fingers brushed through his hair, her nails digging into his scalp. Ignoring the brunette for the time being, he leaned in and kissed Paris, his tongue brushing against the seam of her lips, seeking entry.

She tasted of mint and brandy, but her technique left something to be desired—too little tongue and too much teeth.

"What's your pleasure, my lord?" she asked before kissing a trail to the sensitive curve of his ear.

Blood coursed through his veins, straight to his cock. "I am up for anything."

Her brows lifted as she looked down between them where his cock swelled against the fabric of his pants. "Yes, you most certainly are."

Paris's slender fingers slid down his chest and abdomen, past the band of his pants, to caress his cock from root to tip.

Setting his drink on a nearby table before he toppled it, he kissed Paris again, ever aware of the brunette who watched them intently. Did he have enough money for a ménage à trios?

he wondered, mentally calculating the money he had in his coat pocket. If all else failed, he could always send Jeffries back to the townhouse for more.

"Perhaps you can buy me for the entire night, my lord," Paris whispered against his lips, her hand gripping him tighter. "I will make it worth your while, I promise."

"I think we can do without the formality, love. Call me Sinjin."

"I'd rather call you Sin—because that's what you are— sinful." She bit his lower lip and sucked on it. "I want every inch of your long, thick cock imbedded deep inside my hot, creamy walls."

Aroused by her sensual words, Sinjin could not keep the smile from his lips. "I am more than happy to oblige."

She lifted her skirts a little, and taking one of his hands within her own, guided him to her slick folds. "Do you feel what you do to me?"

"You're hot, sweet Paris."

"I'm on fire, Sin. Shall we venture up to my room?"

He was ready to ask if the brunette could join them when his brother Victor appeared out of nowhere, a concerned expression on his face. "Mother is here."

Sinjin shook his head, hoping he had misunderstood. "Pardon?"

Victor glanced nervously over his shoulder before turning back to Sinjin. "Mother is here, as we speak."

Sinjin laughed, but Victor did not share his amusement.

"I am not joking, Sinjin. Mother *is* here. Jeffries said she has been circling the block for the past five minutes." He brushed a hand through his dark curls, a habit he'd had since a boy, especially whenever he was anxious. "Where the hell is Rory? We've got to find him and get out of here."

Sinjin's heart slammed against his chest. Dear God, he *wasn't* kidding. Jeffries, their trusted valet and faithful servant, would never jest about something as serious as their mother staking out a whorehouse in Covent Garden in the dead of night. "What in God's name is Mother doing in London?"

"Looking for her sons, I imagine," Victor said absently. "We must get Rory and leave by the back way, posthaste."

Sinjin turned to Paris. "Show us the way out."

Paris frowned. "You cannot stay?"

"Not tonight, but I shall return, and when I do, I will make it up to you."

"Promise?" she asked, her lower lip jutting out.

"Of course," he said, having no such inclination. If their mother was in London, it meant his time in the fair city had come to an end.

"There he is," Victor said, relief in his voice as he located their youngest sibling. No surprise, Rory had a redhead up against the wall—his lower body moving in a suggestive motion. The whore's arms were wound tight about his broad shoulders, her fingers messing his too-long hair.

Victor tapped him on the shoulder, and Rory turned abruptly, looking none too happy about being interrupted. "Jesus Christ, Vic! Do you mind?" He glanced at Sinjin. "Bloody hell, you both look like you've seen a ghost."

"Even worse, I'm afraid," Victor said, grabbing Rory's jacket off the back of a chair and handing it to him. "Mother is here."

The color drained from Rory's cheeks as his gaze skipped to something, or rather someone, just beyond Sinjin's shoulder.

Sinjin's gut rolled, and the hair on the back of his neck stood on end. His worst fear was realized when his mother's voice rang out loud and clear from behind him. "You boys will be the death of me, I swear it!"

"What in heaven's name did I ever do to deserve such grief?" Betsy Rayborne placed an age-spotted hand over her heart. "I have been a good mother to the three of you, and what do I get in return—rumors of scandalous behavior, that's what. Do you know you have even acquired a nickname?" She shook her head in disgust. "The Rakehells of Rochester! How utterly humiliating!"

Sitting between his brothers on the only couch in their mother's opulent hotel suite, Sinjin remained silent. A difficult feat when Betsy kept berating him for his brothers' steady slide into a life of debauchery.

"I cannot count the number of times I have heard that deplorable nickname in the past few weeks. And you are in London, for God's sake! Why does all of Rochester know what you have been up to in London?"

"Mother, perhaps you should sit down," Victor said, concern marring his brow.

Betsy ignored the request and leveled him with a look that made him flinch.

"I could have perished from embarrassment last week when Lady Walbery said she had heard the three of you were servicing everyone from a certain duke's own sister to the lowest of servants." Her gaze shifted to Rory. "How many times have I told you not to dawdle with the help, darling? One time is all that is needed for you to regret your actions. Lord knows how many bastards you have scattered throughout England already. I do not desire a constant reminder of your insatiable lust running around one of my estates."

"Mother, they are mere rumors," Rory said, only to receive a ferocious scowl for his trouble.

"I dragged you and your brothers out of a filthy, dirty whorehouse this evening. Please do not speak to me as you would to one of your many witless mistresses."

Rory swallowed hard.

None of them had a mistress at the moment, witless or otherwise, but Sinjin was not about to argue with her.

"And what kind of an example are you setting for your brothers, Sinjin?" she asked in a high-pitched voice that had him recalling a time from his youth when he had drank his father's vodka and refilled the bottle with water. His mother had seen to it, by way of a paddle she had nicknamed "the truth seeker," to give him his due. He had been unable to sit for a solid week.

"I am sorry for any distress I have caused, Mother."

He might have saved his breath, for she did not even hear his apology. "I honestly believed you invited Victor and Rory to London to convince them what mature, well-respected men of good breeding could accomplish with their lives. I had been so proud to hear how active you have been on the family's behalf."

He did not have the heart to tell her the only reason his brothers had traded the city of Rochester for London was because Rory's previous mistress had turned to stalking him whenever he'd leave the estate. "Mother, I am—"

"Instead, you encourage your siblings to live a hedonistic lifestyle I find absolutely appalling."

He glanced at the clock. They were nearing the quarter-of-an-hour mark and she did not look at all ready to stop her tirade.

She cleared her throat loudly and focused her attention on Victor. "When I heard rumors you had become involved with a London actress, I defended you to the end, telling all my friends how preposterous the very idea was, that you, my quiet, studious son, would never consider an actress as a love interest. However, I have recently learned how very little I know about all of my sons." She pulled a kerchief from her sleeve and dabbed at an imaginary tear. "How could you not see through her lies, Vicky?"

When Victor opened his mouth to defend his actions, Sinjin elbowed him, and his brother wisely pressed his lips together.

"And what of you, Rory? True, you are handsome to be sure, as are all of my boys," she said with a smile that did not begin to reach her eyes, "but sometimes looks can be a curse. One day there will be a woman who comes into your life—and God willing, she will bring you to your knees."

Rory took a sudden interest in his boots.

"Looks fade with time, my dear boy. All you have is what is here." She pressed a hand to her heart. "This is what makes you the man you are. And start using *this* for a change," she said, tapping a firm finger to his forehead.

She paced the floor before them, arms crossed over her chest. "I always hoped you would each find the love of your lives one day. Indeed, I had hoped it would happen long before now, especially for you, Sinjin." She took a deep, steadying breath.

Sinjin straightened his shoulders, wary of her next words.

"You are over thirty now, Sinjin, and Victor and Rory, you are not far behind." She sighed dramatically. "I am not getting any younger, nor are the three of you. And that is why I have decided you shall all marry this summer."

Rory came off the couch like it had caught fire. "You mean *Sinjin* will marry, correct?"

Their mother's brows lifted nearly to her hairline. "*Sit* down, Rory."

Rory sat down, albeit slowly.

Sinjin felt Rory staring at him, no doubt hoping big brother would come to the rescue.

When Sinjin could once again catch his breath, he sat forward. "Mother, since I am the eldest, I assume you are specifically speaking to me?"

Betsy's lips split into a mischievous smile. "No, my dearest.

By the end of this summer, *all* three of you will be married and well on your way to making your father and me the happiest of parents—and, God willing, grandparents."

Rory ran a trembling hand down his face. "Sinjin, for Christ's sake, do something," he muttered under his breath.

Taking his life in his hands, Sinjin stood. "It is rather ambitious of you to marry all of us off, wouldn't you say, Mother?"

She arched a brow. "You question my capabilities, dear?"

Oh God.

"Not at all, Mother. You are capable of anything you set your mind to." He chose his next words carefully, knowing full well they could be his last. "But would it not cause suspicion if all three of us became engaged at the same time?"

"Exactly!" Rory exclaimed. "The *ton* would think we were on the brink of ruin."

Betsy shrugged. "Or they would assume your parents have grown weary of your childish behavior—and finally gave you all an ultimatum."

Sinjin tried another tactic. "The end of summer is less than four months away, Mother. Most courtships last that long and oftentimes stretch longer. Then comes the wedding itself. Therefore, perhaps you could give this little venture a bit more time."

"Do not think for a moment I will relent on this matter." She pursed her lips in a way that made Sinjin nervous. "I am tired of waiting for the three of you to settle down, so I have no choice but to put your feet to the fire, so to speak. Hear me and hear me well, my dears. Each of you *will* marry, and you shall do so by summer's end."

"Sinjin is right, Mother. This seems all rather ambitious," Victor said, a slight edge to his voice.

"Ambitious? Yes, perhaps it is," she said, picking an imaginary string from her skirts. "However, I am extremely motivated."

Feeling the invisible noose growing tighter about his neck, Sinjin asked, "Father knows of this?"

Betsy nodded. "Not only does he know . . . he encourages the plan. In fact, it was your father who came up with the ingenious idea to throw a party at Claymoore Hall to find potential brides for each of you."

Rory brushed his hands through his hair. "And what if we refuse?"

Betsy smiled genuinely for the first time all evening. "You will lose everything."